THE VIEW FROM TIGER'S BACK

DAN PELED

iUniverse, Inc.
Bloomington

The View from Tiger's Back

iUniverse books may be ordered through booksellers or by contacting:

iUniverse
1663 Liberty Drive
Bloomington, IN 47403
www.iuniverse.com
1-800-Authors (1-800-288-4677)

ISBN: 978-1-4502-7247-6 (sc)
ISBN: 978-1-4502-7249-0 (dj)
ISBN: 978-1-4502-7248-3 (ebk)

Printed in the United States of America

iUniverse rev. date: 11/15/2010

THE VIEW FROM TIGER'S BACK

To my family: Jordan, Mary Ellen & Steve.
To my grandchildren: Matt, Elizabeth & Stephanie.

CHAPTER 1

Ankara in February was cold, and the iron tables outside the Likya Café on Kavaklidere Street were empty. Inside, the dozen wood tables and chairs held various patrons under ceiling fans that moved in lazy revolutions. Posters in Arabic dotted the walls, most of them tattered movie and airline advertisements. Former Special Forces Lieutenant Eric LaGrange huddled over a glass of mint tea near the warm kitchen while Suleyman Ehmat waited with a newspaper at a nearby table for his guest. Eric wore old man clothes of collarless shirt, gray cardigan, baggy pants, and suit jacket with frayed cuffs. In the bundle of garments hid a law enforcement-grade audio microphone with digital recorder.

Ehmat looked up from his paper when the bell over the café's door rang. A man entered. Ehmat waved to the man who entered and motioned for him to take the chair on his right. Both men had broad shoulders and dark eyes, wore knitted skullcaps, and were clean-shaven with small facial nicks showing unfamiliarity with razors. No true Muslim would de-nude himself of his beard unless the will of Almighty God demanded. Eric identified the other man as Yakir Arvatian, a former colonel in the Armenian army.

"How was your trip, Yakir?"

"Security was very tight at the airport in Istanbul, and the train ride dirty, crowded, and stupid."

Ehmat turned to the waiter and asked for coffee and pastries. Arvatian agreed and waved the waiter away.

"Suleyman," said Arvatian. "Ever since Kamal ibn-Sultan gained the leadership from Abu Abdullah, he's been impossible to contact. None of the telephone numbers or mail drops has been effective. When will we hear from him?"

"Contact was made yesterday. If you had stayed longer in Istanbul, you would have seen the shipments of material for completing the Baku–Ceyhan pipeline. The Turks anticipate the Westerners will share their wealth. Why start now? The oil will run across Georgia from Azerbaijan, to the southern coast of Turkey, and then it will be loaded on supertankers for Western Europe and America. One million barrels a day they expect, reason enough to steal land and destroy communities along its 1750 kilometers. This is a crime, Yakir."

"Yes, but this has nothing to do with us. British Chemical Enterprises are financing the pipeline. The Cleric said our targets were only to be American."

"They will be the final consumers of the oil and not one drop will go to people it is taken from. I have been talking to the Azeri. Kamal suggests we accept their entreaties for our aid."

"To sabotage the pipeline?"

"Lower your voice, Yakir. The Azeri will pay for our intercession on their behalf. We need the money for a new operation."

LaGrange lost interest in the conversation and concentrated on his lokma. Eating with his hands was wrong but he could not get the fork and bite of pastry into his mouth without going through the tangle of his false beard. The spirit gum gave way when he stretched his lips to drink his tea. But his ears remained tuned to the conversation between the two men. *Did the two consipators notice him?* He wondered.

LaGrange had returned to the Middle East after his release from the US Army, and rented a small efficiency apartment in Damascus where he woke in the morning to prayers coming from minarets. He read and walked the cobblestone streets, and took his meals at a local café whose proprietor referred to him as the "reformed infidel."

His days were quiet until CIA case officer Roger Shaw knocked on his door and invited LaGrange to join the spook world. Shaw was a thin and balding forty-seven years old who looked ten more. He officially worked out of the Istanbul US Embassy, but these days everyone shuttled between countries with little regard for borders. Any potential threat of Muslim violence against the United States was quickly met with money and manpower. Shaw needed an asset who understood the Middle East and LaGrange had spent much of his youth in Saudi Arabia, tugged by his English teacher father to Jiddah, Riyadh, and Medina.

"What are you doing here?" Shaw asked.

"Research into sharia, the Islamic law, among other things."

"I heard about the scholarly turn. You embarrassed your professors at Georgetown University by being smarter than them before signing on with the Army."

"The military was a momentary lapse of reason. I thought about being a career soldier until my problem."

"Took your medal and quit is how I heard the story. Ready to retire at age twenty-five."

"Whatever, Mr. Shaw. I don't mean to spoil the day for you, but I'm not interested."

"You're broke and your visa is a day away from being revoked."

"The Army checks have run a little short. As for the visa, I'm depending on Almighty God to provide."

"He won't and we can," Shaw said. "Along with enough tax-free cash to raise your standard of living. This joint is a dump."

"What happened to doing this for my country?"

"My patriotism is weak after the bureaucrats at Langley sent me analysts with one week of weapons training and called them agents. They're hell on PlayStation and know squat about gathering intelligence. I need a man with the language who's not afraid of what we're up against."

"In all the reading I've done, I know less about who is the enemy and who are the righteous."

"The bad guys are the ones killing innocent people."

" 'Innocent' is a relative term."

"Standing by when you can stop the bad guys is complicity."

"You sound like a Jesuit. I've made mistakes."

"The bastards I want are the Followers of the Cleric and they are planning something big. Web sites and cell phones have been burning in this part of the world faster than we can shut them down. When they struck in the past, they killed more civilians than soldiers. Take a look at my personal rogue's gallery." Shaw dipped into the inside pocket of his suit jacket and pulled out a sheaf of black and white five-by-seven photographs. "See here? Suleyman Ehmat, a real sleazy number who arranges payments. Reza Deghani gets the arms. This is my favorite, Kamal ibn-Sultan, the number one guy."

LaGrange stabbed a finger at the picture. "Ismael," he said. "I knew him in Baghdad. He's had the growth on his right eyelid removed. I'd like to see a little justice pay him a visit."

"This is intelligence gathering, not a vendetta. No targets."

LaGrange agreed and floated around Syria, Afghanistan, and Iran on various assignments. Shaw pointed and LaGrange tailed and recorded and photographed who he was told, and learned the tradecraft as needed. This week was Turkey, a country he liked less than his native Wisconsin.

———

The two men sipped their coffee until they were joined by a third. LaGrange recognized Reza Deghani by his rimless glasses and goatee, an Iranian counter-intelligence officer and bio-weapons expert. Arvatian rose as Deghani limped to the table and they embraced, and kissed twice on each cheek. Ehmat stayed in his seat.

"You're looking well, Reza," Arvatian said.

Deghani smiled. "Except for my damned wound from the war with the Iraqis. Any news on the *smoothie*, Yakir?"

"We await further communication."

"Good. Order me a coffee."

Ehmat signaled the waiter. "One for the gentleman and bring the menu."

"Tell me about the *smoothie*," Deghani said.

"Later," Ehmat intervened. He turned to look in LaGrange's direction.

LaGrange finished his tea and rose from his chair by leaning on his cane. He walked slowly, aware of the attention the men gave his departure. LaGrange continued down the street until he disappeared into a crowd and headed for the Embassy.

A *"smoothie"* was an ambassador or diplomat. The three men at the café could have been referring to any country's representative. China had interest in the Azerbaijan oil fields to support their military ambitions against Taiwan. The Russians hosted the only pipeline in the region and did not want to share revenues with the British. They had registered complaints at a meeting of the World Bank, as did the Iranians who hoped Iran would be on the route any new pipeline would take. Then there was the American ambassador to Kazakhstan, Elizabeth Paige. The gossip mills in Washington considered her a legend for her relentless pursuit of the Baku–Ceyhan project. If she could get British Chemical to divert some crude to the Chinese or Russians, the payoff would finance a run for the Senate. Who would suspect the Western oilmen's darling?

———

The Embassy building on Furmanov Street in Almaty, Kazakhstan was made of gray stone and barely missed being depressing as the surrounding chunky Stalinist-era architecture. When the light from the many leaded glass windows faded into dusk, wall sconces and chandeliers illuminated the rooms. Carpets lined the red tiled floors and heavy oak doors kept the curious to the public areas.

"You're crazy on this one," Shaw said to LaGrange as they walked the hallway to the main reception room.

"Four hours ago I was in Turkey. I've been debriefed until I can't remember my own name and flown on military transport to a town I like even less than Ankara. You forced me into a black market Armani tux to meet Ambassador Paige and tell her my suspicions. Who's crazy?"

"Point taken. Just don't strong-arm her. This gala is for US Energy Secretary Martin Holbeck's tour of the region."

"In these clothes I can't even scratch my nose. Next time find a suit not so tight in the shoulders."

Shaw laughed. "I'll settle for a promise of no verbal abuse."

"She must be as attractive as her photograph for you to be so protective."

The reception line for Holbeck and Elizabeth was long and more guests continued to arrive in their formal finery. LaGrange knew the ambassador's history from Shaw. At forty-five, Ambassador Elizabeth Paige was at the top of her career. She joined the Foreign Service in 1985, had an extensive background in Soviet and Russian affairs, and stationed at the US embassies in Prague and Moscow. Paige served four years as ambassador to Uzbekistan before her assignment to Kazakhstan, and spoke Russian, French, Italian, Armenian, and Arabic, some with and others without an accent.

She was born Elizabeth Gretchen Tooler in California and held a degree from the University of California's Hastings College of Law. Two years of Soviet and Eastern European studies at Harvard speeded her acceptance in the Foreign Service. Paige had a daughter, Amelia, and remained single after her husband, Thomas, died from leukemia several years earlier. None of this information gave an indication of what kind of woman Elizabeth Paige was, and she preferred the distance.

Waiters in black linen jackets carried trays of champagne flutes among the attendees. LaGrange watched Ambassador Paige shake the hands of her guests. She had long auburn hair twisted into a chignon, and wore a burgundy Versace evening gown that complemented her fair skin and slim figure. Above her high cheekbones were steady green eyes, and below a determined mouth tinted with coral lipstick. She turned to Chinese Ambassador Xiang and his wife.

"You have done wonders in supporting the pipeline, Madame Ambassador," Xiang said.

"America is committed to helping the former Soviet bloc countries develop their own economies. We've worked with the Kazakhstan government on a wide range of issues, but I believe encouraging the pipeline is our best effort. Many new jobs will be created."

Xiang smiled. "You sound like a press release. The Iranians are certainly unhappy about losing their chance of becoming the Caspian oil conduit to world markets. There has also been talk of stolen land and drinking water pollution."

"Progress is always bitter to some," she replied. "The prosperity brought to the region cancels out any reservations about the pipeline. As we speak, construction teams are installing the pumps to fill storage tanks at the Ceyhan port. We are going ahead."

"My country has a great need for oil and eager to participate in this new resource."

"Not until China cleans up its human rights violations. You're still under the United Nations embargo for what has been done to the opposition in your country."

"Where there is money, conscience is replaced by pragmatism."

"A quote from Chairman Mao, Ambassador Xiang?"

Elizabeth Paige noticed Roger Shaw talking to a young man wearing a tuxido.

The line thinned and Ambassador Paige took Shaw's hand. "I see you're still with the cloak-and-dagger squad."

"The Peace Corps refused my application. Madame Ambassador, this is the man I've been praising, Eric LaGrange."

"A pleasure," LaGrange said.

She offered her hand to the young man in the uncomfortable tuxedo. "What brings you gentlemen to my reception?"

"We'd like a private word. Tonight."

"Is anything the matter?"

"Maybe."

She turned to the corridor behind her. "I'll meet you in my office down the hall in the next hour."

Elizabeth Paige excused herself and departed. A tall man carrying a tray of drinks approached them. LaGrange helped himself to a glass.

"What do you think?" he asked Shaw.

"She's not aware of anything."

Two men stood in the doorway. One had a shaven head and his dark eyes were fixed on Elizabeth. The man's companion wore a traditional wool cap and a large, black mustache, curled upwards.

"Ambassador from Uzbekistan and his bodyguard," Shaw said and tilted his head toward the newcomers. "Let's go to the office."

LaGrange watched Elizabeth greet the latest arrivals with her signature cold charm. No one who witnessed her working the room could refer to Paige as a *"smoothie."*

———

Burt Strauss arrived as the party wound down. He got himself a glass of champagne from the bar and studied the guests. Well-dressed politicos and their wives chattered in small groups. Elizabeth was tied up with people in the corner. She waved to him but did not break away from her conversation.

Strauss at fifty-two sported a full head of light brown hair with gray at his temples. His lean figure attested to the many hours he spent on the tennis court, as did his tan. Even in Baku where he lived these days, the Connecticut resident managed a tennis game at least twice weekly despite his busy schedule.

He was the board member of British Chemical Enterprises in charge of the Baku–Ceyhan pipeline, and did his best to stay in Elizabeth's good graces. They had been lovers more than twenty years ago, though Elizabeth refused to acknowledge the shared past.

Strauss saw in her the young woman he loved, an athlete, a beauty, a feisty debater, and a brilliant scholar. He recalled seeing her dark hair bounce from her shoulders as she ran across a tennis court or galloped across a meadow on a horse. He loved to watch her catch a pop fly or put someone out on base in those informal, spur-of-the-moment softball games Sunday afternoons with her friends at Harvard.

Not in the mood for small talk or politicking, he stood with his drink by the bar. Finally Elizabeth came over to him. "Burt, what happened to you? People were asking."

"What people?"

"Energy Secretary Holbeck, the Shermans, Abe Altmeier, Ambassador Xiang, and the Vandewetterings."

"Sorry, I was tied up."

"You look stressed. We're still ahead of schedule."

"Yes, but I'm concerned about the Iranian backlash. Be careful."

"You needn't worry about me."

He would never break through to her. "Iran lodged a protest at the UN over NATO moving its operation base from the Adana Incirlik Air Base in Turkey to Azerbaijan."

"There have been complaints from Moscow as well."

"I'm not surprised with our forces in the Persian Gulf. The Caspian has been floating free since the collapse of the Soviet Union. Leaders are anxious for ties to the West and damn the consequences."

"Five years from now we'll be heroes for saving the economies of Kazakhstan and Azerbaijan."

"In the meantime we're the villains. I'm going to the port of Ceyhan for the opening of the pipeline. Will you join me?"

"I'll be there with the Energy Secretary."

"If not for all your hard work, this project would still be a dream."

"I'm not blind to your contribution, Burt."

"Just to me."

His remark caught her off guard and she blushed.

"Excuse me. I must join Roger in my office."

"Shaw sticking his nose in the dirty laundry of the world?"

Elizabeth swept away and he excused himself to the wake of her perfume.

———

The office walls were decorated with the usual portrait of the President. The spare furnishings included matching severe chairs of leather and chrome, and standing lamps. An oak desk held telephones and computer, and a television with VCR sat on a credenza. The only human touch was hidden in the bottom left drawer of the desk, where Elizabeth kept the Barsetshire novels of Anthony Trollope.

LaGrange studied the spines of the books on the shelves and Shaw stared at his drink. Elizabeth came through the door with exasperated urgency. "Let's keep this brief."

"LaGrange uncovered intel we believe was a threat on you."

"Speak English, Roger."

"He overheard a conversation in Ankara between the bad guys. The Azeri are going after a diplomat. After considering the Chinese and Russians and anyone else out here, you're the only viable target."

"The Azeri have registered their complaints through the proper channels. They're satisfied we are addressing the concerns as best we can."

"Madame Ambassador," interrupted LaGrange. "The men I overheard are followers of Kamal ibn-Sultan. International courts for the victims of Islamic terrorism have frozen their bank accounts. They need money to continue the jihad against America and the Azeri are willing to hire them for an attack against a diplomat who supports the pipeline."

"Don't give me the government line about ibn-Sultan's hatred of our way of life."

"I won't. He's angrier at our foreign policy. We've consistently messed and muddied the Arab world since becoming a world power."

"My friends at the National Security Agency sent me a brief on you, Mr. LaGrange. There's not much in your war record to give me confidence."

———

Three years earlier, Lieutenant Eric LaGrange lay on the rooftop of a warehouse and looked through the viewfinder of the laser acquisition marker. The crosshairs focused on an airshaft atop a large office building across the Tigris in downtown Baghdad. Ismael, LaGrange's Iraqi contact, had said the airshaft led to the main artery of a bunker where the remainders of Saddam Hussein's regime were hiding with enough armaments to retake the city.

LaGrange sweated under the weight of his fifty-pound pack on the hot windless night. A layer of pollution lay over the ruined city, rancid with the acrid odor of explosives, chemicals, and burning debris. He longed to finish and get out.

Nearby his team lay restless, though they were used to bunker busting. LaGrange zeroed in on the airshaft half a mile across the river with the viewfinder and squeezed the trigger of the designator. "It's a go," he said.

Private Walsh radioed the C–130J transport aircraft more than 20,000 feet above them. "Bright sky on dead zone." The transport descended to 6,000 feet and the Daisy Cutter, a BLU–82 designed to clear helicopter landing-zones, fell from doors.

LaGrange heard the whisper of the bomb seeking out the target projected by the designator. First came a cloud of dirt and building debris, then the roar of explosion. The bomb hit concrete deep below ground and shook the soldiers before the concussion bounced them into the air and made a rolling wake on the river. Baghdad lit up in shadows as fire rose like a tower of light. Modern steel and concrete rubble poured down over the city as computer guided Tomahawk missiles completed the mission.

The Special Forces team left the roof in the following silence. They ran through empty streets and met the camouflage-painted Hummer. Ismael leaned against the vehicle door.

"Mission accomplished, sir?"

"The evil have been vanquished, my man. All in a day's work."

LaGrange gave his men the thumbs-up sign and they climbed in the vehicle for the thirty-mile ride into the desert for extraction. Ismael stayed silent until the Hummer rolled to a stop.

"I must speak with you alone," he told LaGrange. He motioned for the men to go on and paid Ismael from a large roll of twenties.

"Americans call this blood money, yes?"

"Among other things. Less of Saddam means your country will soon be free."

"Coca-Cola, Marlboros, and DVD in every home."

"If you want." The conversation with Ismael grew tedious. LaGrange disliked the man from their original meeting. Ismael had a mole on his right eyelid, large enough to close the lid shut, and too lazy to have the mole surgically removed.

"Do you know my name in the Hebrew Bible?"

"Sure, the illegitimate son of Abraham, born of Hagar the housemaid. 'He will be a wild donkey of a man; his hand will be against everyone and everyone's hand against him, and he will live in hostility toward all his brothers.' "

"Precisely. You hit the wrong target."

LaGrange stopped. "What do you mean?"

"I gave you false information. The building had wounded traitors leaving the city with their children. Those bunkers were empty."

The hot air pounded in his ears.

"What will the world say about the Crusaders now?" Ismael pulled a 9 mm pistol from his waistband and shot LaGrange.

The bullet slowed during its journey through LaGrange's camo gear and a copy of Gavin Young's *Return to the Marshes,* and lodged near his liver. He collapsed and woke up in a hospital bed with peritonitis. A kind nurse knocked him out with shot of morphine into one of the many intravenous units hanging around his bed. LaGrange was sent stateside to a perfunctory tribunal where he was charged and cleared of the murder of 37 Iraqi civilians, and awarded a Purple Heart. As soon as his health permitted, LaGrange left the Army and flew to Damascus where he studied Islamic law as penance for his part in Ismael's treachery.

———

"I was found innocent, Ambassador," he said.

"Then you should have stayed in the Army."

"Being raised among Muslims gives me a different perspective on them as a people. I couldn't see them as targets and the next time I had to call in a strike, I knew I would hesitate. Wars are lost by hesitation."

"This viewpoint you have extends to the Azeri?"

"In this situation."

"I have checkpoints and metal detectors and Marines in the Embassy. If I'm to be safe anywhere, it's here."

"The threat is very possible," said Shaw.

"Call my office when information comes from a reliable source. Good evening, gentlemen."

CHAPTER 2

Petrova Ivanovna Verkhovtsev was a young Eurasian woman with almond-shaped eyes and light tan skin, and the figure of a runway model. High cheekbones gave her a regal aura back in fashion and blond hair fell to her shoulders. Behind her beauty was a master's degree from the London School of Economics. As sales representative of Caspian Works, Petrova had negotiated the deal with British Chemical Enterprises to provide the steel pipes, drilling equipment, and pumps for the Baku–Ceyhan pipeline.

Her home in the medieval old town of Baku was hidden in the narrow alleys and serpentine passages near the fortress walls. Petrova lived among the history of the Palace of the Shervan-Shahs by preference, and admired the age-worn Maiden Tower with its view of the Caspian Bay. In private moments she dreamed of a return to the aristocracy of centuries past, but only if she was included in the elite.

Petrova answered the door dressed in a light silk blouse and beige skirt, and black silk stockings. Strauss regarded the daughter of a retired Russian general and Uzbek mother. On another woman, her outfit would seem plain. Petrova wore the skirt and blouse with sensual promise.

"Good evening, Ms. Verkhovtsev."

"Come in, Mr. Strauss. Where will be dining tonight?"

"Call me Burt. I wasn't sure what you'd prefer, so I made reservations at the Hyatt's Delicias restaurant and Ragin' Cajun on Mammademin Rasulzadeh. Your choice."

"Petrova." She took his hand and pulled him into the foyer. "The Hyatt will be fine." The delicate scent wafting from her ignited a familiar sensation through him.

"How have you been?" he asked.

"Very well. We have achieved the impossible with the pipeline."

"Caspian Works did a great job, and you."

"My father is responsible for my success. He encourages me in all my undertakings."

Strauss accompanied her down a long hall. "I understand he's retired."

"He went through hard times during the Soviet withdrawal from Afghanistan and is now a consultant to the military. The free market economy has not reached public service, according to him. They can barely afford his experience."

"So I hear."

"You have been studying me."

"I must confess we, that is, British Chemical, investigated Caspian Works."

"Likewise," she said. "Not only your company but we investigated you."

"Should I be worried or flattered?"

She did not answer. They entered the drawing room. Dark wood floors were covered in thick rugs. Petrova motioned to a large sofa with too many paisley jacquard pillows and a Mozart concerto played from concealed speakers. Books filled the shelves behind the sofa and the fireplace held copper pots of green ferns instead of fire. The rosewood writing desk showed no signs of clutter or use. A copy of *The Politics of World Economy* lay face down on the coffee table.

"My home," Petrova said in a soft voice. "Shall we sit down?"

The couple was silent as they looked out the picture window to the lights of Baku spread below. "Can I offer you a drink? I have an excellent

Polish vodka." She pointed to the small wet bar at the opposite end of the parlor.

"On the rocks, please. I haven't been young enough to drink it straight for many years."

Petrova went to the bar and produced a bottle of Luksusowa from an ice bucket, and splashed liquor into two glasses. She handed Strauss his drink and raised hers. "To our success."

He leaned forward and put the glass down. Petrova touched his knee. "I wanted to celebrate this occasion privately with you."

She withdrew her hand and the sensation of her warmth lingered. She crossed her legs and he noticed the curvature of her calf sheathed in silk. "I have a proposition. My partners and I would like to make a deal with you."

"Do I know them?"

She took a sip of vodka. "You might have heard of one or two."

"What do you have in mind?"

The vodka was smooth and Strauss relaxed. He leaned back against the sofa. She moved closer.

"I like you, Burt. You are very generous." She placed her hand on his knee again, slightly higher in the direction of his groin. Petrova's seduction made Strauss wary. Woman as the aggressor was never easy to get his mind around. Her lips parted and revealed small, white, even teeth.

"We can make you a rich man."

"How?" he asked. He reached for his drink.

"We can talk business later." Petrova poured more vodka into their glasses. "Who is she, this woman?"

"So much for not being obvious. I gave up sexual entanglements for work. I'm much better at work."

"Our investigation showed you had been a womanizer in the past, but you do like your work. My intuition says there is a woman you cared for deeply, and perhaps still do."

Strauss allowed himself to be charmed by Petrova. "There was someone. Unfortunately I was married at the time and lost the woman once she found out."

"You overlooked this little detail and like most men realized you loved her too late."

"I was young and foolish."

"You are divorced. What stops you now?"

"The story gets worse. She was pregnant and I sent her money for an abortion she didn't want to have. She got married and had the baby."

"Maybe the baby belonged to the husband."

"Nope. The child had to be mine."

"Is the husband a complication?"

"He's dead and she doesn't know I'm aware she kept the baby."

Petrova shook her head. "You Americans have messy lives."

"I'm over it. I regret having a daughter I've never met. She wants to go to medical school and is applying for scholarships. How about you? Don't you have anything messy to share?"

"Only that I would like to make love with you."

She slid next to him, and reached for his hand and stroked his fingers. Strauss was unnerved. The smell of her overwhelmed him and her closeness made him ache.

"No one is going to bite you, except me," she said.

Petrova kissed him and put her tongue into his mouth. Then she straddled him and pulled at his necktie and shirt. He threw several pillows out of the way, damned by her Dior eyes and Chanel lips. Strauss tore at her blouse and her braless, erect nipples brushed against his lips. He cupped one and sucked on it. He released her breast and lifted up her skirt to tear off her underwear. She cried out and slid alongside him. That made him wild and he pulled her beneath him. Her tongue moved along his neck and her nails dug into his arm.

Strauss was yanked off her and she screamed. He struggled as his arms were jerked behind his back and he was pulled to his feet. He had a glimpse of several shadows in the lowlit room. Petrova made muffled sounds as though she had been gagged.

"Blindfold him."

Strauss' eyes were covered and his mouth stuffed with rag. "Dress naked boy," said the same voice. One man held him while another lifted his right leg and jammed it into his pants, then the left. The rough handling continued until he was clothed. He felt assembled like a puppet. They did not bother with shoes. What were kidnappers doing at Petrova's home?

Letting a woman seduce you was always dangerous. Had she set him up or was she a victim too? He no longer heard her muffled protesting. Someone had turned up the stereo and the concerto boomed as they dragged him out the door. The heavy door banged shut and left the music and Petrova behind.

———

Petrova was enraged and dialed a telephone number. "Let me speak to Grigory Parfenovich Pluchenko," she demanded.

"He is not here," said a male voice.

"Mikhail Osipovich Kalgonov, then."

"He is not here either."

"Tell Mikhail Osipovich I said to get right over here as soon as he gets in."

Mikhail arrived late the next morning, tweed cap in hand. The slight man shivered at Petrova's words.

"Do not ever invade my privacy or interrupt me when I have company, you idiot. For two kopeks I would have Grigory send you back to Siberia with the wolves."

"I am sorry. Our orders were to pick him up. We did not know how we would find him."

Kalgonov released a snicker hidden behind his words. This infuriated her. "Who gave the orders?"

He paused. "Grigory Pluchenko. He is a jealous man, Petrova."

"I had Burt Strauss without the violence."

"Grigory prefers persuading with force rather than seduction."

"How will you explain Burt Strauss being taken from my home?"

"No one saw him leave, rest assured."

"Get out of here. Tell Grigory what you saw if you think that will help you. I do not give a damn." She ushered the man out and slammed the door.

Petrova walked the streets of the Inner City, known as Ichari Shahar by the Azeri, in attempt to work off her anger. Few of the estates and courtyards held greenery, an odd tradition of keeping to stone. The tangle of streets saved the residents from the mean north winds of winter and the closely fitted buildings cooled each other with their shadows in the summer. She played the tourist walking by the minaret of Mohammad ibn Abu Bakr's Mosque and Maiden Tower, Gyz Galasy. Baku was Petrova's chosen home, the petro-dollars waiting to be shoveled into numbered accounts in Zurich and Luxembourg. For its wealth, the water of Baku held more bacteria than liquid. The only consolation was its uneven dispersal. No water meant no bad water.

She returned home and met Grigory Pluchenko standing by her door. He was a hairy man, curls of dark hair from his toes to his heavy beard, and came of age in a tattered Moscow where crime had replaced Stalinism as the state religion. Pluchenko moved among the thugs and thieves and soon worked in the arms market. Where his parents had Marxism, Grigory embraced money and followed it to Baku. The city had not changed him. He wore a black leather coat regardless of the season, and underneath a dark blue Brioni suit tailored to his wide imposing frame. The ensemble was completed with black shirt and matching tie, black Ferragamo wing tip shoes, and a Cartier wristwatch. Some of the items were purchased legitimately, but only a few.

Petrova was still livid. "Why did you take Strauss from under me?"

"Business. Calm down."

"Your men yanked him out of here and I want to know why."

Pluchenko sat on the sofa. "Ehmat paid us ten thousand hard currency for Strauss. That damn Turk is kissing ibn-Sultan's ass by doing a freelance job for the Azeri."

"Where is my half?"

He took a thick envelope from his inside jacket pocket. "Where is our trust?"

"In the pipeline." She turned on the stereo and hefted the table lamps to look underneath, and took down a picture from the wall to feel its back.

"There must be electronics, otherwise Ehmat's men would not have known when to enter. Help me turn over the sofa."

The two looked behind the books, under the coffee table, and through the wet bar. Finally she sat down, exhausted.

"No bugs. If they are none, I have information no one else has."

Pluchenko dropped into an overstuffed chair across from her. "What information?"

"He has a daughter."

"Really."

"Yes. The Chinese want oil and I need him to make the deal. If he has any scruples, he will refuse and I can blackmail him. It's better to dangle a subtle carrot."

"Like sex?"

Petrova glared. "I do not dangle sex. I either do it or don't."

"No need to be defensive."

"With Strauss, you have to suggest things, like maybe he could provide the funds his daughter needs to go to medical school."

"What else?"

"His stock portfolio. He heavily invested in commodities and lot of it on margin. The man is broke. By convincing him to sell oil to the Chinese before Western Europeans and Americans, and get him out of his trouble, the man would talk himself into the deal. Ehmat kidnapping Strauss will spoil everything."

"I'm not going to fight with Ehmat, or ibn-Sultan. They are mad with religion."

"Remind him you control access to Vozrozdeniye Island. Grigory, do business with Ehmat carefully, my love, with a promise in one hand and a pistol in the other."

"You are right, but he's been cooperative enough in the past."

" Then you had the explosives he wanted and he behaved." Petrova sighed. "Did you ever consider ibn-Sultan might want us to take the blame for his dirty work here? He might blow up our oil pipeline—our money pipeline."

"We'll do it your way."

"Good," she said. "Let me see if I can still salvage this. The first thing we have to do is to keep ibn-Sultan from killing Strauss. We need him and British Chemical."

The fifth floor of the CIA headquarters in Langley, Virginia was given over to the Counterterrorism Center, part of the Directorate of Operations. Sheets of rain pelted the office windows on the gray evening, followed by sudden thunder. Chief CTC John Devine sat behind his flat government-issue desk desolately watching CNN on the console television. A secure e-mail message from Roger Shaw came on Devine's computer screen.

"Confirmed meeting in Ankara between Iranian spy Reza Deghani, and Yakir Arvatian, Armenian terrorist, hosted by Suleyman Ehmat, confidant of Kamal ibn-Sultan. Possible threat to Ambassador Paige involved."

"What are you boys up to?" Devine said to no one. He typed a reply, shut off the lights, and drove the Dulles toll road home as the rain intensified. Shaw would read the terse message while Devine slept.

"Keep asset in motion. Protect Ambassador Paige."

Forty-seven-year-old John Devine had served two tours of duty as a Green Beret, and joined the Agency when they offered him a steady desk job. He traveled the bureaucracy until promoted to the CTC and chief of the section. Devine learned quickly the levels of deniability demanded by the current administration and probably the previous ones as well. Do the job and don't tell us how. He took Zoloft to keep his ulcer under control, and Viagra for date nights with his wife.

While other men fussed with fly-fishing gear, Devine's passion was for his wife, Stephanie Ireland. They met at a Knicks game at Madison Square Garden in the spring of 1995. Devine had the seat next to her and from the moment she spilled beer on his leg, he was intrigued. Stephanie's hazel eyes, freckles, and carelessly cut chestnut hair caused a crack in his usually hard exterior. "I'm so sorry," she told him.

"No problem," he said, and shook off the Millers Light. "I always allow for damage to clothing when I come to the Garden."

She looked at the man with gray-green eyes and a mop of dark hair speckled with red. He wore jeans, sweatshirt, and a pair of running shoes, and stood over six feet tall. His hands were large and steady. "Bulls fans are particularly clumsy," she said.

"You noticed, too?"

"I'll be glad to send those jeans to the cleaners."

"Not necessary. I'll wear them swimming the next chance I get."

She turned her attention to the scoreboard. The game had yet to start.

"What's a Bulls fan doing in Knicks seats?" he asked.

"I'm sponging off a friend's season ticket."

"You're a welcome substitute, even if you are rooting for the wrong team."

"Not tonight. Chicago rules."

"Nah, Jordan's lame and Rodman is being Rodman."

"And then some."

He laughed. "You from Chicago?"

"Sort of. I go to school there."

"Let me guess. Parsons."

"Do I look like an artsy Bulls fan? No, the University of Chicago. Journalism."

By now the Garden was packed. The regular season game was a sell-out. "You want to make a friendly wager?" Devine held up a dollar. "This greenback says the Knicks win."

"I'll see your dollar and raise you four."

"Five bucks it is. But I hate taking money from students."

The game began and the people she had come with might as well have vanished. Stephanie hardly spoke to them, though the game was too noisy to talk anyway. It was a fast-paced game and she smiled and clapped for Pippin, Rodman, and Jordan. Her seatmate hooted, whistled, and stomped for Lohaus, Mason, and Ewing.

"You're going to lose," she said before the fourth quarter. "Jordan's on a roll."

"Hey, we're kicking ass, despite losing one coach and four players."

"Whine if you must."

Michael Jordan with his own contribution of 55 points, set up a slam dunk for Bill Wennington that gave Chicago a last-second victory and brought the crowd to its feet.

John Devine produced a five-dollar bill and Stephanie accepted. "I hope you won't hold this against me."

"Let me buy you a cup of coffee. I can afford it and you can't."

The coffee led to Devine's hotel room at Essex House across from Central Park, and the use of every frequent flyer he had collected to shuttle between Washington, DC and Chicago until Stephanie graduated.

With little prodding, Stephanie moved to Washington, DC and hired on with WJLA-TV, Channel 7 News on Wilson Boulevard in Arlington, Virginia. She pulled copy from the wires and distilled them to one-minute bites for local broadcast. They married and bought a house in Georgetown, made the mortgage payments, and planned for a family until a doctor's test showed Stephanie to be infertile. They had each other, and celebrated their anniversaries by taking the train to New York and seeing a Knicks game at the Garden. When Agency technicians installed the STU–III secure telephone in their home, Stephanie made one request.

"Never tell me what you do."

CHAPTER 3

The port of Bandar-e Anzali on the Caspian Sea in northern Iran had a wharf, oil depot, and fishery buildings where state monopoly black caviar was produced. Heavy security and refrigeration did not hold back the smell of dead sturgeon stripped of their eggs. Though very much Iranian, Bandar-e Anzali has been influenced by Russia since the establishment of a trading post in the nineteenth century. Store windows, the dusty promenade along the west bank, failing architecture, and fair-skinned citizens look Russian.

Suleyman Ehmat rode the ferry to Bandar-e Anzali two hundred miles south from Baku. He mingled with the merchants and construction workers on the passenger deck making their way home for Ashura, commemorating the martyrdom of Imam Hassan, grandson of the Prophet. Wearing a shabby coat, work cap, and soiled overalls, Ehmat passed for another worker as his passport declared. A month-old ragged beard completed the Turk's disguise.

Kamal ibn-Sultan leaned against the dock railing and watched the oil slick on the waters of the Caspian change colors waited at the dock. The short man with the thick black beard was dressed as road-worker with wool cap and dark glasses. He had missed the Afghanistan war against the Soviets, but was ready for invasion of Iraq. The Jordanian street thug renounced his former criminal self and became a devout Muslim to follow the Cleric's command for jihad. Ehmat put his cap under his arm to signal all was clear. They met and embraced, and kissed twice on each cheek.

"I am glad to see you," ibn-Sultan said.

"This is quite an honor. The Crusaders have set a bounty on your head for one hundred thousand dollars."

"Let them shake their rusty sabers. Is Reza coming?"

"He is waiting for us at the Hotel Iran."

"You may do the negotiating. I have no patience for the flattery he requires."

They walked the port split by the outlet of the Anzali Lagoon, across the Pol-e Ghazian bridge to the city center on the opposite bank. After the empty promenade, the two men continued to Khomeini Square, past the bazaar, and finally the restaurant at the Hotel Iran. Reza Deghani sat in conversation with the owner, a beefy man sporting a black beard and black turban. People crowded the tables almost to capacity in anticipation of the fast for Ashura. Deghani motioned to a table at the corner of the airy room, where two patrons were preparing to leave.

The men greeted each other and shook hands.

"Welcome, my friends. I trust you are hungry," Deghani said. "They serve a very fine kebab made of lamb from the north."

"A good choice for hungry men," ibn-Sultan said.

He surveyed the busy eatery with suspicious eyes. Waiters hurried among the tables with large trays loaded with steaming pots of chai and brass plates heaped with food. The scent of grilled lamb wafted toward the table and teased ibn-Sultan's mouth. A waiter in long white apron took their order.

"Now then, Reza," ibn-Sultan began once the waiter left. "Your estimated costs on the latest project we discussed seems high to me, especially since this coordinates nicely with our work for the Azeri. What do you think, Suleyman?"

"I'm concerned about the price, too. An American television news program said the product we're interested in could be produced in someone's home in a five-gallon bucket. They said if the particular item were released from a boat on the Hudson River, four hundred thousand or more deaths in New York City would result."

"Yes, that," Deghani answered. "It was also written in American papers that for around $20,000, those such as our people could eliminate thousands with this same material. This was not accurate either, only propaganda to get Americans to overlook an increase in money and power allowed to their military and intelligence agencies."

"What is true?" asked Ehmat.

"To use the material effectively, it must be converted to a powder that can be inhaled. In liquid form it turns into globules that cannot remain airborne when sprayed. The product must be made into an aerosol.

"In order to do that, the particles have to be washed several times in various large and expensive centrifuges, then dried and sprayed in mist form into a vacuum. This is how powder is made from liquid. Otherwise, everything coagulates and hardens. The equipment has to be cleaned in a pressure chamber and steam-sterilized for several days. Such an operation is costly. Only two countries have succeeded in doing this, America and Russia. Iraq found the liquid form most ineffective."

"Has the product on Vozrozhdeniye Island been through the procedure?"

"Exactly, and why so valuable."

"All you have to do is arrange transport."

"Oh, no. At the present stage the material is not powerful enough to give the effect you described earlier. An individual must inhale ten thousand particles to produce the results you want. However, a scientist of my acquaintance found that by adding a certain combination of chemical substances, the number of particles needed to cause the desired effect is greatly reduced."

The waiter brought a tray of plates loaded with skewers of kebab, steamed rice, warm pita bread, and bowls of green olives to the table. Conversation temporarily slowed and Deghani watched ibn-Sultan eat with displeasure. The man who was named successor to the brave Abu

Abdullah, who fought the Russians and gave his inherited wealth to his brothers in the struggle, had the table manners of stable boy. Ibn-Sultan shoved chunks of lamb into his mouth and made terrible sounds as he masticated the food. He licked the grease off his fingers and ignored the finger bowls. That the radicals of the Muslim world followed this man was beyond comprehension.

"Once other things are added, the amount will be enough?" asked Ehmat.

"Yes and no," replied Deghani. "The Russian scientists put test animals into gas chambers during the dispensing of these materials to insure the desired intake. What you must create for your project is something similar. Make your target a crowded building of some kind."

"We have friends experienced in heating and cooling systems for large public facilities, and access to a number of foreign buildings."

"What kind of buildings?"

"Perhaps American ones."

"Praise God, praise the jihad, and praise the Cleric," Deghani enthused. "If the materials are going to America, I know how they can be delivered."

The Iranian went on to describe the route. A trawler would take the container across the Aral Sea to the best route across Uzbekistan, then unloaded and driven overland to Iran and refined further at a laboratory to make the particles more lethal, durable, and easier to disseminate. The new mixture would be packed into a load of rugs and taken by truck to a private port west of Bander Abass on the Arabian Sea, and placed into a Eurobox for shipping.

"Eurobox?" asked Ehmat.

"This container is deeper than the eight-by-nine twenty-footer," explained Deghani. "We'll load this on a repainted and renamed bulk carrier, and go across the Red Sea through the Suez Canal to Port Said. From there the carrier will sail for Gioia Tauro and wait for a legitimate carrier. The container of rugs and your merchandise, along with a bill of lading, a commercial invoice, certificate of conformity, documentation for the consignee to clear customs, and any other required goods-for-transit papers, will be loaded onto a ship going west via the Mediterranean through the Strait of Gibraltar to the Atlantic. I can guarantee its docking in New York, though the ship will probably be diverted to Port Newark to be checked for any illegal materials such as those used in 'dirty' devices."

"Like uranium and plutonium oxide."

"Exactly. When no such substances are detected, the vessel will unload at the docks. Your cargo container can then be picked up and taken anywhere by truck, even lower Manhattan."

Ehmat and ibn-Sultan exchanged glances. "We will contact you on the specifics once we confer with our Russian friend, Grigory Pluchenko," said Ehmat. "He is providing access to the island."

"Why do we need you for more than arranging the shipment?" asked ibn-Sultan.

"I will insure you get the final materials you want. You see why this project is so expensive."

"This is now clear," ibn-Sultan said. "Can you store the materials in case our distribution includes locales other than New York City?"

"For a small extra charge."

Reza Deghani rose to leave. "Please allow me," he said and put down money for the meal. "We will call you."

"Until then." Ibn-Sultan remained seated while shaking Deghani's hand. Ehmat stood and did likewise.

"What did you think?" Ehmat asked once Deghani had gone.

"Nothing matters if we are successful. The fear Reza suggested the Americans have evoked in their own people will work to our advantage. Like a mass hypnotic suggestion, the stories may do as much damage as the product itself."

"Is Reza necessary or should we go directly to Pluchenko?"

"We will work with Reza so he does not become a liability. He also gives Pluchenko someone to turn on, should he need."

"You don't trust the Russian."

"He will help fulfill our contract with the Azeri, but is an infidel without any higher purpose than the accrual of money." Ibn-Sultan paused. "What building did you have in mind?"

"There are several possibilities. Airport terminals and indoor sports arenas are the best targets. They have many people, confinement, and easy access for us."

"Go over likely buildings with your team and research the possibilities. When you decide, we'll need the necessary contacts, identification, and our employees in place six months before. Consider vendors and concessionaires as well."

"Right away."

"Very well. I have something else I wish to discuss with you."

The men strolled through Khomeini Square and the public garden following the coast road. On Fridays the garden was crowded with people, but tonight the men only encountered trysting couples unable to afford the privacy of a hotel room. Ibn-Sultan turned from the lovers with disgust, a puritan in worker's clothing.

""You are the only one I trust with the project I have in mind," he began. "This must not be compromised."

"You can depend on my devotion, ibn-Sultan."

"I want to have a dozen videos made of me and the same number of you, and both of us together. Should anything ever happen, the survivor will use these as live broadcasts to our fellow Muslims. The tapes will encourage our friends to continue our cause and keep fear in the hearts of our enemies."

"I see."

"A writer is needed for scripts on financial depression and war, the death of certain world leaders, even the unlikely possibility of American victories. The scripts must be vague so the world will project its own appropriate interpretation."

"Sounds like quite an undertaking."

"The scripts are the most challenging aspect. We need the help of a politically astute writer."

"What if one of us is killed and our identities are made positive in the newspapers?"

"Our medical and dental records have disappeared. The Americans could kill us on CNN and our people would not believe what they see. The Muslim world mistrusts anything the Americans do, and most of the Europeans as well. Once they see one of our videos, any American claims will be scoffed at. The videos should suggest our people not to be mislead by Western propaganda or photos easily generated by computer."

"What if something should happen to us both?"

"We are going to be very cautious about meeting again. Meanwhile, I want you to find me cell members with certain specialties."

"The number of men involved in our plans is growing."

"I want a cameraman experienced in video production, a makeup artist, and a expert at editing on computer. Find me nondescript locations that could be anywhere. We will also need a cook and driver for a van or small bus. The locations should have no landmarks. We do not want anyone dating the videos by something that may no longer exist."

"You mean because of American bombing."

"One more thing. Find people who have no families. They have to travel without taking any leave for the duration of the project."

———

Elizabeth lingered over breakfast and coffee at her desk, dressed in a severely cut brown business suit. She pushed aside the plate and read a chapter of Trollope's *The Small House at Allington* before replacing it with a week-old *New York Times* article recapping recent Washington budget revisions to augment Homeland Security forces.

She put the novel in the desk drawer and checked her notes for the week. Today she had to meet the Chinese ambassador to discuss the delicate issue of the Kazakh oil sale. The Chinese wanted her support to buy trainloads of crude from Kazakhstan and could affect the amount of oil available to the new pipeline between the Caspian and Ceyhan. Currently the oil production in the Azeri fields was 75 percent less than projected and weakened oil prices threatened to make the Ceyhan pipeline commercially unfeasible. Even without the Chinese drain on supplies, the pipeline required an additional billion barrels of reserves added to the volume, likely from Kazakhstan, or British Chemical would have to spend another billion dollars on the project.

Elizabeth also had the forthcoming journey to Ceyhan with the Energy Secretary. She penciled the date in the staff meeting agenda scheduled for later in the week. She liked morning meetings, a routine from her early days in the diplomatic corps.

Her secretary, Sarah Edwards, leaned in the doorway. The young woman looked dowdy in long tartan skirt and shapeless white blouse with wide collar, and needing fashion tips if she planned to advance in the Foreign Service. "There's a call for you from the Turkish commerce attaché."

"Okay, Sarah, I'll take it."

Elizabeth picked up the telephone. "Madame Ambassador," the caller said, "my name is Osman Yanbou. I am the new Turkish representative here in Almaty."

"Welcome, Mr. Yanbou. How can I help?"

"I would like to meet and discuss the forthcoming event at Ceyhan, so we may coordinate the details of the ceremony."

"A good idea, Mr. Yanbou," Elizabeth agreed. "Check my schedule with my secretary."

"I have already done so, Madame Ambassador, with your approval, I hope."

"You are steps ahead of me. Is my schedule full?"

"Not this afternoon around two, Madame."

"My secretary seems to be running my affairs. How is two o'clock for you, Mr. Yanbou?"

The Turkish attaché laughed. "Two is fine."

"All right, Mr. Yanbou, we'll meet at two."

"I look forward to our introduction, Madame Ambassador."

She heard a click and returned the telephone to its cradle. Elizabeth called Sarah on the intercom and told her to come to her office. She read her mail and her secretary entered fidgeting with a ballpoint pen.

"You have committed your first mistake," Elizabeth said sternly.

"What have I done?"

"Relax. It's not the end of the world, Sarah. I need you to be aware of office protocol."

"Are you referring to the call from the Turkish attaché?"

"My schedule is my own business. You should have checked with me before telling him I was available."

"It won't happen again, I promise."

"We're vulnerable in a foreign land. There are lots of problems here," Elizabeth said, softening her tone.

"I apologize."

"Let's get back to work. Cancel my appointments next month from the 19th through the 27th. I'll be traveling to Baku and meet Mr. Strauss on the 19th, then to Ceyhan for the ceremony."

"I'll have your airline tickets and your hotel accommodations confirmed, Madame Ambassador."

"Thank you, Sarah." She might have been too hard on the girl, but Shaw and his friend had scared her the other night with their warnings. The Azeri would never abduct anyone, especially not an American ambassador.

———

The Golden Gate Bridge in San Francisco glimmered in the sunlight of a false spring. Ali Massouf walked down Hyde Street with his knees straining and shins aching from the steep slope to the Embarcadero. Tourists shivered in tee shirts printed with "Alcatraz Swim Team" and avoided the silver painted mime. Sea lions barked mournfully from the piers. Massouf ignored the homeless people looking for handouts.

Several fishermen lined the wharf ahead. Vietnamese, he realized when he got closer. Ahead of him the dark shape of Alcatraz Prison rose like a dark scar on an otherwise beautiful view.

A merchant vessel moved slowly past and left a noisy wake that slapped at the pilings. Massouf raised the collar of his tan topcoat against the fog, facial scars from fighting in Afghanistan livid in the chill. He walked along Pier 45 until finding Minnelli's Italian Restaurant promising fresh seafood. A man near the entrance stretched and turned his gaze toward him. FBI? Massouf went ten feet past him and watched two seagulls fight over the remains of an abandoned crab salad sandwich.

The man was not a federal agent, made obvious when a woman came out of the restaurant and took his arm. Massouf turned into the restaurant for his meeting with Samir Mohammad, working under the name Sammy Hammond. He stood at the hostess stand and strained to see Mohammad among the waiters inside or on the patio setting out silverware and condiments for the dinner rush.

Four women in a booth in the corner of the dining room were the only customers. He had come an hour late for lunch, and an hour early for dinner.

The hostess appeared. "Table for one?" she asked. "Inside or out?"

Massouf hesitated until he saw Mohammad coming around the corner with a tray. Mohammad gave him a nod of his head and put the tray down on a cart near the four customers.

"Inside," Massouf told the hostess. Mohammad was at his table a few moments later.

"Ali," he said. "Good to see you."

"Are you enjoying San Francisco, Samir?"

"Very much. Even with the temptation in this city, I keep my prayers."

"We need to talk."

"I will be off within the hour. Wait for me and I'll bring you something to eat."

"Something light. Minestrone."

Massouf picked at the vegetables in his soup and watched diners straggle in. Outside a waiter lit the heat lamps among the patio tables. Samir Mohammad grew up in Baltimore, the son of a Turk father and Kurd mother. He went to high school and went on to the Massachusetts Institute of Technology, where he graduated with honors in chemical engineering. His parents had dropped their devotion to Islam, and Mohammed converted to the religion while visiting Saudi Arabia. He had been a respected scientist with a teaching position in Amman. Now the nervous man with the large nose and small ears dressed in waiter's whites to serve infidels.

Mohammad finished his shift and brought a bottle of Pellegrino sparkling water with two glasses to Massouf's table. He poured the water and the men talked quietly.

"I was surprised when you left the university."

"Jordanian security had me under close observation and my colleagues told them of my affiliation with ibn-Sultan. I could not do my duty to jihad."

"No matter. Our fight is everywhere."

"Mine was a case of their bigotry and racism. Shi'ites and Sunnis read a different *Qur'an*. What brings you here?"

"We need your help to distribute certain materials in an enclosed area to create a gas-chamber effect.

"Powder or liquid?"

"Powder."

"Small chamber or large?"

"Large. We have in mind an indoor sports facility."

"We will need a way to get the material into the air vents directly in front of the blowers. For what you have in mind, there must be high airflow rates and a large quantity of source powder to insure an extended delivery in high concentrations. This takes hours to distribute enough for significant damage in a space that size. We can use a propellant such as butane or Freon to push through the air system. Of course, the access should be unlimited."

"Of course."

"At the school research lab, I worked with dust feeders and several types of nebulizers to simulate aerosol exposures. For simulating large particle inhalation and sampling, we used a low velocity wind tunnel to distribute main and side-stream smoke and gases into various testing chambers. I can design some technical instrumentation that might serve your needs. What kind of schedule?"

"What kind do you need?"

"Six months, a laboratory, and money for supplies."

"Very well. You have to relocate to New York."

Mohammed drank the last of his water. "Let's go."

"You're not going to say good-bye?"

"I think not."

"Then we will be on our way."

CHAPTER 4

Damascus showed the signs of being 3500 years old: black streaks on buildings from decades of smog, streets lumpy from patched potholes, and exhibits in the National Museum speckled with dead flies. For Eric LaGrange, the decay of the city held more honesty and mystery than any Illinois strip mall. He renewed his affection for Damascus in the taxi ride from the airport, soon as he saw the walls and dome of the Omayyad Mosque. LaGrange paid the driver and walked upstairs to his apartment. Paint chipped off the arch leading to the truncated kitchen and revealed pink beneath the aquamarine. On the table near the one window were his books, the sunned and broken spines of *Muslim Jurisprudence and the Quranic Law of Crimes* and the *Bibliography of Islamic Law,* and the *Qur'an* in Arabic, English, and French. His studies were more important than the Agency's targets, problems, and threats.

Sunni, Shi'i, Alawites, and Ibadi Muslims agreed on the principles of Shahada, "No God but God, and Muhammad is his messenger;" Salat, the prayer said five times a day; Zakat, the giving of alms; Sawm, fasting during Ramadan; and Hajj, the pilgrimage to Mecca. How the hadiths, stories about the life of Muhammad, were interpreted by centuries of theologians caused the different divisions. LaGrange read the texts with glasses of mint tea and became confused. "Islam" translated as submission to the will of God, and the Arabic root word gave "salam" or peace, and "salama" or security. How could orthodox clerics call for jihad from this source?

The cell phone rang from the soiled clothing still in his black duffel bag. "Ooh baby, now let's get down tonight/Baby I'm hot just like an oven/I need some lovin'," sang Marvin Gaye as the tone. LaGrange rummaged in his dirty shirts for the Nokia and pressed the green telephone icon.

"I've been home for all of twenty-four hours, Shaw. The possibility of traveling for you again is slight."

"Elizabeth Paige is missing, abducted we think. Maybe you want to jump in here."

"When and where?"

"Our embassy in Almaty, yesterday afternoon. I have a car coming to take you to the airport."

"I'm there."

———

Roger Shaw had finished interviewing the Marine guards the Embassy when LaGrange arrived. They escorted Sarah Edwards into an office off the reception hall. She wore another of her tartan skirts and a tan blouse with a flopping bow. Sarah twisted a sodden cambric handkerchief around her knuckles and sat in a heavy club chair.

"Tell us what happened, Ms. Edwards," said Shaw.

"This isn't my fault. I know my job and always have good evaluations. Sure, I haven't been promoted as fast as I'd like, but I'm learning. Ambassador Paige was always kind to me."

"You're not under suspicion. We need facts to figure out who took her and why. If you want a moment to compose yourself, we can wait."

"I'm fine. Ambassador Paige had an appointment in the afternoon with Mr. Yanbou Osman. He's the Turkish commerce attaché. I knocked on her office door when he left and she didn't answer and I went in."

"Is this customary, to go into her office if she isn't there?"

"No, maybe. I had papers she wanted and thought she'd just stepped out. The garden door was open so I left the papers. Her three o'clock appointment arrived, Ambassador Xiang. I went to her office and the garden door was still open. Then I saw her reading glasses and silk scarf on the grass."

"When did you alert security?"

"Right away. I told Mr. Xiang the Ambassador had a family emergency. He was nice enough but he stank like he needed a bath for weeks. I know this sounds wrong, except if you've spent any time around the man. We have to air out the building after he visits."

"Show us the papers you put on her desk."

"They're in her office."

Sarah led the men to Elizabeth's office and handed Shaw the papers. He flipped through the press releases, itineraries for the Baku trip, and pipeline reports.

"Thanks, Sarah, for being so helpful."

"There's something else," she sniffled. "Earlier I told Mr. Yanbou she had time at two. Ambassador Paige bawled me out for giving him the information. She said I should be careful about her schedule. This is my fault."

"You saw Yanbou?"

"Yes, and his assistant."

"Good. We'll have you can go over a few photos and talk to our sketch artist. Eric, any questions for Sarah?"

"Not until later. Will you excuse us?"

Sarah backed out of the room apologetically. Shaw leaned against the Ambassador's oak desk and sighed. He patted his jacket for cigarettes he had quit three years ago.

"Don't take this personal, Shaw. Elizabeth ignored our warning and now she's missing, and we'll find her."

"A man would be easy. Look for the parlor maid, intern, or secretary with the big eyes and there he'll be, fat and happy with lust. I've run to ground I don't how many diplomats who've taken a flyer on a woman.

Paige? She's a machine, government flack all day, every day. Someone had to grab her."

"Who was in charge of the security detail when the ambassador disappeared?"

"A young pup named Lieutenant Lind who saw Yanbou and his assistant leave. I'd put my money on Yanbou for the snatch. The timing works. He came in for his two o'clock with the Ambassador and went outside to the garden where an accomplice or several were waiting."

"Involving the gardener and his helpers. The visitor's parking area faces the tree line and the subdued Paige could have been shoved in the trunk. Where's the gardener?"

"He hasn't come in today."

The telephone on the oak desk rang. Shaw answered and rattled questions at the caller. LaGrange tapped a pane of the garden doors with a fingernail and turned the Paige problem over in his mind. The telephone conversation ended with a slam of the receiver.

"The attaché Elizabeth Paige met with was a fake. They found the real one dead in his shower with two bullet holes in his head."

———

The faded yellow Econoline van struggled along the narrow mountain road leading to Kzyl-Orda and the Sea of Aral. Nine hundred kilometers of bad or nonexistent road made the men restless while their cargo remained in drugged sleep. The vehicle passed a small village of mud huts and yurts scattered among the dark boulders on the slope of the mountain. Yakir Arvatian tapped the driver on the shoulder and asked him to pull over.

The men emptied from the van, stamped their feet for circulation, and pissed on the barren soil. They had followed Arvatian's incursions into Azerbaijan to sabotage oil production. The brothers, Hassan and Anatoly Abratov, were Khirgiz mercenaries who learned warfare in Chechnya, Ali Massouf had fought alongside Abu Abdullah and been credited with several operations against the Soviets in Afghanistan, and Suleyman Ehmat, the Turk.

Tea was made over a small brazier in a copper pot and the driver handed plastic cups around. The six sat on their haunches and listened to Arvatian.

"Our mission begins when we deliver the Azeri baggage. Let me bring a little history into our discussion."

"We need to know our roles in today, not yesterday," said Ehmet.

Arvatian turned to meet the Turk's gaze. Hassan took a sip of his tea and held the liquid in his cheeks. The taste was terrible and he contemplated whether to swallow or spit. He swallowed.

"Yesterday decides today," Arvatian said, raising his voice. "In 1988, Russian scientists transported hundreds of tons of anthrax bacteria out of the country in stainless steel canisters, enough to destroy the world's population many times over."

Hassan moved closer to Arvatian. "Transported by train?"

"Yes, two dozen cars. They sent the cargo a thousand kilometers across Russia and Kazakhstan to the Aral Sea." Arvatian pointed at the map spread out on the dirt in front of him. He rapped his knuckle on the Caspian region. "This is where they brought the bacteria, to Vozrozhdeniye Island, or Rebirth Island, right here." He drew a circle with his finger around the location.

"Once they arrived on the island, soldiers dug huge pits and buried the canisters. The island was the major Soviet Union open-air biological testing site. Russian scientists had a whole complex of laboratories there to test anthrax and typhus, botulism toxin, and smallpox, anything that might be useful in warfare. Thousands of animals were killed in the tests. We are going to Rebirth Island, the world's largest anthrax burial ground, and shared by Uzbekistan and Kazakhstan."

"We're the search and recovery team?" asked Anatoly Abratov. He was a big man with a drooping mustache. His large hands and thick fingers toyed with a string of beads.

"Exactly. Central Asian and American officials have always feared that if access to the island becomes easier, the buried anthrax will be dug up by thieves."

Ehmet frowned. "Or the righteous fulfilling the Cleric's call for jihad. Are we safe to dig?"

"Of course, the anthrax can't escape the canisters. The laboratories still exist, but the buildings are empty of any staff." Arvatian rose from the dirt. "We shall talk logistics later. Suleyman and Ali, come with me. The rest of you check on our passenger and be ready to leave."

The stars were bright and a pale quarter moon neared the horizon.

"Did Reza Deghani explain everything?" Arvatian asked the Turk.

"In broad terms only," said Ehmat.

"We have anthrax to retrieve on Rebirth Island. The passenger goes to the Azeri," Arvatian said, and began detailing the task.

Elizabeth Paige woke alone in the dark of the van. Her head ached and her body was stiff from being cramped in one position for so long. They had drugged her with sodium pentothal, Elizabeth familiar with the indiscrete euphoria of dental surgery. She heard voices and tried not to move. One of the voices belonged to Osman Yanbou, the man who claimed to be the commerce attaché.

The van's engine strained as it climbed the steep road and she assumed they were going up a mountain. A blindfold tied tightly around her head explained the headache. She felt helpless in complete darkness. How was it possible to have been abducted in daylight? Elizabeth had bragged about the Marine guard. Where were they now?

Osman's credentials had checked out before his visit. The identification papers must have been stolen from the Turkish commerce attaché to gain entry to the embassy grounds. He had been admitted to her office and his assistant waited outside. They chatted about several issues around the pipeline and he stood at the window to admire the garden. Elizabeth decided to finish their business while walking the grounds. A third man had waited for them. What happened afterwards was a blur. They had taken her into the building through another door and then out the service entrance on the other side of the building where the delivery trucks pulled in.

Sarah must have alerted security at the embassy and everyone knew she was missing. Maybe Roger Shaw had been called. She heard a man say "Yakir." The name Yakir Arvatian had been in an intelligence report on active followers of the Cleric. What reason would he have to abduct her? She considered her work on the pipeline, and how she persuaded several heads of state in the Caspian region to join Turkey in the construction of the pipeline. Perhaps her kidnappers were supporters of the proposal to build a network of pipeline under the Caspian between Turkmenistan and Kazakhstan.

Her critics complained her favoring of the Baku-to-Ceyhan route stole the oil from the Russians and added to the growing friction between the United States and the Caspian basin's superpowers, Iran and Russia. They warned the pipeline could ignite an arms race in the Caucasus, and force the American government and US corporations deeper into the Turkish campaign against Kurdish insurgents. Elizabeth believed a conflict with Russia was always a possibility, no matter the issue. If Russia controlled the route of oil, the disputes over the division of seabed borders among the respective Caspian states would continue, because Iran and Russia were claiming the right to veto any partition they deemed unfavorable to their own interests.

Elizabeth fought for the longer 1100-kilometer route from Baku to Ceyhan despite the fifty percent cost increase from not taking the oil from Kazakhstan to Novorossiysk. The Baku route bypassed the narrow busy shipping lanes on the Bosporous Strait between the Black Sea and the Mediterranean. Oil spills along the course would cause major problems to the most heavily populated region of Turkey and the Ceyhan port already had the capacity to handle large tankers. Unlike the Russian route, the Baku pipeline would not have to shut down for two months of the year because of weather. The Ceyhan port's proximity to markets in Europe was a huge advantage.

With the pipeline practically finished, nothing would be gained by her abduction. Elizabeth had her position and hard work, but no real political power to influence any other outcome or the money to pay a ransom. Why bother abducting her if they were going to destroy the pipeline? Many factions opposed Western interests in the region.

I'm in real trouble, she told herself, and wanted to weep. The fear overwhelmed her. She might never see her daughter Amelia again. She might be tortured and killed. Elizabeth could not give way to the fear. If she could think about something else for a few minutes, she would survive. She focused on how her bones and muscles ached, and relaxed into the pain. Next she tried feeling through the fear. Stop thinking about what you fear, see this as an interesting sensation in the body like adrenaline, a knot in the solar plexus.

Elizabeth counted her breaths until the panic had passed. She moved on to her immediate environment. There was the smell of sweat and another odor, like dirt or muddy shoes. A window was cracked and the outside breeze slipped into the vehicle. They passed vegetation, she knew, because there was a hint of mustard in the air and fresh basil. She listened to the men, maybe Turkish, and they broke into laughter as though setting off on some great adventure. They were having fun like old friends going on an expedition or a fishing trip. She hated them for enjoying her capture, hated how the locals refused to see the growth guaranteed by the pipeline, and hated Burt Strauss for offering to pay for the abortion.

No more hate. Elizabeth accepted her death was imminent and pain extremely likely. She wanted to make peace with her life.

Northern California in 1979 was agriculture and lumber, and fishing boats on the coast filled their nets with salmon. The peaked-roof and columned Tooler house in Redding buzzed with chaos for Elizabeth's going-away party. Elizabeth had come home for the summer after graduating from Hastings College of Law, ready for her next move to Boston and Harvard. Her parents argued upstairs, and the caterers setting tables on the brick patio were irritated with each other. The gardener cursed in Spanish at the electrical cord strung across the lawn he had run over with the mower. Elizabeth called into the house, "I'm off to the cabin. I'll be back for the party." After a pause, her mother shouted back the warning a geologist had rented the cabin.

She jumped in her red Toyota and backed out of the driveway. Some geologist was always using the cabin. This one would have to camp in the woods or find a motel in town because she was spending the night. She turned the radio on to a classic rock station and listened to Credence Clearwater Revival ask if she had ever seen the rain. Elizabeth tapped the steering wheel to the bass line as she turned west on Highway 299.

She breathed easier once in the Six Rivers National Forest and protected by the sequoias. Driving through the huge trees, Elizabeth was awed by the magnitude of such living things at least a thousand years old. The forest made her feel insignificant and important at the same time. She would miss the trees at Harvard.

Elizabeth parked the car outside of Willow Creek and sat under one tree, her favorite. The sequoia was like an old friend. Today the sun filtered through branches shimmering from a light breeze at the top. She leaned against the cool bark and closed her eyes. Juncos called across the forest, squirrels chattered, flies buzzed, and then a snap of dry twigs.

She sat up startled. A tall, brown haired man said, "Sorry, I didn't mean to surprise you. The name's Burt Strauss." In his jeans, boots, and faded sweatshirt, he exuded a quiet energy, an irresistible gentleness.

They talked in the way strangers do when attracted to each other. Strauss was the geologist her mother warned her about. They walked to her car and she gave him a ride to the cabin. He cooked steaks over a fire and shared his only bottle of wine. Being the child of former flower children, Elizabeth welcomed him into the cabin's single bed with no questions or expectations.

In the morning she took him to the corral and pasture, a few miles south of the Hoopa Valley Indian Reservation. The smell of the earth and air and woods made her hungry for more. They galloped on horseback over a path through the grand sequoias, reveling in the intense pleasure of being new lovers.

Elizabeth had to leave for her party and she and Strauss parted. She drove home, showered and dressed, and greeted her guests, not expecting to see him again. Later that night she saw him on the patio, drinking beer with her father. He worked for Standard Oil and wanted to recruit Strauss.

"Thanks for the offer, Mr. Tooler, but I'm already signed on with British Chemical Enterprises. Overseas is where I want to be, next to the fields instead of the office."

Elizabeth excused herself and left them talking about the petroleum industry and the ongoing quest for new and richer oil fields. Their conversation was nothing new to her. Before the party was over, Strauss approached her. "Can I see you again?"

Behind him her mother waved from where she was sitting with a young man in a tweed jacket.

"I'm leaving tomorrow," Elizabeth said.

"My business takes me even to places like Cambridge."

"That's where you'll find me."

He touched her hand and she left him. When she looked back, he had a look on his face she mistook for love.

She and Strauss spent time together when he came to town, and lovemaking played counterpoint to her studies. Over chowder in a tavern near the campus, Elizabeth told him she was pregnant. She had grown from the young girl without expectations who asked for nothing. Strauss told her of his marriage and three children. For two years he had lied. Elizabeth ran out of the cafe, down the street into the Harvard Square Bookshop, through the rows of books, out the back door, and up the alley to catch a cab a few blocks away.

Her best friend at Harvard was another political science major, Thomas Reardon Paige, a Scotch–Irish Catholic homosexual rejected by his family for his sexual preference. God bless Tommy. A letter came from Strauss and Paige held her while she cried. Strauss sent news he was leaving for the Saudi oil fields, and money for an abortion.

"Sweetie," Paige said. "It's not the end of the world. Most men don't do this much."

She scheduled the abortion and Paige went with her. They stopped at a park not far from the clinic. Elizabeth held her tears as he hummed under his breath, a habit that annoyed her, but this day gave comfort.

She had not told her parents. They would worry their daughter had jeopardized her scholarship status. The sexual revolution was still being contested at Harvard. Elizabeth sat on a bench, not thinking for she had done all the thinking she could stand.

Paige stopped humming. "Sweetie," he said, "Say you have the baby. We could get married and give the child a name. Paige isn't such a bad one if you don't count all the thieves in my family history."

She stared at him in disbelief. "Okay, you don't like Paige. How about Reardon? We'll live together and I'd help with the baby, then after you graduate, we'll get a divorce."

"I want the baby, I do. I can't give it up."

He put his arm around her and she leaned on his shoulder. "Shall we have the child baptized Catholic?"

"Let's not," she said.

Her parents accepted her pregnancy and even were excited. They had no idea Strauss was the father of their beautiful granddaughter, Amelia Reardon Paige. They did look askance at Thomas Paige, but never said a word, former hippies they were.

For five years Elizabeth and Amelia lived with Paige and his lover, Peter Hankshaw, named Petey Pete by Amelia. Between the three of them, they finished college and graduate school, took care of Amelia through diapers, teething, colic, day care, toddler-hood, and preschool. They found good jobs and generally had a good time. Elizabeth loved the two men and remained good friends even after she got a job in Washington, DC with the Foreign Service. They continued to spend time with her and Amelia. They were family.

Six years after Elizabeth settled in Washington, Paige died of leukemia and the grieving Hankshaw moved to Europe. She and Paige never filed for the divorce they had planned. "You're still Catholic," she had teased him. Paige held on to every commitment he made.

When Strauss appeared in her life again, he did not know Amelia was his child and how Elizabeth sustained herself for years on the anger she had for him. She developed an indifference to Strauss, and being in the same business, saw the wisdom of getting along. They had a strained friendship, though he would have taken more had she let him.

The possibility of dying made her think about Strauss. To die with him not knowing his daughter made her sad. She wanted to forgive him and herself and tell Amelia her biological father lived. She would have to tell Strauss the truth, too.

A man spoke from the front of the vehicle. There was the sound of a zipper, the rustle of paper, and the click of plastic hitting plastic as though someone searched through a bag of cosmetics. A man grabbed her shoulder and manhandled her into a position to accept a jab in the arm. The cold liquid of the drug entered her vein.

CHAPTER 5

Rebirth Island was hot and stripped of plant life, the landscape blasted into the muted browns and grays of desolation. The division settled on by the two countries made the north Kazakhstan territory, and the south in Uzbekistan. Since 1936, when the island came under the control of the Red Army, the island had been used for biological experiments. A test site known as "Aralsk–7" was built in 1954 and included a military settlement of warehouses, barracks, schools, and power generator. Earthmovers brought by ship leveled the hard ground into landing strips for the Barkhan Airport, and a seaport and docks were built at Udobnaya Bay.

Surrounding the island, the Aral Sea is fed by the depleted Amu Darya and Syr Darya rivers. Irrigated cotton farms on the mainland took most of the water and what was released carried chemical fertilizers. The Aral Sea has shrunk by half since the 1960s. New islands poke out of the sea inhibiting navigation, but few vessels have need of the Aral. Russia quit Rebirth Island in 1991, and dismantled the laboratories and sealed the remaining buildings. Kazakhs and Uzbeks stripped the island of any remaining equipment and abandoned the land to the poisons.

The blue and yellow fishing trawler was an anachronism from when the sea supported commercial fishing, the processing plant on the mainland having fish shipped by train to keep the conveyors rolling. Aging Captain Velikanov watched his lone crewman tie a thick rope around the decaying capstan as Yakir Arvatian walked the creaking boards of the Udobnaya dock.

"Stay here," he warned. "I want to see inside."

The corrugated iron facings of the warehouses were torn and stained with rust. Signs had been replaced with Cyrillic warnings of contamination, and the doors chained and padlocked. Arvatian stopped at a door newer than the others and unlocked the chain from a ring of keys. He opened the cargo doors to stacks of wire animal cages scattered through the warehouse, some tipped over as if by a giant hand.

Arvatian called to the crew, "Bring the box." The Abratov brothers, Ali Massouf, and Suleyman Ehmat hoisted the coffin-size box on their shoulders and up the gangplank to the dock. They hastened their pace despite the weight. The warehouse was quiet inside and the men could hear the wind howling through the cracks in the walls.

"Over there," ordered Arvatian. "Be gentle with her."

The men placed the container next to a large cage. Captain Velikanov studied the open crates containing dirty metal canisters in a neat line against the wall.

"They have poisons here, Mr. Arvatian?"

"No, the labs are on the other side of the island. The cages are from testing biological weapons on animals. When the Vozrozhdeniye site was operational, monkeys, sheep, and even horses and donkeys came through these docks. The cans are harmless. That's what we're taking back with us. Suleyman, have the crates nailed shut and take them to the trawler. I want to sail in under an hour."

Arvetian put his hand on Anatoly Abratov's shoulder. "You and Hassan are in charge of our prisoner. Don't trust the Azeri," he warned the Khirgiz. "With plenty of weapons and ammunition, they should keep their promises."

"Any tricks will be answered by my Kalashnikov. I spent enough time fighting the stinking Soviet army to know how to use the unexpected as a tool of defense."

Arvatian smiled at him. Anatoly Abratov was his most loyal

lieutenant. Their acquaintance spanned several years, from before Arvatian joined the Followers of the Cleric.

A noise came from the box.

"The woman is waking. The drugs are wearing off," Arvatian said. "Let her out for the moment. Don't harm her. She's no good if you scare her to death. Do you have your cell phone?"

"Yes, colonel," Abratov said.

"Keep the phone with you day and night. We must be in communication at all times. Wait for my instructions and keep the woman healthy."

The men pried open the lid of the wooden container and helped Elizabeth Paige to her feet. She was weak and held on Ali Massouf to steady herself. She wore a blindfold and her mouth was wrapped with silver duct tape. Her brown business suit and blouse were filthy from the box.

Arvatian took a digital camera from the pocket of his windbreaker. "Remove the blindfold and gag."

She winced when the tape came off and touched her mouth. Abratov noticed her hazel eyes, and judged her to be late thirties or early forties. The other men turned away, not wanting to see her uncovered legs. Elizabeth looked at the man holding the digital camera. He snapped several pictures of her and the flash blinded her momentarily.

"You are in good hands, madam," Arvatian said.

"Where are we?"

"On an island."

A chill coursed along Elizabeth's spine by the thought of being surrounded by water.

The cell phone in the man's windbreaker chirped. He turned his back to her and talked to the caller in Arabic. The large cages in the warehouse frightened her. Smaller ones were for animals, but the big cages had to be for humans. Smells of dried fecal matter and ammonia reminded her of dog runs and rabbit warrens, and judging by the crusted waste material, they had never been cleaned. They were going to put her in a cage.

Aravtian snapped his phone shut and spoke loudly to the others. The men hefted the crates on handcarts and began carrying them to trawler.

"Are you leaving me here?" Elizabeth asked.

"Do not be concerned, Madame Ambassador. I leave you with Anatoly Abratov. He is a capable, experienced man and will see to your needs."

"Could I have some water?"

"Anatoly will take care of that shortly."

Arvatian spoke with Abratov and pointed to a rusty cage less bent than the rest, and a working lock mechanism on the door. Elizabeth tried not to react as Abratov looked at her curiously. Arvatian barked more directions at the men, and Abratov opened the cage and pushed Elizabeth inside. Her acquiescence puzzled him. He disappeared and she stood in the middle of the cage, afraid to touch the rusty sides or sit on the dirty floor. Arvatian took another picture of her before leaving with his men.

Abratov returned with a straw mat and covered the floor of the cage. Elizabeth sat on the mat, glad to be off her feet. She shivered. The Khirgiz mercenary offered her a blanket, plate of unfamiliar stew, and a cup of water through the wires of the cage.

"You are so kind," she said.

"It is my pleasure," he said, without sarcasm. "Would you like to use the facilities?"

"Please."

"Follow me." She walked behind him to a door at the far side of the warehouse. "In there," he said. The bathroom windows were sealed tight with sheets of plywood nailed to the outside wall. Toilet and sink still worked, despite the negligence and how old she guessed they were. More men than women had been using them. The smell was definitely like a latrine.

If nothing else had been good since her capture, she could be thankful for this bathroom and her guard's fair treatment. She would dwell on the luxury of a dirty bathroom and the kindness of a stranger.

———

The STU–III secure telephone rang in the bedroom of the Devine home. John groped for his eyeglasses and cursed the buttons of the telephone. Stephanie rose from the bed, put on a dressing gown, and went to the kitchen for coffee. John rarely slept after a call.

"Devine here. Identify yourself."

"Roger Shaw. This connection is lousy."

"Complain to tech services. What's important at three in the morning? Anything about Elizabeth Paige's whereabouts?"

"Noon where I am, John. Complete silence about the Ambassador," Shaw answered. "Except for a rumor an American oil executive has gone missing as well, and not with his cooperation."

"How about the phony Turkish attaché?"

"Sarah, the secretary, gave our sketch artist a good description. I'll have a copy faxed to you."

"Tell me your location."

"Driving up a mountain in Uzbekistan. The view is incredible. I can see the Aral Sea from here. I'm going to Moynaq to meet locals who knew the Embassy gardening crew. There's an island in the sea where Soviets scientists did biological testing and stored a pile of viruses."

"Rebirth Island, home of the largest biological weapons testing facility. The Aral Sea used to be beautiful. Call me after your meeting."

Stephanie handed her husband a mug with "World's Greatest Spy" stenciled around the sides, a goofy Valentine's Day gift from her. "Bad news, baby?" she asked.

"Worse. No news or not enough to do anything about."

"Remember our pact. Don't tell me."

"I won't. Let's see if CNN is as awake as we are."

Shaw neared the small village of Moynaq, perched on a mountain plateau. The countryside was scattered with goats, camels, yaks and horseback riders. He stopped the Renault sedan for a better look. Shaw took out his binoculars and scanned the sea from the high ridge called

Tigrovi Hvost, translated as Tiger's Back. He could see what used to be the Aral Sea's southwestern shore.

The view from Tiger's Back was a window on the devastation in the Middle East. The remaining waters of the Aral were calm, as in dead, and the land so white with saline looked like a snowfield. The once huge seabed was largely a great saltpan cavity strewn with beached fishing boats.

A vessel anchored off the island caught Shaw's attention. Activity on Rebirth Island? He zeroed in on the ship. A trawler in near shallow water that no longer sustained fish was definitely a red flag. He got out his cell phone and punched in LaGrange's number.

"Yo," LaGrange answered.

"Hey, bud. Still at the Embassy?"

"A couple of people are hoping for a ransom call. Not me."

"Always the optimist. I need a satellite scan of the Aral Sea. Walk down the hall and ask the boys to produce."

"On it," LaGrange said and hung up.

After finishing the interviews in Moynaq, Shaw headed down to the Aral Sea. He called John Devine.

"Almost thirty-six hours and no trace of her," Devine said. "The news is going to break soon."

"I'm running down activity on Rebirth Island and LaGrange has requisitioned a scan on the area. Did biological testing cause all this devastation to the Aral?"

"Russians siphoned water from the two rivers that feed the sea to irrigate cotton. Thirty years later and you have the world's largest environmental disaster."

"Damn if you don't have an encyclopedic mind."

"Any more news on the rumored male American captive?"

"Nothing. The embassy gardener only recently hired two helpers, both Uzbek."

"They live in Moynaq?"

"Evidently the gardener spent some time there. According to reports, he was seen at the local coffee house several times with the Uzbeks. All three disappeared when Elizabeth Paige did." Shaw watched the twisting road, and the map spread on the passenger seat fluttered in the breeze coming through the open window.

"Pull in your favors and get me solid information I can make into a brief. The bureaucrats need a stronger supposition, if nothing else. Should we hope to hear from the abductors in the next twenty-four hours? The silence has been too long."

"I'll do what I can," Shaw said, turning to avoid a goat blocking his path. The animal ran to a ravine alongside the steep narrow road.

"Roger, you with me?"

"I'm listening."

"There was a meeting in Baku between your suspected Russian arms dealer Grigory Pluchenko and Reza Deghani, the Iranian intelligence agent. An Agency operative spotted them at the ferry dock after getting a tip. How's that for bad tidings?"

"Yes," Shaw said. "Any meeting with Pluchenko is not good."

"I don't know if there's any connection to Elizabeth Paige's abduction. We have to consider the possibility."

"Pluchenko works for money. Snatching an ambassador is too political for him."

"Have you talked to Burt Strauss recently?"

"Last I knew he was heading for Baku. I'll get in touch with him when I return to Almaty."

"Tell him about Elizabeth Paige. They've worked together on the pipeline."

Devine signed off and Shaw made a third call. "Eric, get Burt Strauss on the line, then get a hold of me."

He was halfway to Almaty before LaGrange called.

"About Burt Strauss. I haven't been able to run him down. No one has seen him in days and he's missed his appointments. Strange behavior this close to the pipeline opening."

"Thanks, Eric. Ask the staff to scare up a photo of Strauss."

"You placing him into the rumor you've been hearing?"

"I am."

———

After days inside a dark and drafty room smelling of chemicals, the man who delivered his food came for Burt Strauss. He shoved him with a rifle barrel jabbing his back across graveled grounds. Strauss counted the 182 very cold, sharp steps. He had been barefoot since his abduction at Petrova's flat and the rocks cut his feet. They stopped and he was pushed into a dimly lit warehouse to what looked like cages. They stopped at one and the man with the weapon shone a flashlight inside. Strauss looked at a figure on the floor, dead or asleep. "Elizabeth!"

"Get him out of here," Anatoly Abratov told his associate and waved them out. "Put the American back where you got him, and bring whoever decided he should be moved without consulting me."

The first light of dawn bathed the rusted structure with a soft pink color. As the sun rose higher, the building returned to its former rust. Light penetrated through the broken windows and the cracks in the walls. Abratov sat with his back to the wall, thinking about his prisoner. Her bearing reminded him of his grandmother, her smile of his mother before the days of invasion and war. His mother had smiled little those weeks before she died and had made him bitter. His prisoner? The woman harbored no ill will, and might have been a cleric instead of a politician. Her composure spoke well of the Americans. Abratov got up to make tea and passed the guards sleeping nearby.

———

Elizabeth opened her eyes and shifted her aching bones on the straw mat, careful not to touch the floor. She could see sun on the window through the bars of the cage and was grateful for another day alive. Two guards slept a few feet from the cage, their Kalashnikovs next to their bodies. One guard snored loudly and Abratov was not around.

Elizabeth yearned for a hot shower and a soft mattress. She dreamed Strauss had called to her from her bedroom doorway as though he had urgent news. She lost count of the hours she'd lived inside this cage. Elizabeth spent many of them thinking about Amelia, particularly the last time she had seen her in Paris.

The day had been bright, a temporary respite from winter's pewter skies, and they decided to go to lunch. In a cab heading down the wide boulevard of Avenue de l'Opéra, Amelia turned from the window to her mother. "What sounds good?"

"Anything. You decide."

"Les Deux Magots in Montemarte."

"Promise me you're not reading Simone de Beauvoir."

Soon they were sitting in Les Deux Magots with menus and Elizabeth was undecided. Nothing appealed to her. Amelia made a few suggestions and Elizabeth ignored each of them. "I'm not very hungry."

Amelia slammed down her menu. "You always do this, expect me to read your mind."

"What are you talking about?"

"I asked you what sounded good and there you are pouting."

"I am not pouting."

"You expect me to know what you want and choose to please you."

"I do no such thing."

"You always do."

"Give me another example."

Amelia was angry. "I can't think of one right now."

"The next time, let me know."

They ordered and peace was restored for the length of the meal. They paid the bill and were about to go off to the shops. "You're going to need some new things for the fall term. Let's go to Jacques."

"About the fall term. I've decided to take the year off."

"If you drop out now who knows what will happen. Going back after a long break is always so hard."

"We've discussed this a hundred times and you said the final decision was mine."

"Yes, but I thought we agreed you would go ahead and finish."

"Mom, you're pouting again. You say this is my decision, then you're disappointed and disapproving if I don't agree."

"I know what it is to struggle through school. I don't want that for you."

"This is my choice."

"You've never struggled. You don't have a clue."

"I'm never going to get one if you keep pushing me. Goodbye, Mother."

"My plane doesn't leave until this evening. Aren't we going to spend the afternoon together?"

"I can't." Amelia walked out of the cafe in tears and left Elizabeth stunned. Weeks went by before Amelia would accept Elizabeth's telephone calls. Ever since, their conversations had been guarded and strained. Amelia had been right. Elizabeth had planned Amelia's life in her own mind. She wanted to heal the rift between her and her daughter, and have Amelia know she trusted her no matter what she decided.

Elizabeth heard a commotion outside the warehouse. The two guards woke and jumped to their feet, weapons at the ready. Arvatian entered and moved to her cage. Elizabeth stood up. Anatoly Abratov shouted his name went on loudly in a dialect Elizabeth could not understand. Arvatian turned his attention to Elizabeth. He stared at her in the cage, her matted hair and filthy clothes.

"Are my men treating you fairly, Madame Ambassador?"

"Yes, thank you."

"I must apologize for the lack of beds or mattresses. Have you eaten?"

"No," she answered.

Arvatian turned to Abratov. "You are feeding her regularly, yes?"

"We share our meals with her."

"Good. Come with me, Anatoly. I have news. Let us walk outside and watch the sun rise."

"I have a question," said Elizabeth. "Is this the island where the Soviets tested their biological weapons?"

"Yes," Arvatian said, and the men walked out the door.

They returned later and approached the cage where Elizabeth sat cross-legged, her back away from the rusty bars. Her face looked gaunt and her eyes listless. Arvatian spoke to Abratov, who hurried outside.

"Here we are again, Madame Paige. I have ordered a cup of tea. Do you need to use the bathroom? I will escort you."

She stood while he unlocked the cage. She walked stiffly and her legs hurt. He followed her. She knew where she was going. Arvatian waited patiently until she emerged, her hair looking neater from a brisk finger combing. Elizabeth was an attractive woman for an infidel, and with a figure of a young girl. He admired her poise and unbroken spirit.

"Come," he said. "I will take you back."

"Do you think I could have daily walks in the sunshine for half an hour?"

The Ambassador seemed to have no animosity toward him. No wonder she was popular in Almaty. Elizabeth Paige was not what he'd expected. She stood tall with her shoulders pulled back and chin up.

"I will discuss with Anatoly."

"Thank you."

They were back at the cage and Arvatian held the door for her. Abratov came in carrying a tin cup of tea and the two men talked until Arvatian excused himself. Anatoly Abratov handed Elizabeth the steaming cup and she let the tea cool before taking a sip. It was delicious and warmed her.

The manila envelope sat face down on John Devine's desk. Inside were two photographs of Elizabeth Paige looking haggard behind bars. The photos had been sent overnight from London to the CIA's Counterterrorism Center without a name or note.

John Devine looked at the blank computer screen in his office. What had been mentioned in conversation had to be written into a brief, especially now he had proof of life. He hated writing briefs, the distillation of fieldwork into easy-to-digest chunks for those who wanted action without taking on responsibility. Devine took another sip from his coffee, scratched the bridge of his nose, and began typing.

"Operatives believe Ambassador Elizabeth Paige is being held on Rebirth Island, a former Soviet biological weapons testing facility in the Aral Sea.

"British Chemical Enterprises executive Burt Strauss has been missing since the evening before Ambassador Paige's abduction. He may also be on the island.

"The identity and political affiliation of the abductors are unconfirmed at this time. Two Uzbek men possibly helped in the abduction.

"Satellite scans show increased activity around Rebirth Island. A trawler has been spotted at the Udobnaya Bay dock.

"Ambassador Paige and Burt Strauss are American citizens who have been instrumental in the Baku-to-Ceyhan pipeline. Following our mandate of protecting Americans abroad, the military option must be considered.

"A Special Forces unit can be mobilized for a jump-in-jump-out rescue without loss of life. If this option is approved, complete discretion is advised for the continued safety of Americans overseas."

The signed document made the rounds of the CTC. Meetings were held and alternatives vetted until finally a decision was reached. Devine called Roger Shaw.

"We don't need another shock and awe spectacle," Devine said. "People are tired of war."

"Then keep the goddamn press away. That's all the current administration needs, pictures of a well-liked diplomat standing captive inside an animal cage. Anything we try to do will be a thousand times harder."

"Any word on who is behind the abduction?"

"Could be terrorists protesting Western interests in the region, or the Russians or Iranians. If the region appears physically unsafe and politically unstable, Westerners will be wary of investing. More than one nation is mad about Western financial support for the Baku-to-Ceyhan route, and we have a Turkish faction who does not approve of Turkey throwing in with the United States on this. Petro-National, the San Francisco-based company who thumbed their nose at Washington when they partnered on the Russian route from Kazakhstan to Novorossiysk, also has an interest in seeing the pipeline fail."

"There are lots of players. Whoever owns or controls the flow of oil will also control the global economy and the means to govern it long into this century. We already have border disputes and claims to ownership have turned into armed conflict and aggressive separatism throughout the region."

"In the meantime, we have to move. Make no mistake. Whoever abducted Ambassador Paige may kill her. The satellite scans should be enough to push the bureaucrats into action."

"Jesus, John, Rebirth Island is full of weapons-grade anthrax. Besides the toxin, the island is a diplomatic nightmare with Russia, Uzbekistan, and Kazakhstan. You're asking we use the Special Forces to piss off three countries."

"We get along with Uzbekistan and signed an agreement to help them remove all trace of anthrax from the island. Russia and Kazakhstan can fall into line."

"Tell them. According to the scans, the shrinking of the Aral Sea has uncovered a peninsula that allows anyone interested to wade to the island. No one's been keeping watch. De-commissioning the nuclear and rocket bases in Kazakhstan had the priority."

"I have a Special Forces team ready in Baku. Give me the go ahead, John."

"Is a successful rescue possible?"

"Not without bending the rules. Every minute we waste talking, we risk their lives."

"My brief has been sent to the White House as part of tomorrow morning's session. You have eighteen hours before the diplomatic solution is tossed around. Make me a believer in the covert option."

CHAPTER 6

Grigory Pluchenko reached across the prone nude form of Petrova for the ashtray and stubbed out his Dunhill cigarette. "Not a single gentle bone is in your Muscovite body," she said.

"To your pleasure, my dear slut. I prefer not to be weak like the other men you invite into your bed."

Petrova sat up from the tangled bed sheets and examined her bruises from the afternoon ordeal of lovemaking with Pluchenko. He bit, chewed, and clawed during sex. The thrill of orgasm was replaced with relief when the battering had stopped. She accommodated him for now. Her father, General Nickolai Pavlovich Verkhovtsev, had introduced them. The street thug wanted to smuggle large shipments of small arms from Russia and Petrova provided space in Caspian Works containers. More business opportunities followed.

"I have heard a rumor Ambassador Paige is missing," said Petrova. "Do you know about this?"

"Kamal ibn-Sultan's man, Yakir Arvatian, has taken her. She is probably with Strauss."

"Xiang is desperate for oil. He told me this morning if we do not find a producer to accommodate him, he must contact other sources. We have to get Strauss out of there. I will call Arvatian."

"Are you out of your mind, woman?"

"To deal with the Chinese, this is what must be done. I know how to approach Yakir."

"Go ahead, call him."

She picked up the cell phone and dialed a number. The phone rang a half dozen times before she got an answer. "Yes?" Arvatian answered.

"Petrova Verkhovtsev, Mr. Arvatian. I will come right to the point. It's about the American, Burt Strauss. I need him for a very lucrative oil venture and would appreciate your assistance. My appreciation comes with cash."

"We have already been paid and very well. The kidnapping of Strauss is a contract with the Azeri, who have been forced by the West to take extreme measures to have their voices heard. Talk to them and they might give you the American."

"You can name your price."

"I do not oppose this but my priorities take precedence."

"The oil deal is of paramount importance to us. Have the Azeri make their statement by killing Ambassador Paige and leave Strauss to me."

"I have in mind to kill them both."

"Think how Strauss can best serve your cause. If he sells out to the Chinese, the Americans lose political control of the region and the pipelines, and money will stay in the area. Followers of the Cleric have left us alone but the Americans have notions about making Muslims the world's villains. You have also obtained Russian armaments through my partner, Grigory Pluchenko. A businessman such as yourself knows the supplies can be stopped for any reason."

Arvatian made Petrova wait while he considered different actions. Whatever he said now could be ignored later. He needed time to consult with ibn-Sultan. "I understand, Miss Verkhovtsev. We will give you Strauss and keep the Ambassador. You may even use our humble fishing vessel to take him home."

"I will be at the island and retrieve him."

"Tomorrow then. My men expect you."

Petrova closed the cell phone. She could live with the bargain. Ambassador Paige had used what power she had in getting the Baku-to-Ceyhan route. The money could shift toward another route and Petrova wanted a finger into the Russian pipeline after completing the deal with the Chinese.

———

The team Yakir Arvatian had assembled for securing the Rebirth Island prisoners was under the command of Anatoly Abratov. More than forty men were scattered around the former Russian laboratories. Twice already, Abratov had encountered locals scavenging what was left of the laboratory equipment and structures. The bodies of these intruders rested at the bottom of the Aral Sea.

Other teams were busy as well. The Turkish contingent headed by Suleyman Ehmat prepared for an upcoming assignment at the Mediterranean port of Ceyhan.

Arvatian had fought in Afghanistan during Operation Enduring Freedom. Kamal ibn-Sultan had led his mercenaries and local fighters against the combat units, and killed scores in night raids and daily skirmishes. Arvatian had heard of ibn-Sultan's daring attacks and saw him as the next leader of the Followers of the Cleric. He had been right in his assessment.

The cell phone in his coat pocket vibrated. Arvatian stood on a hill overlooking Baku and the oilrigs dotted along the Caspian shore.

"Did Ali Massouf arrive?" ibn-Sultan said. He was always a man in a hurry.

"Yesterday."

"I tried to call him on his cell phone. I instructed you and your men to carry those phones day and night."

"I spoke to Ali barely thirty minutes ago. He'd been awake for almost thirty-six hours. He must have fallen asleep."

"Hear me, Yakir. There is much work left before we deliver another blow to the infidels."

"Perhaps I can help."

"Find Ali. Have him call me. I need him to travel as soon as possible."

"I should be the one."

"Stay in this region and direct the operation from here. Ali has lived in America for many years and best suited for this particular job. He has a legitimate American passport."

"I will locate him right away. Petrova Verkhovtsev wants the American man released for an oil deal with the Chinese. She might also bargain for the American woman."

"Let her have both and kill all three, along with whoever Verkhovtsev brings with her. Do not start a battle in the laboratories. I have plans for them."

"Did you say to kill Miss Verkhovtsev as well?"

"You know how passionate Russians can be. Pluchenko is likely to side with a seductress like her over a Muslim like me."

"Understood." He turned to the sound of footsteps on rock. "Here comes Ali now." He motioned to him and handed him the phone.

"Yes?" Ali Massouf said.

"Did you get the information?"

"Yes, I have it right here." He pulled a notebook from his pocket. "Madison Square Garden has its cigarette machines, vending machines, and restroom and cleaning supplies stocked by Apex Supply. City Casuals sells sports clothing, Triborough Distributing has the beer and pop concessions, and Starbucks serves coffee and snacks. Belvedere does the food concessions except for Viola's Gelato, Nathan's, and Del Taco."

"What was the gelato?"

"Viola's Gelato, an Italian company. Baskin-Robbins is trying to buy the New York franchise."

"Get me everything on the company and the owner, and I mean everything."

Ibn-Sultan signed off. Massouf held the silent phone and shielded his eyes from the glare of the Caspian Sea in the noonday sun.

———

Petrova Verkhovtsev arrived on Rebirth Island dressed in dark slacks, high boots, cotton pullover matching the color of her eyes, and an oyster Aquascutum overcoat. The sun arched over the scarred and stripped laboratories as the blue and yellow trawler docked at Udobnaya Bay. She did not trust ibn-Sultan and arranged for three of Pluchenko's men to meet her. Where and when? Anatoly Abratov greeted the trawler carrying a Kalashnikov and wearing a pistol and commando knife strapped on his web belt. He helped Petrova maneuver the wobbly gangplank from the vessel to the quay.

"Welcome to our once beautiful island," Abratov said.

"We have been smelling your paradise miles in advance."

"Be glad there is a breeze."

"I have come for the American. Has Yakir Arvatian informed you?"

"Yes, I've been told."

"Where are you keeping him?"

Abratov pointed at a warehouse with gaping holes in its decaying roof. "There."

"He is well and fed, I trust."

"We share our food with him and the ambassador. How was your journey aboard the luxury cruiser?"

"Captain Velikanov took good care of me."

Outside the warehouse, five men huddled in a circle holding tin cups of afternoon tea. Abratov and Verkhovtsev entered the building. The interior was dark except for the light from the sun almost to the horizon coming through broken windows and gaps in the walls. The large cage next to the wall contained a man who leaned against the cage bars as though asleep. Strauss opened his eyes and looked at Petrova with surprise. He struggled to get to his feet.

"I have come to help you," said Petrova. "The abduction was a mistake. I will explain later."

"Ambassador Paige is also here. We have to take her with us."

"Impossible. I used every favor I had negotiating on your behalf and told them I would pay a handsome bribe."

"Not a dime to these creeps, Petrova. I'm broke except for my salary."

"Promise me your aid in supplying the Chinese with oil and money will not be a problem. Afghanistan will gain from a deal, as will the whole Middle East. Not any extremist organization, but the Afghan people themselves." In a roundabout fashion, this might be true, she reasoned.

"I'll agree to your terms if we take Elizabeth."

"That is another negotiation."

"Then count me out. We can't leave her here."

"What is this woman to you?"

"She's the mother of my daughter."

Petrova sighed. The Azeri wanted Strauss to get their message out. She could use Elizabeth as a negotiating point with him and worry about the Azeri later. "Agree to the Chinese deal and I will try to get her released."

"Do it."

The cage Strauss sat in had a straw mat spread on the bottom and a bucket filled with water. Verkhovtsev touched his hand through the bars and he pulled away.

"Do you realize what this cage was used for?" he asked.

She took a step back in fear of the plagues and toxins still lurking inside the cage.

"Don't worry. The testing wasn't administered to the animals in these cages. Nevertheless, I'm not fit to touch at the moment. I need a shower and clean clothes."

"Anatoly!" she shouted. "Unlock this man and the ambassador. We'll depart immediately."

Abratov hurried over with a kerosene lantern. He removed the shade and struck a match to the wick, and weak yellow light dispelled some of the gloom. Abratov flipped through a key chain. He found the right key, and then unlocked the cage door, as Hassan entered the building.

"Is everything quiet outside, brother?" Anatoly Abratov asked.

"Yes. I put some of the men to guard the trawler."

"Thank you. Get the ambassador and meet us on the dock. Our guests will be leaving shortly." Abratov, Petrova, and Strauss trailed with the dim light of the lantern through the darkened warehouse. Except for their footsteps on the stones, Udobnaya Bay was dead quiet.

"We will be in Baku in a few days," Petrova told Strauss. "I have arranged for all the necessary transportation."

"Do you have a cell phone?"

"No calls until we are safe in Baku."

They were soon to the fishing trawler and Anatoly Abratov held the light for them while they boarded. Strauss and Petrova stepped into the cabin with Abratov to wait for Elizabeth to be brought on board.

"What can be taking so long?" Strauss asked.

"I will go and see," Anatoly Abratov said. "Do not worry about the ambassador being safe."

They heard a commotion on deck, and then a low whistle.

"Come," Petrova told Strauss. "Time to leave."

He followed her outside. The sky looked unusually dark, like a storm was soon to arrive. A man stepped from the shadows and motioned to Petrova. She pulled on Strauss. "Mikhail Osipovich. He's a friend."

"What about Elizabeth?" he asked.

"Anatoly will bring her."

They followed the man off the boat along the shore in the opposite direction of the dock. The boards turned liquid and Burt walked in water. Osipovich pushed Strauss and Petrova through the shallows and the only sound was the swish of waves as they moved. The smell was awful, a stink of chemicals and offal. They kept going until Strauss stepped into a hole and stumbled. The water was chest high and Strauss walked carefully, ready to start swimming. He did not want to put his head in the contaminated water. Petrova and Osipovich were barely discernible as the moon sank deeper into dark clouds. Strauss saw Petrova swimming, and he prepared to do the same.

A bare flicker of moon crept through the cloudbank and he looked up to see parachutes like a scene from an old war movie. Strauss sank. He had been preoccupied with the sky and neglected to pay attention to the water depth over his head. He struggled to swim weighed down by his clothes and the mud beneath him. After 300 yards, he stood and was behind Petrova and Osipovich. *Had they seen the parachutes?*

Twenty minutes later they were out of the water and climbing uphill on rough terrain and Strauss felt the squish of mud between his toes. Osipovich helped Petrova and Strauss stayed to the rear. He looked at the sky but the moon was deep into dark clouds again. He fell several times, and was chilled and hot at the same time.

After what seemed like hours, they rested at the top of a hill.

"Where are we going?" Strauss asked.

"Moynaq, on the ridge called Tiger's Back," said Petrova. "Below us used to be the delta of the two rivers that fed the Aral Sea. The river beds are barren from the water siphoned off upstream and the sea is drying up."

Osipovich said nothing and Strauss and Petrova were silent as well. "What's in Moynaq?" he finally asked.

"There is house we can stay in tonight. We will clean and continue our journey tomorrow. My friends will drive us to Tashkent, the capitol of Uzebekistan, and from there you can fly home to Baku."

"What about Elizabeth?"

"She's safe. Trust me, I know."

"The deal I made was based on getting Elizabeth out too."

"Don't worry. Your ambassador will be home safe by the time we are in Tashkent. Hoa Lin, Xiang's representative, wants to talk soon. I prefer you do not look like you have had a harrowing experience on a polluted island."

The woman Strauss had been drawn to weeks earlier scared the bejesus out of him.

———

Elizabeth lay awake listening to the noises coming through the broken windows of the warehouse. A guard talked to his companion and water hit rock, a one man dumping his tea outside the window.

The trawler rocked on the gentle waves. Two guards standing on the dock were telling dirty jokes. A light breeze blew off the water and one guard raised the collar of his jacket. The other guard pissed over the railing into the sea.

Commandos in black combat gear without markings gripped them from behind, blocked their mouths, and slit their throats in economical, fluid movements. The commandos dumped the bodies into the Aral Sea. Two splashes hit a salty brine of chemical runoff from the mainland.

One commando held up his hand for silence and more appeared from the darkness. Eric LaGrange motioned for two men to cover the trawler and waved his companion to accompany him to the warehouse. The other two advanced toward the aft where the sleeping cabin was located. Willie Hanson shone a penlight on the stairs leading to the cabin. His companion, Tom Singer, covered him with a Heckler & Koch submachine gun, the fat suppressor ready to spit fire.

Gunfire came from the warehouse and people shouted in excitement. A stray bullet hit the deck of the trawler.

"I'll check it out. You stay here," Tom ordered.

"Got your back, farm boy."

Hanson cursed for not bringing the night vision goggles. He could barely see. There were distinct sounds of shouting, machinegun fire, and hand grenades exploding. Footsteps raced across wooden planks. Hanson scanned the blackness, his weapon poised. A man crouched on the deck behind the fishing net reel. Hanson moved right and fired at the slight movement of a shadow. His weapon flew through the air and his body hit the deck. The man had not been alone and another gunman rose out of the water and fired.

Elizabeth heard the disturbance from her cage and hoped against all probability for rescue. When the gunfire started, her heart began pounding wildly. Her calm had disappeared and she feared for her life. Shouting and explosions moved closer to the warehouse. Abratov was soon inside directing his men. The kerosene lamp was extinguished and Elizabeth prayed silently.

"Elizabeth Paige, can you hear me?" asked an unexpected voice. The shooting and shouting raged again. A man shoved the sliding bay doors open and ran to her. "Elizabeth, are you in here?"

"Over here," she said. The beam of a flashlight shone in on her. "Madame Ambassador," Hanson said. "Over here, Eric."

Elizabeth recognized the friend of Roger Shaw who visited the embassy before her abduction.

"As long as you don't say the banal 'I told you so,' I'm glad to see you again, Eric."

"The pleasure is mine, Ambassador. Stand back and I'll have you out of there." He shot the cage door lock and pulled her out. "Stay low," he whispered. "We have a ways to go yet."

Bursts of rapid fire came from the direction of the dock. LaGrange passed Elizabeth to Tom Singer. "Guard her with your life." He ran in a crouch for the doorway lit by the rising moon and heavy machine gunfire followed. LaGrange raced to the deserted trawler in hopes of finding Burt Strauss.

He stepped inside the empty cabin. Through the smells of cordite and the Aral Sea, he smelled perfume.

"Anything down there?" a commando asked from the top of the stairs.

"Not a damn thing. Where is Strauss?"

"We got a body here."

LaGrange stepped on deck and the commando pointed to a body against the rail.

"Goddamn, Willie. Hold on. We'll get you out of here." Before he finished his words, the body he held was lifeless. More gunfire hit the trawler and LaGrange dove for cover with the dead soldier.

———

Stephanie Devine heard the mechanic trill of the STU–III secure telephone before her husband. She gently nudged John awake and went to make coffee as he fiddled with the switches and buttons.

"What went wrong?" he asked.

"Everything," Shaw said. "They had more men than we thought and an arsenal of weapons. Out of our eight-man team, four are dead. We lost Kowalsky, Jones, Hanson, and Baranko. Tom Singer was wounded and the team had to withdraw."

"Tell me part of the action went right."

"Elizabeth Paige is safe, but Burt Strauss, if he was there, disappeared. What a hell-hole."

"Where is Tom?"

"In the military hospital in Almaty. He was lucky. A bullet pierced his shoulder and missed the muscles. There was no injury to the bone. The surgeon says he'll be fine."

"Everyone's accounted for by this report."

"The dead and the living. We brought home the bodies. The ambassador was advised to go to the hospital for observation and she refused. I'm going to see her today and ask if she knows Burt was on the island."

Devine tapped at his front teeth with a jagged, chewed thumbnail in reply. The brief on this action would be filled with apologies, prevarication, and outright lies, and the Administration would still be angry.

"John, are you okay?"

"Distracted is all. We asked a lot from those men. I should give more credit to LaGrange for going along. For a burnout, he stayed with them."

"Eric demanded to go with his old Special Forces outfit. He couldn't wait in the embassy while pushing for the operation. He's got brass balls."

"Mine are made out of paper mache."

"We need you in Langley to deal with the politicians or we're all in trouble."

"I'm fucking old. I've never gotten used to losing men, and telling their wives and mothers never gets easier."

———

Elizabeth Paige put down her copy of *The Small House at Allington* when Roger Shaw entered her office. She had lost weight from the ordeal but her cheeks were rosy and she radiated her usual confidence.

"Are you feeling as great as you look?"

"I'm fine. I've had three showers today and anticipating the fourth."

"Rebirth Island is a nasty place."

"They treated me surprisingly well. We need to talk about your business, Roger. When I arrived on the island, the kidnappers loaded metal containers on the trawler they had dug up on the island. They were caked with dirt."

"Anthrax. Do you know where the containers were headed?"

"The men taking them out were the same crew who brought me in, though I was very drugged. The voices were the same."

"Elizabeth, we have reason to think Burt Strauss was on the island, too. There were several other buildings they could have kept him."

"Why would he be there?"

"The pipeline."

"Those people made no demands and asked no questions. The only disturbing thing they did beside keep me in a cage was to take my picture."

"We received the photos and suppressed them."

"That is good news. I was not looking my best."

Roger laughed. "I'll be in touch."

"If they had Burt, where is he now?"

"We don't know. If you hear from him, call me."

"I fear something has happened to him. More likely, he's off touring somewhere."

Shaw left Elizabeth at the Embassy and called Devine.

"John, new development. Elizabeth Paige claims that there was a large stash of anthrax moved off the island."

"We'll look into it. What about Strauss?"

"She's drawing a blank."

———

Shaw spent the afternoon at the US Army hospital where Tom Singer nursed his wounds. He sat by Tom's bedside drinking bottled water and listened to his version of the commando raid.

"The high altitude–low opening jump from the C-130 was no big deal. Oxygen masks worked fine and we'd been worried because we got them on the black market. Once we hit the ground, all hell broke loose. They were trained fighters, those men guarding Ambassador Paige. They fought a sophisticated battle with a blocking force of at least thirty. They overwhelmed us.

"The enemy was everywhere and we scattered, some of us looking for the ambassador, others for Strauss, trying to watch each others' backs. The worst mess I've ever been in."

Singer raised himself from the bed and grimaced with sudden pain.

Shaw got up. "I'm going to let you rest."

"Eric was great out there, like he never left. We need him back in the outfit."

"I'll pass along the compliment."

"Before you go, hand me those painkillers on the dresser."

Shaw gave him the pill bottle. "Sorry about Hanson. I know you two were friends."

"He died doing his job, and that's how a commando lives. I'm only concerned we didn't find Burt Strauss."

Shaw walked the hospital hallways to the sun outside. Elizabeth had been captured two weeks earlier and said the people who dropped her off picked up containers of anthrax. He needed to figure out who and where they took the material. Europe or the United States or both? They might take it overland to the Black Sea, then by ship through the Bosporus and across the Mediterranean to an Italian port, or overland across Iran to the Gulf of Oman and around via the Suez to the Mediterranean. Other routes were the Eurasian Silk Road into Europe, or into Yugoslavia to the Adriatic and then to the Mediterranean. They could have gone across Russia to the Baltic and around to the Atlantic, or through Siberia to the Arctic and over to the Bering Sea.

Wherever the canisters went, he bet they had arrived at their intended target. Shaw took out his cell phone and punched numbers. Devine was not happy to hear he had to run down every overland route possible and any ship to dock anywhere in North America and Europe in the last two weeks. The Counterterrorism Center had enough work without having a new threat by persons unknown.

CHAPTER 7

⎯⎯

The Tashkent airport needed work, even after the European Union's multi-million dollar loan for improvement in the late 1990s. Weeds pushed through the rough resurfaced tarmac of the two runways, freshly painted fuel trucks had rusted connections with hoses tangled on the ground, and the modern control tower looked less modern than should have for the money spent on its refurbishing.

Petrova went to secure tickets for the flight back to Baku, and left Strauss to drink whiskey and eat beef kebabs alone in the airport bar. He was glad to be admitted to the bar considering how he was dressed. His suit ruined by his stay and escape from Rebirth Island, Petrova had found him a dark blue polo shirt missing its alligator, plaid trousers worn thin at the knees and backside, and plastic flip-flops too small for his feet. A red windbreaker smelling of diesel fuel served as a coat.

"Buy me a vodka," demanded Petrova on her return. "I have made a call while arranging our transportation. Ambassador Paige is safe at home."

"I'm relieved. Good news is always worth a drink."

"My apologies for the ill-fitting clothes. I only notice one size of a man."

"His wallet makes two."

After a short delay of four hours, the Uzbekistan Airways flight bumped into the skies. Strauss ignored Petrova's attempts to cheer him out of his funk. He settled into a half-whiskey stupor and slept without bothering to fasten his seat belt. They hailed separate taxis at the terminal in Baku.

Strauss came home to dozens of messages on his answering machine, including several from Roger Shaw. He dialed the Almaty embassy and the receptionist put him through to the ambassador.

"Burt!" answered Elizabeth. "Where are you?"

"Home in Baku. We need to talk about something. I'll be in Almaty in the morning."

"Come to the office. I've taken so much time off I won't get another vacation for five years."

She laughed like she was happy and Strauss laughed, too, at the joy in her voice. What had gotten into her? Elizabeth sounded unusually warm and friendly, and just when he had to give her bad news.

———

Strauss arrived at the embassy the following day, barbered and brushed, shaved and showered, wearing a chocolate brown Brioni suit with starched white Egyptian broadcloth shirt and blue and bronze striped tie. Elizabeth had forsaken her usual professional clothes for an unbleached cotton blouse and muslin Bohemian skirt. She kissed his cheek, a rare and unexpected offering.

"Let's go outside where we'll have more privacy. I'll show you the flowers."

Strauss followed her into the garden. "I'm sorry about your experience on the island."

"I'm fine, really. My guard told me the Azeri had arranged for the abduction to stop the pipeline. They were expected when the commandos showed up. The Azeri fear a mismanagement of resources like Rebirth Island, and the travesty of the Aral Sea."

"Our kidnappings were political."

"More like environmental. I don't want anything like Rebirth to happen because of the pipeline. I love this country. Groves of wild apple trees used to grow here. Between the mountain regions in the south and Lake Balkhash in the north, Almaty was on the medieval caravan route connecting Asia and Europe. In fact, ruins of an ancient town were found west of here."

"I'd like to see them."

"I'll show you sometime. Historians think Mongol invaders destroyed the original town in the ninth century. Later, the Russians took over the area. I have a great-grandmother who was among the colonists who came here around 1850."

"About the time gold brought settlers to California and drove out the Spaniards."

"According to my family history—the Russian one, not the California one—each family to colonize here was given hardware for building a home including nails and panes of glass, a cart and horse harness, and 55 rubles in cash to buy cattle."

"No horse?"

"I guess you had better already have one. When my great-grandmother's family arrived, they were also given a year's supply of flour and seed grain for sowing."

"You probably still have relatives here."

"None I can find. My great-grandmother's father was killed when the local Kokand Khanate tried to drive the settlers out. Her mother and other relatives died a few years later in a catastrophic earthquake."

"She moved on."

"Not on, back. She married a Cossack and returned to Russia."

"This is why you love this land so much."

"Not only the past, but the possible future with the oil pipeline. Outsiders from Genghis Khan to Hitler have waged war to control the Caspian region. The pipeline will give them autonomy no army can conquer, and an infrastructure in place to protect the environment. Let's go upstairs to my quarters for lunch."

"I'd like that." They walked through the office, down the hallway, and up the stairs to her private apartment. "Your great-grandmother's story is fascinating. After all these years, I didn't know any of this about you."

"My official government biography leaves out many things." She opened a large door and ushered him into the living room. Except for the elaborate gold filigree and white lacquer furniture, the woodwork, French doors, and high ceilings in the room might have been from an old mansion back home.

Strauss and Elizabeth sat at opposite ends of the long, overstuffed rose sofa. He compared the room to her cabin near Willow Creek. Elizabeth had come far without changing her basic simplicity and poise.

"I've kept a secret from you, Burt."

"You gave birth to my child instead of having an abortion."

"Damn you. Why haven't you said anything?"

"My shame stopped me. I approached Shaw in Washington when you were being checked for the first posting, and asked if he would speed the process along. He came back with photocopies of Amelia's birth certificate. Since your husband was O positive and Amelia AB negative, no way could Thomas Paige be the father. Shaw found out Paige was what he called 'a private fag,' " Strauss said with an obvious distaste. "I despised the little spook after reading the report. I didn't want anyone to interfere in your life."

Elizabeth turned pale as her blouse and walked to the tall windows.

"To think of Shaw examining me is disgusting. He's supposed to stick to international affairs, not domestic."

"The lines blur in the diplomatic corps. Background checks are part of the process."

"When did Shaw do his digging?"

"About the time Amelia started school in New York. She's not the reason I've been friendly and tried to maintain a good business relationship. Whether or not you had my child, I've always loved you. I really have."

She was silent for a moment. "I don't know what to say. I've been angry for so long."

"I know."

"Being in the cage made me realize I've been unfair to you and Amelia. I want to put aside the past and tell the truth."

"We have other concerns now."

Her smile vanished. "I'm not going to like what's coming."

"No. Amelia could be in danger."

"That's impossible. She's not part of my political career. Does someone besides Shaw knows she's our daughter?"

She got up again and paced in front of the sofa. "You told a lover of yours."

Burt stared at his dumb and useless hands. "We were interrupted before we went that far. Petrova Verkhovtsev."

"She's head of the Caspian Works and I've heard rumors of her being associated with the Russian mobster, Grigory Pluchenko. I don't care who British Chemical is in bed with to get the job done, but my daughter is everything."

"Please listen. I don't think Petrova will tell anyone."

Elizabeth moved away like she had been struck. "Because she loves you?"

"She's blackmailing me to divert part of the Caspian oil to the Chinese."

"And using Amelia as a pawn in an international barter." Elizabeth sat across from Strauss. "I want Roger Shaw to help."

"Not the spooks. The fewer people who know, the better."

"You don't trust Shaw?"

"Even with their current inefficiency, the Agency tends to go in with a raging posse and do more harm than good."

"I can't leave my daughter's life in your hands, Burt, even if you are her biological father. I'll be honest. I'm not sure I can ever forgive this."

The Elizabeth in a younger woman's summer clothes left the room and the hard Ambassador Paige picked up the telephone. Whoever messed with either persona would be in for a shock. Strauss watched the transformation.

"Shaw is at the embassy in Baku," he said. "We should talk to him in person."

———

Clean-shaven Ali Massouf traveled under the name Albert Marshall and passed the customs inspection at the Milan international airport with American papers. The customs inspector leafed through his passport, looked once at the tanned tourist, and waived him through.

Marshall smoothed the lapels of his pinstriped business suit and smiled to the other passengers as he picked up his luggage from the conveyor belt. He wheeled the bag to the exit and hot air hit him outside the door. Marshall loosened his tie and walked to a white BMW sport van parked at the curb.

The driver was a big man, too big for the BMW, and wore dark wraparound sunglasses. He clumsily emerged from behind the wheel, and stored Marshall's single piece of luggage in the back. "How was your flight?"

Marshall settled in the rear seat. "Fine. Are we going straight to the factory?"

"Yes. Signor Viola is waiting for you."

"How long is the drive to Bergamo?"

"Less then thirty minutes if the traffic is clear."

To his relief, the driver was silent and Marshall closed his eyes. He was exhausted.

The swerving of the car jolted him awake. "Fucking maniac!" the driver shouted. He waved his fist at a black Mercedes cutting him off in the fast-moving left lane of the autostrada. The Mercedes picked up speed and Marshall's driver moved to the center lane while cursing under his breath.

"What's your hurry?" Marshall asked. "Don't get us killed before I have a chance to taste the product."

"The autostrada, sometimes she is crowded with drivers like this all the way to Venezia. Only another twenty kilometers. I am sorry, Mr. Marshall. That mad man pushed me out of the fast lane."

"Let him have the lane."

The Viola Gelato factory was a low concrete and steel building not far from the winding streets of Bergamo proper. Marshall gave his name to the receptionist in the lobby of comfortable leather chairs and startling red carpet. Signor Viola quickly appeared, a trim older gentleman in dark gray suit with thinning brown hair and an uneven gait. Thick eyebrows crowded deep-set dark eyes above a large Roman nose. He wore bifocals kept safe by a slender chain around his neck.

"Mr. Marshall," he said, extending his hand. "Welcome to our factory. Here is home to the finest gelato in all Italy. I am glad you could come."

Marshall matched Viola's powerful grip. "Please call me Albert."

"The famous American informality. Would you like a tour of our facility?"

Marshall and Signor Viola entered the factory through the doors off the spacious lobby. Two rows of tall silver tanks stood as sentries over the factory, and pipes frosted with condensation kept the batch freezers at the proper low temperature. Workers in white coats and cloth caps on an assembly line pressed different mixtures into stainless steel containers headed for refrigeration and shipment. At the rear of the factory, three men loaded Euroboxes for shipping.

"The secret to Viola gelato is simple. We make ours here and only ship the finished product. The dedication enables us to guarantee the quality wherever Viola is sold. This shipment is going to Tuscany and that one to Venezia. Over there is part of the shipment for Paris. Once the containers arrive at the gelaterias, anything can occur. My favorite is ricotta copetta, made with our goat's milk ricotta gelato, figs poached in red wine, and candied walnuts."

"America's taste buds are not so adventurous."

"A pity. Gelato is the perfect solution to the problems of obesity. We have only 12 percent butterfat compared to your ice cream, and every flavor we offer is made from natural sources instead of chemicals. *Perche' il nostro Gelato e' fatto con ottime materie prime.*"

"I can see your gelato is made with the finest ingredients, and that's why we are anxious to buy the New York franchise."

"You know the Italian language?"

"Some. My mother was from Firenze, God rest her soul," Marshall lied.

"And your father?"

"American. I grew up in Brooklyn."

Signor Viola smiled. "I have been to Manhattan, everyone in a hurry. Is your novelist Thomas Wolf correct in only the dead know Brooklyn?"

They watched the workers. "We've been gentrified since his time."

The cell phone in Marshall's suit pocket vibrated. He took out the device and extended its stubby antenna. "Excuse me, Signor Viola, I must take this call."

"Are you in Milan?" He recognized the caller as Kamal ibn-Sultan.

"No, I'm touring the gelato factory outside of Bergamo."

"I understand. Be charming, Ali. We need this deal."

Marshall cut the connection. "My secretary," he explained, and tucked the cell phone back into his jacket pocket. "Have you looked over our offer?"

"Yes, I did and I was pleased your people have no problem with having Viola gelato sent from here. Many would say this is a silly affectation, but having the equipment does not guarantee the same gelato. We have spent many resources to develop the shipping route and customs brokerage. Viola gelato must always come from Bergamo."

"We see this as an aid in marketing the higher-priced product, not a hindrance."

"Mr. Marshall, I am glad to be talking with a man who understands. There are two other Viola gelaterias, in Miami and San Francisco. Baskin-Robbins has expressed interest in acquiring all three."

"A big ice cream company will use your name and reputation for the same old American thing. Any promises made at the beginning of the deal would be broken by their lawyers."

"For me, the ignominy would be painful. This is why I must ask you to consider the purchase of the three to keep those wolves from our doors. We already have a gelato concession in place at Madison Square Garden. The other two gelaterias can pursue the same business model and you will make back your investment very quickly."

"This is unexpected. I will have to consult with my partner."

"Certainly. I have profit and loss statements on the other operations to show their viability."

Marshall punched in the number for ibn-Sultan. "Baskin-Robbins is bidding against us. There are three franchises, not the one we believed."

"Buy them. The others may prove useful."

Signor Viola returned with a stack of computer printouts and Marshall gave him the good news.

"My grandfather would be pleased. Follow me."

The elegant man showed Marshall into his office. Tall windows looked out at the city of Bergamo in the distance. He pointed to a burgundy leather chair facing the desk. "Sit down, my friend. May I offer you an aperitif?"

"No, thank you. My doctor says I have a poor liver."

They talked about payments, shipments, and deliveries until Signor Viola announced a break for lunch. "Coming to the factory, you have seen only the modern part of my city. We shall dine at the real Bergamo, Bergamo Alta, our ancestor. I have a table reserved on the Piazza Vecchia. I trust your doctor allows the local specialty, polenta con gli ucceli?"

"Quail," translated Marshall. "I would enjoy the change from airplane food."

The deal with Signor Viola dragged through the afternoon. Sometimes ibn-Sultan came up with the strangest ideas. Couldn't they have gone with a coffee or hot dog concession?

———

Roger Shaw finished the last of his report on the Paige abduction at the US Embassy on Azadlyg Prospecti in Baku. The recounting had more suppositions than facts. Azeri nationalists had hired mercenaries to grab the Ambassador, but canceled the contract from fear of their own drastic action. The mercenaries were identified as possibly Jordanian, a fine bit of government doublespeak. Either they were from Jordan or not. Shaw's contacts in the Dairat al Mukhabarat, Jordan's General Intelligence Department, had found no new activities among the roster of Islamic extremists they regularly tracked. Only the Followers of the Cleric had the arms and men to pull off such an operation.

Let someone else do the brainwork, he decided. A quick trip to the airport and he would soon be home in Istanbul. Shaw took his topcoat from the rack. Every year and every day, intelligence work got messier and harder. He should have stayed in law, hung out his shingle with a decent Washington firm, and grown fat on lobbying dollars. The telephone on the plastic wood veneer desk rang with a nasty insistence. He picked up the receiver.

"Roger, it's me, Elizabeth. I'm in town and need to see you privately."

"Meet me at the Terrace Disco on the Boulevard. Take a taxi, a real taxi with a meter so you won't be robbed like a foreigner, and stay off the metro."

"We're a bit old for a disco."

"You're following my thinking. The place is so loud we'll have no worries about being overheard. See you there."

Traffic was heavy leading to the Boulevard and many people walked the broad, shaded pedestrian walkway at the edge of the Caspian Sea.

At the center across Neftchilar Avenue squatted the dour former House of Soviets, now home to the Azerbaijani government. Why did the ambassador want to meet him among the people responsible for her capture? This would be Shaw's first question to her. Along the water Azeri children rode carousels, and single men and women loitered at the outdoor cafes and pool tables.

Inside the Terrace Disco, couples crowded the dance floor under splinters of light tossed by the mirror balls hanging overhead. Sweat mixed with cigarette smoke and alcohol fumes dominated the club. Vacant chairs circled small tables holding ashtrays, beer bottles, and glasses. Elizabeth sat at a table and looked like any other tourist in a denim skirt, tee shirt, and sunglasses. She had a thick wool sweater over her shoulders, the sleeves knotted below her neck.

Shaw took a chair and sat next to the ambassador. "Come here often?"

"The only song I've recognized is U2's 'Vertigo' and the rest has been nothing but techno. I thought that music belonged to the 1990s."

"Baku believes in tradition. What's the reason for the meet?"

"Let's wait for a moment."

Burt Strauss arrived at the table with a drink in each hand. "Hello, Roger."

"Nothing for me?"

"Pardon my lack of social graces. I've never been a fan of yours or the Agency. What Elizabeth and I tell you goes no further. I'll get to the point without the details. Elizabeth can fill you in later."

"Okay," Shaw said.

"I'm being forced to divert oil for the Chinese. The go-between is Petrova Verkhovtsev of Caspian Works."

"What is she using as pressure?"

"Petrova helped me escape from Rebirth Island under the condition I secure the oil. I didn't want to bring you in, but Elizabeth assures me you'll keep all the parties involved safe. I'm willing to do anything you want."

"Even find information for us?"

"Tell me what you want and I'll get it. I have to meet with a man named Hoa Lin tomorrow. He's Ambassador Xiang's aide."

"Tell me the terms of the blackmail."

"No definite threat. Petrova knows I took a bath playing the commodities market and she's told the Chinese my reluctance is about money. She expects a percentage of the deal. Petrova will probably also make more from the Chinese side. She's been as subtle as hell."

"Agree to the terms from Hoa Lin, but add demands of your own. Don't let him know Petrova is coercing you. Keep talking about the money. If Hoa Lin believes your sincerity, Petrova will let down her guard. Stall."

"Jesus, Roger. This is a complete mess."

"I've covered up worse for senators and admirals. An oil executive is easy."

"Thanks. I'll be going. Take good care of Elizabeth."

Strauss staggered around the tables and out the door of the Terrace Disco. He walked until he found a street open to traffic and hailed a taxi. "All is vanity," he muttered to himself after giving the driver his home address.

"What, sir?"

"Vanity, one of the seven deadly sins. The greatest stupidity man ever visited on himself."

Shaw picked up the drink abandoned by Strauss and tasted the whiskey. American bourbon, he guessed, and not a good brand. The club's disk jockey switched from Euro pop to an old standard.

"Recognize the tune, Elizabeth?"

"The Rolling Stones, 'Gimme Shelter.' My parents played the album when I was growing up."

"Junkie or not, Keith Richards' opening licks still make my feet itch. I danced to this song a thousand times through college at house parties and clubs."

"We had 'Radio Free Europe' and REM."

"Enough of the backward glance. Tell me who Burt is protecting."

"Our daughter, Amelia."

"I remember the report I gave him. He's treated me like an unnecessary evil ever since. My guess is he told Ms. Verkhovtsev."

"During the tender moment before sex when couples do that wound-revealing crap and call it romance."

"Madame Ambassador, I detect a definite bad attitude."

"This is about Amelia, not me."

"I have a few outstanding favors stateside. Give me everything you have on Amelia, where she lives and where she goes, boyfriends and girlfriends, anything you can. I'll pull together a private sector security detail so no government clerk can get their hands on any dirt about her. This is going to cost you."

"I'll spend whatever is needed. Protect my girl, Roger."

CHAPTER 8

Strauss dressed carefully in his Park Residence flat the following morning. The Brioni had to pull duty for another day until his housekeeper, the squat and ill-tempered Madame Ahmadbayov, returned from her annual vacation and caught up with the laundry. He made a full Windsor knot in his red tie, a power color according to the lecturer at a silly retreat for British Chemical Enterprises executives.

Park Residence came about after the "Contract of the Century" was signed in 1994, and Azerbaijan joined the international oil community. Great construction projects were built with the hard currency pouring into Baku, and the Residence's steel, concrete, and glass was one of many housing complexes reserved for the foreigners who brought the gospel of the free market economy to the former Soviet state.

The company leased the flat for Strauss as part of his perks and left the furnishing to him. He kept the high-ceilinged rooms spare of clutter. The living room had a sofa constructed of dark leather rectangular cushions on a teak frame, and a glass coffee table. A widescreen plasma television stood where a fireplace might have been, and a small wet bar held several bottle of liquor, glasses, and a bookshelf stereo system. The only room he had paid attention was the bedroom, where he had arranged a series of dumbbells, a barbell, and weight bench. A photograph taken of him and Elizabeth sat in a pewter frame on top of his five-drawer dresser.

Madame Ahmadbayov kept the kitchen her domain, and Strauss allowed this since he never had interest in domestic chores. A water heater and filters helped make what came out of the taps less unreliable and almost potable. When he found a woman for the night, he rented a room at the Hyatt. The "womanizing" Petrova had alluded to consisted of prostitutes, secretaries, and au pairs, and once an Azeri bureaucrat. Not one had been invited to his home. He had already lost a wife and a lover, and a therapist he visited said his avoidance of another relationship bordered on the pathological. Strauss quit seeing the therapist.

The doorbell rang and he looked at his image in the bedroom's full-length mirror. How did Shaw take the stress of lying for a living? He was likely a secret drunk, dope fiend, or sexual predator, or he really enjoyed the work. Strauss did not want to know.

Petrova Verkhovtsev waited at the door in a light blue dress made professional by a gold scarf covering her décolletage, covered by her oyster overcoat.

"Are you ready?" she asked. " I have a car waiting."

"Let me grab a coat and we'll be off."

They rode in a white Volvo through the Baku streets until coming to a broken-down hotel missing a sign and a star rating five kilometers from the city center. Petrova took his arm and guided Strauss up the stairs to a red door on the third floor. An Asian man in casual tan slacks, Nike running shoes, and a mottled orange pullover opened the door.

"Miss Verkhovtsev," he said. "Right this way."

Inside the room, a bottle of Johnnie Walker Red whiskey and three glasses were on a card table bordered by four straight-backed chairs. The iron bedstead held a sagging mattress covered with a patched comforter. A sink in the corner had its white enamel overtaken by rust stains. The windows shades were drawn, the only illumination came from two lamps with bare bulbs, and the room stunk of mildew.

"Greetings," the man said. "You must be Mr. Strauss. Please forgive the surroundings. Ambassador Xiang suggested our business is better discussed away from both our countries prying eyes."

"I agree with him, Mr. Lin. Petrova tells me you have a business proposition."

"I do. And how are you, Miss Verkhovtsev?"

She took his hand. "Very well, thank you."

"Please sit down. Mr. Strauss, I trust Miss Verkhovtsev has outlined our desire?"

"I want to hear the offer from you."

"We need oil and are prepared to pay well for any assistance."

"Everybody needs our oil, and most without political ramifications. The Chinese have not made many friends. There are those in the West who voted against having your country join the World Trade Organization. Somehow the problems were circumvented and now you're creeping slowly toward a free market economy. Since the standard of living and wages are lower in China, the country will take manufacturing jobs away from other countries."

"One complains about having sweatshops, the other that the sweatshops are moving. I am unsure whether to be amused at the irony, or saddened the world has turned from ideologies to profit margins."

"More oil means more manufacturing capabilities for China, and will also aid your already formidable military. There are rumors the Chinese plan to invade Taiwan."

"Taiwan will fall when ready and without much prodding. These subjects make for interesting conversation, but in the end we are talking about the purchase of oil. Our offer will be the highest, I assure you."

"I have no doubt. What do you have in mind, Mr. Lin?"

"We will establish a company in Geneva for the purchase. Your fee will be paid to any bank you wish. The amount we have in mind for your services is $500,000."

"This might seem like a princely sum to you, but not nearly enough for my risk. I want one million dollars deposited in a Luxembourg bank, half now and half when the oil is delivered. Ms. Verkhovtsev expects to be paid for her role as a middleman, or in this case, middlewoman. You take care of her."

Hoa Lin hesitated and Petrova cleared her throat to interrupt either man's thinking processes. "The pipeline will be ready for operation very soon."

"I'll have to appeal to the British Chemical Enterprise board of directors. Most of the money invested in the Ceyhan pipeline comes from the West and they rightly expect the oil. The only leverage I have is the mandate of every corporation to make the greatest profit for their shareholders. Your bid has to be no less than forty percent higher than the current market value of crude oil," Strauss added.

"Ambassador Xiang has told me of an event happening soon to convince the West of our needs," Hoa Lin said. "Your people will be looking for a supplier and not be troubled by diplomacy."

"Fair enough, as long as Xiang knows my price is not negotiable."

Hoa Lin rose and poured liquor into the three glasses. "Let us toast to our new venture."

"My pleasure," Strauss said.

The driver and Volvo were ready for Strauss and Petrova as they left the hotel.

"Are you mad?" asked Petrova.

"No, I'm pissed off. The Chinese will have to pay for the oil, and me."

"Do not play Hoa Lin or Xiang for idiots."

"This is going to look strange to the consortium. I've helped develop the architecture of getting the oil to Western Europe and beyond, and here I am touting a shadowy new buyer. I prefer to retire and not get fired because I'm being investigated for trading improprieties."

"You were ready to do this for free when Elizabeth Paige was threatened."

"Leaving anyone on that island would have been inhuman. I like sleeping nights. As the situation turned out, your people were not her rescuers."

"You are different from anyone I have ever met, Burt Strauss."

Petrova kissed his cheek as the Volvo stopped in front of Park Residence. The driver remained behind the wheel.

"Why did you demand a million dollars if you're not interested in the money?"

"An ego thing. This male competitive crap automatically kicks in. Men always like to know how far they can push."

"I am not going to let you get away easily. I find you immensely attractive."

———

Slight tremors from cars and trucks rushing through the Brooklyn-Battery tunnel registered in the brownstone near the Red Hook Recreation Area. Ali Massouf and Ramzi Zaidan lounged in the kitchen with the morning edition of *The New York Times*. Zaidan was an angular, hyperactive young man with sunken cheeks and bulging eyes. He repeated to anyone who would listen the story of how Islam had saved him from crack addiction. His devout and dead Uncle Essam appeared to him during another stay in rehab, and demanded he dedicate his wasted life to freeing Muslims from the oppression of the Crusaders. At a mosque in Queens he met a man recruiting for a cell to perform various tasks in defense of Islam. The man also offered a small sum of money so Zaidan could afford an apartment instead of living in his parent's Ashbury Park home.

"Listen to this," said Massouf over the sports section. " 'Madison Square Garden's All Access Tour allows fans to get an insider's view of the inner-workings of the World's Most Famous Arena.' "

"Like what?"

"According to the ad, the locker rooms, backstage of the theater, and the dressing rooms. You get to see players practicing, rehearsals, crews staging events, and how a basketball court becomes a sheet of ice. Read for yourself." Massouf threw him the paper.

" 'The legendary showplace,' they call it."

"Get tickets for Samir and whoever he wants to accompany him. He will also need blueprints. Try the library or city records. Steal them if you must."

"They even have dog shows at the Garden."

"Ramzi, forget about the dogs."

The small television on the counter tuned to CNN showed more battles in Iraq, Iran, and Afghanistan. Massouf had the volume turned low. Why listen to the Western lies?

Two men, known as Michael and David, entered the house and tracked Massouf's voice into the kitchen. They were the faithful who had renounced the families and material possessions to follow the Cleric. Both had made out the wills of warriors committed to jihad, ready to sacrifice their lives for a place in heaven with the Prophet. The men were dark, slim, and taciturn. Massouf shook their hands and thanked them for being prompt. Once everyone had met, he pointed to seats at the table.

"You have been recommended for this operation for your intelligence and skills, your loyalty to the cause, and for courage under pressure. Each is a team leader and your members will depend on you for guidance.

"The war is coming home to the infidels and our target is Madison Square Garden. Kamal ibn-Sultan has sent a message he wants passed along to the members of your cells: 'The Crusader world has rallied for the despoiling of the Islamic world. All we have left for fighting, besides Almighty God, is you young men who have not been weighed down by the filth of the Crusaders. They have entered our land and holy sanctuaries, and plundered Muslim oil. We are called terrorists when we offer resistance. The fight will once again cross the ocean and come to America. My brothers, do not waver. We are waging jihad for the sake of Almighty God. The Cleric prays for our success every day, as we pray for his long life and the blessings of Almighty God on all his works.' "

The two men listened without comment. Zaidan tapped the linoleum tabletop and jiggled in his chair. Massouf rested his throat for a moment before continuing. The rhetoric made Massouf uncomfortable, but he followed his leader. He relaxed going into the practical aspects of the operation.

"Our plan is to introduce anthrax in aerosol form through the Garden during a crowded evening event. We will install the equipment we need to send the gas into the air-conditioning vents. Much of the scouting can be done during the 'All Access' tours or the upcoming Asian Jewelry and Watch fair. We have the gelato concession in Food Court 61, down from the Team Store. There is an air-conditioning vent in the men's room and above the nearby water fountain. The security is probably very light during the tours, and we can have our janitors close the men's room and access the vent."

Massouf explained the need to have their own people working inside the Garden and find out the plumbing and heating contractors. Air-conditioning and heating experts loyal to the cause were necessary. If not among the local followers, they would be imported. Identifications, uniforms, and a false plumbing and heating truck were needed, and a man in the managerial offices would be excellent, someone like a secretary, janitor, or clerk.

"Check on employment opportunities at the Garden, even at other concessions. Become familiar with the Garden and the surrounding neighborhood, and Penn Station for the train and subway schedules and parking garages."

Massouf unrolled a map and tacked it up on the wall. "The Garden is bordered by 7th and 8th Avenue, between 31st and 33rd streets. The Expo Center is on the 31st Street side of the arena, the Penn Station entrance on the 7th Avenue side, the loading door on the 8th Avenue side. The taxi underpass is one way, so drivers get used to entering from 31st Street. Seventh Avenue is one way going downtown, and Eighth Avenue one way going uptown. We'll be practicing escape routes, so pay attention. Keep in mind vehicles will not be able to make turns from 36th and 37th Streets between Second and Sixth Avenues between 10 am and 6 pm."

"We need clothes to look American," Zaidan suggested. "Should we shop at the Gap?"

"Part of the mission is not to draw attention. Be invisible. Be any man on the street. Obey their laws. Be discrete. Is the importance of this understood?"

The men nodded in agreement.

———

The USS Ross, an Arleigh Burke-class guided missile destroyer out of Norfolk, Virginia, cruised the Straits of Taiwan during another day at sea. On board the Navy's latest and most sophisticated ship was the AEGIS air defense system with SPY-1D phased array radar, and 90-cell vertical launching system able to fire standard, Tomahawk, and vertically launched ASROC missiles.

Four LM2500 gas turbine engines drove the 8,300 tons, 506 foot-long ship through the Chinese waters length at a stately ten knots. The Ross was made of all-steel construction, with topside armor around the vital combat systems and machinery, and double-spaced plates around the bulkheads. Originally designed during the last years of the Cold War, the Ross and other Arleigh Burke-class destroyers were now assigned to keeping the world's uneasy peace. Thirty officers and over three hundred enlisted men and women made up the crew.

Under the sign reading, "In God We Trust, All Others We Track" and barely discernible in the blue light of the Combat Information Center, Sonar Technician Brown sipped his instant coffee. The nasty stuff required three sugars and still retained its bitterness.

"I'll be a son of a bitch," Brown said to the backlit screen. "We have a submarine not a thousand feet from the ship. Someone wants to play tag and I think we're it." He hit the button on his communications link. "Peters, tell the captain a Russian Kilo submarine has surfaced off the stern."

"We should have heard them," replied the radioman.

"Not this baby. Here's the best part: damned if they aren't marked as Chinese."

Peters called for Captain Redmond Nichols on the bridge and relayed the information. "I'm coming down to have a look. Send what you have to the electronic warfare technicians and intelligence specialists."

He joined the busy Combat Information Center and watched the submarine registering on his chart screen. Captain Nichols had read about the SSK Kilo class, but this was his first encounter with the

3,000 ton, 240-foot long ship. The Komsomolsk shipyard had built the Kilo until construction was transferred to the Admiralty Shipyard in St Petersburg. An anti-submarine and anti-surface ship, the Kilo was powered by two diesel generators and main propulsion motor that drove a seven-blade fixed-pitch propeller. This guaranteed a silence under the sea even the USS Ross could not detect. A Kilo class ran at 11 knots on the surface and 20 knots underwater. For weaponry, the submarine carried eight surface-to-air missiles, and six forward torpedo tubes capable of firing mines along with the torpedoes stored in the racks. Her crew of 52 could stay under for 45 days.

The ship maneuvered around the Ross like a flying fish. Nichols buzzed the radioman. "Peters, advise vessel to back off immediately and identify." He punched in a security code and identifiers on the computer to send a flash dispatch to Norfolk: "Chinese Kilo pop-up. Circling at five knots. Locked on radar. No apparent threat. Advise."

Nichols called Peters again. "Transmit the draft on the Kilo as a flash dispatch."

"Transmitting as flash dispatch, sir."

The screen revealed the unidentified sub moving along the straits at eight knots, north into the East China Sea.

"The sub identifies itself as SSK Yizhou on a training mission," Peters reported. "The commander extends an apology."

You mean, fuck you, Captain Nichols thought, and drafted another flash dispatch to update the earlier one. Twenty years of service in the Navy and Nichols had yet to be involved in any conflict. Yizhou was an ancient name for Taiwan. The Ross had a ringside seat to a renewed One-China campaign.

———

Analyst Howard Crumbly had the markings of career drudge, his dark hair lightened with a dusting of dandruff, bad skin, thick eyeglasses, and a pocket protector stuck in his short sleeved white shirt. His black necktie was not a clip-on, the only grace in his appearance. The brief he worked on through the night sat on top of the disarray on John Devine's desk.

"Tell me again why I should give a shit," said Devine. "Counterterrorism has enough messing around in another department's business."

"A Chinese Kilo class submarine in the Straits of Taiwan challenged USS Ross a few hours ago. According to my Navy source, they posed no direct threat to the destroyer or other vessels in the water."

Crumbly shoved two satellite photographs at Devine. "See here? Two Chinese army divisions are moving to the straits. We think the Chinese are preparing for war over Taiwan."

"This is military stuff, not intelligence. We have our part in the President's morning briefing and they have theirs."

"I read Shaw's report on China attempting to extort oil from British Chemical Enterprises. They have enough fuel for their ships and jet fighters, and are using this as a bargaining chip. We help them get the oil they want, they back down. For the Agency to hold the facts until after the event would knock us down again in the Administration's eyes."

"Like the fall of the Berlin Wall. You've got my interest."

Crumbly found his rhythm and began a recitation about where the Chinese army divisions were headed being only a diversionary move. By appearing to American naval vessels, the ships would leave the Straits of Taiwan under pressure from an American public wary of another prolonged Cold War. Once they succeeded in clearing the Straits, an attack on Taiwan with conventional weapons was next and, if needs be, strategic nuclear weapons.

"Quite an assumption, Howard," said Devine "The Chinese would risk a confrontation for a pissy island they gave up on years ago?"

"They took delivery of two submarines from Russia last week. One went directly into the Straits four days ago. Our Navy has extended patrols in the area to include two nuclear subs."

"What am I supposed to do?"

"Sir, the report is incomplete and I don't want this in the White House pouch without all the information and scenarios for the President and the Joint Chiefs of Staff to make a rational decision. Taiwan has been an extremely sensitive issue since the Korean War. China sees Taiwan as Chinese. How would we feel if another nation occupied the Olympic Peninsula?"

"Grateful, I think. Maybe they could get the rain to stop."

Crumbly slapped the desk. "I'm serious, sir. There's a connection with British Chemical and the Ceyhan pipeline and lord knows what else."

"We've kept the oil from the Chinese so far. There's no reason to believe they will get enough for their plans of expansion. Whatever the case, no one can deny a peaceful solution worked out here will go a long way to peace throughout Asia. There's a broad consensus all over the world that US support for Taiwan is slowing the progress regional peace in Asia. Other potential areas of conflict, including Korea, can be handled with relative ease if the US and China cooperate.

"Coffee," said Devine. "I must have coffee." He walked to drip machine set on the credenza and pulled out the full carafe. "We'll both need a lot of coffee if we're going to rewrite and flesh out this brief."

"You'll help?"

"What has saved the United States more times than 'enlightened self-interest' is some guy in an office somewhere who is loyal to this country's ideals of life, liberty, and the pursuit of happiness. This is our turn to be 'some guy.' Grab a mug and let's get to work."

Alternatives and justifications were considered. Even a limited economic blockade would anger American businesses with manufacturing plants on the mainland, but China's record of human rights abuses, and selling arms to Pakistan and Iran could be used as justification. On the other side, China made major contributions to arms control and nonproliferation regimes and treaties in the past decade while the US ignored basic nonproliferation principles. Whatever Devine and

Crumbly's final brief said, the Administration had to decide the only option was diplomacy.

"Damn," said Devine. "The diplomatic solution went out with Kennedy. Look where that got him."

CHAPTER 9

With an Arab kaffiyeh draped over his head and aviator sunglasses, Shafique Al-Zeitun drove the dented Land Rover in the Jordanian countryside. The half-eaten package of figs on the seat beside him was covered in the same road dust invading every crease and surface of the vehicle. Kamal ibn-Sultan had entrusted him to perform small but important annoy-and-destroy missions. He was on one now, the fourth to this area in the past year.

Al-Zetun stopped at Medba, the ancient mountaintop in Jordan where, according to the early Christian monks of Saint Aaron, Moses had seen the Promised Land. Here he drove to an old church on the plateau overlooking the Dead Sea and Jordan Valley to meet a young gunrunner. The smuggler supplied him with a 9mm Beretta, ammunition, hand grenades, and wax paper-wrapped blocks of Cemtex explosive. They packed the materials into black bags and loaded them into the Land Rover. Once done, Al-Zeitun drove south to Petra.

The Desert Highway wound through a bleak, rocky landscape missing any plant or animal life. Al-Zeitun followed the signs to Amman and turned left at the black and white notice for Wadi Mousa-Petra. Not far from the narrow canyon entrance to the Nabatean city of Petra, he stopped at the terraced Mövenpick Resort and parked the Rover himself to the valet's dismay. Rose-red Petra had been lost for hundreds of years until uncovered in 1812. Towering hills of rust-colored sandstone surrounded the city and its building had been carved from the same material. The luxurious Mövenpick Resort had been built to fit into the landscape with cast concrete tinted the same color as the hills.

Al-Zeitun grabbed a camera from the compartment between the seats and left the black bags. This was not his first visit to Petra, for he had relatives in the highlands nearby. According to family lore, his father and mother met in the village once called El-Ji and later renamed Wadi Mousa, Valley of Moses, by early Christians. His mother was the daughter of a Bedouin trader and silversmith. The young couple went to the father's home in Baghdad where Shafique Al-Zeitun was born. Al-Zeitun spent his childhood in the souks of Baghdad where his father had a stall frequented by Arabic nomads who talked with reverence about Petra.

Al-Zeitun mingled among the tourists and students touring the old city.

"Petra was first established around the 3rd century BCE by two early Arab peoples, the sedentary Edomites and the nomadic Nabatean traders," a clean and pressed guide lectured to his attentive group.

"This synthesis produced people whose combined strengths in technology and commerce to found an empire extending into Syria. Despite attempts by Herod the Great, Antigonus, and Pompey to make Petra part of their empires so they could control the trade route from ancient Egypt to Babylon and beyond, Petra remained in Nabatean hands until 100 AD."

"What happened?" asked a man wearing a wide brimmed straw hat.

"The Romans finally succeeded in taking over the city. Eventually they moved east to Constantinople and this area was forgotten by the outside world until the Crusaders built Shobak Castle here in the 12th Century."

The guide pointed to a temple carved into the red rock. "Above is the resting place of Rebaal II, the last of the Nabatean kings ruling Petra."

Like the other tourists, Al-Zeitun took photographs of one ancient facade after another, their ages ranging from the third century BCE to the fourth century AD. He focused his Nikon camera on Jasr-el bint, the temple of the goddess Doshra, and the Chazane, the most photographed burial temple in Petra. The group tagged behind the guide along the red canyon road, the Siq, to the village of Wadi Mousa.

———

The telephone rang in the Counterterrorism Center's chief of section office as John Devine was leaving to get breakfast. He had been at his desk since dawn and needed the break.

"Devine here."

"Shaw coming at you. I have the data on ships receiving and dropping off cargo at the port of Gioia Tauro since the anthrax left Rebirth Island. A Sicilian carrier accepted a cargo container headed for New York, and unloaded at Newark for Marco Polo Imports, a Manhattan freight company. I'm faxing copies of the goods-for-transit papers from the shipper."

"I'll have a man investigate Marco Polo immediately. What else?"

"Look up Al-Zeitun on your watch list."

Devine punched the name on his keyboard. "Got him. Full name Shafique Al-Zeitun."

"He's been spotted in Petra of all places, disguised as a tourist. The General Intelligence Department thinks he's there to blow up a sacred site along with some American tourists for fun."

"Al-Zeitun has the credentials. Born in Jordan and raised in Iraq, trained with Hezbollah in Iran. Mother is Bedouin. He'd blow up his mother's country?"

"Remember Timothy McVeigh. Destruction rules, not sentiment."

Devine watched the screen. "I have recent stuff. Al-Zeitun was named by two Afghan citizens arrested crossing into Jordan from Iraq as a contact for Kamal ibn-Sultan. The Afghanis admitted to being couriers and are suspected operatives in a plan to attack American and other Western tourists in Jordan."

"That's my confirmation."

"A cheap diversion to distract our attention from what is really going on."

"I agree, John," said Shaw. "Meanwhile, Al-Zeitun has disappeared somewhere in Jordanian territory. With help from family and friends, no doubt."

"How about ibn-Sultan?"

"Nothing. The Energy Secretary should be told not to attend the pipeline inauguration ceremony."

"Unfortunately, we would lose lots of prestige if the Secretary fails to show. America has to give visible support to the pipeline. A telegram won't do."

"Okay, keep me informed."

"When are you leaving for Ceyhan?"

"The fifteenth. The ceremony was postponed because of mechanical problems with the main oil pumps."

"Is Ambassador Paige still going?"

"Yes, she's arranged transportation with the Embassy. I'll put someone special on her."

"I want you and LaGrange."

"But I'll be running the Special Ops."

"You can do both. Find a safe house where you can work and live so she won't run off shopping or whatever women do to cause nightmares for a security detail."

"Paige is not the type. I'll get a big place as close as possible. My guys will be in and out, and need crashing space."

"How is our Special Forces team mending?"

"Tom Singer is still recouping from his wounds. I'm going to Almaty for a few days to check things out."

"Keep a tight watch on the ambassador. We can't afford another mistake."

"Will do."

"The Secret Service is sending a small army to Ceyhan and the

Turks have moved their best forces into the port area. Energy Secretary Martin Holbeck needs to be assured of protection."

"What's happening with the Chinese?"

"Naval presence in the Straits of Taiwan has gone up a notch and no one's talking."

"The current crop in the White House regards diplomacy as weakness. Let's hope a cooler head can prevail."

Devine hung up and headed out the door for scrambled eggs, but no sausage. The CIA cafeteria sausages tasted like wood putty.

———

Al-Zeitun had been hiding for almost twenty-four hours in the stone hut that served his cousin Hamid as shelter for his precious goats. The hut on a rocky outcropping faced Jebel Haroun, the mountaintop above the canyons and desert road leading to Petra. Moses' brother Aaron once stood atop the plateau of red rock and gazed at the Promised Land. Prophet Mohammed saw much more.

"Shafique," Hamid called from behind the red-hued boulders. "I am coming in."

Al-Zeitun relaxed and lowered the Beretta. The young man appeared in the cavity of the door, wearing a sun-bleached skullcap, wool vest, and cotton blouse and pants stained with red dirt. Behind him goats climbed among the rocks on a steep rise on the other side of the canyon.

"Did you bring water?"

Hamid handed him a plastic bottle and Al-Zeitun eagerly poured the water into his mouth Bedouin-style. His thirst satisfied, he set the jar on the earthen floor. Hamid reached into the bag hanging from his shoulder and took out pita bread and a flat clay pot. "Best tahini in Jordan," he said. "Soldiers are looking for you, Shafique."

"Only below, not with the goats."

"Petra and Wadi Mousa are ringed with soldiers, as are Bedouins under direct command of King Abdullah."

Al-Zeitun dipped the soft flat bread into the tahini paste. "You worry like an old woman."

"There is one route open. We can smuggle you out to Wadi Ibn-Hamid and the Wadi Arnoon canyon. Cross to the waterfall where a jeep will be waiting. The driver will take you to the King Abdullah Bridge. From there you can go to the Jordan River and into the Palestinian enclave at Jericho."

"I have a mission to complete."

"You are gambling with our lives, my cousin."

"I am willing to take the risk."

"We can leave after dark. The sun is almost gone."

"Kamal ibn-Sultan will hunt me down if I do not deliver on my promise."

"The security forces are going to kill or capture you."

Al-Zeitun watched the shadows lengthen outside. Daylight faded quickly and there was a chill to the mountain air. "Maybe I should leave. But I need a favor before I go."

"Tell me, my cousin."

"I have a Land Rover at the Mövenpick Resort. Send your brother Fuad to the hotel parking lot."

"He tends the goats and they do not know anyone but him."

"Leave those fucking goats on their own for a few hours."

"They are everything we have."

"Many apologies, cousin. Do this for me and half of the money hidden in the vehicle is yours. You can buy more goats and I will be able to fund my escape."

"Let me do this errand."

"No. Fuad spends most of his time with the goats and should be unnoticed. Call him to join us."

"He is an innocent. This is not dangerous, Shafique?"

"I would not put Fuad in danger and worry your mother, who is as dear to me as my own."

Hamid went through the door of the hut in darkness. He heard the jingle of the small bells attached to the necks of the goats, invisible on the slopes of the canyon.

"Brother! Are you near?" Hamid's voice echoed among the rocks.

Fuad stepped from behind a boulder. "Quiet. Shouting scares the goats."

"Sorry, brother. We have an emergency." Hamid took Fuad into an embrace and led him to the hut.

"Why do you need me?" Fuad asked.

"For a mission," Al-Zeitun said. "Here are the keys to my Land Rover in the last row of the Mövenpick parking lot. Drive to the hotel entrance and when the attendant comes, give him the envelope from the briefcase under the passenger seat. The money is in there as well. He will see you get back here safely."

Fuad accepted the keys. "I can do that."

"Keep half of the money to increase your flocks, my cousin."

"You are very generous and I thank you in advance."

"Meanwhile, your goats will be fine. I will sing to them should they miss you too much."

Fuad embraced his brother and cousin, and went out the door. Al-Zeitun's cell phone vibrated in the pocket of his leather jacket, and he ignored the call. This was not the moment to be talking to Kamal ibn-Sultan.

How much money was in the briefcase? Fuad wondered. He hurried along the arid desert road through Wadi Mousa, though he had to rest several times. An ailing kid had kept him awake the previous night. He reached the Mövenpick Resort before sunrise. If not for his mission, he would like to meander through the old ruins again. His promise to his cousin came first.

The parking lot hand many Land Rovers, the rental vehicles of tourists, and archeologists and volunteer excavators. Fuad tried two before one opened for him. By now the sun was rising and he watched the color of the rocks turn red with the light. The morning display of color always struck him as magic. Sundown was the same,

majestic and astonishing. He knew few other vistas and longed for
no other.

Fuad turned to the task at hand. Would the friend of his cousin be
on duty? He saw no one coming or going from the hotel, and tilted his
head back on the driver's seat to sleep a few minutes.

A security guard in dark uniform and matching cap banged his fist
on the Land Rover's hood. "Open the door!"

Fuad rolled down the window. "Good morning," he said, "This car
belongs to my cousin. Is there money owed for parking?"

"Get out," the man said, and Fuad did as he was told.

"Please, my cousin is concerned about his car."

The man struck Fuad and backed him against the fender. He
searched under the front seat of the Land Rover until he found the
briefcase.

"That belongs to my cousin," Fuad protested.

"Let's see what he keeps inside."

A flash of light greater than the morning sun engulfed Fuad, the
man, and the Land Rover.

———

At the Almaty Embassy, Elizabeth tossed and turned in her bed. The
wind outside the window rustled the leaves in the garden. She turned on
her night table lamp and tuned the radio to the Armed Services Network.
Elizabeth wondered how Amelia was reacting to the bodyguards Shaw
had arranged. Bad tempered, she guessed, if she knew her daughter.

A bolt of lightning outside the open window followed with the roar
of thunder and a strong gust of wind drowned out the radio. Heavy
raindrops pelted the screen and Elizabeth got up and closed the window.
She stood there watching the unexpected downpour. Even the sound
was energizing and God knew she needed a boost to drive away her bad
dreams. Soon she would head for the ceremonies at the Port of Ceyhan
where the new oil pumps would be activated in front of the presidents

and prime ministers of Turkey, Azerbaijan, Georgia, and Kazakhstan, and the US Energy Secretary.

Finishing the pipeline was a significant achievement for everyone involved, including Strauss, and he would be there. She hoped to be gracious but she was still angry with him for putting her daughter in danger. Shaw would accompany her and serve as a buffer between them.

Elizabeth hated to be so bitter to the father of her only child. She had more reason to be thankful. The repeating memories at night of her time on the island happened with less frequency, and her medical tests for chemical toxicity had come out negative.

She tried to think of anything else at the late hour. The storm's thunder and downpour continued. She flicked the television remote to catch a French or German movie. The late news on CNN had a reporter in front of the State Department building in Washington. Elizabeth turned up the volume.

"In Jordan, a bomb intended for a hotel went off in its parking lot at dawn. The early morning blast destroyed many vehicles and thought to have killed a security guard. Officials at Jordan's General Intelligence Department believe the bomb to be the work of Shafique Al-Zeitun, a long-sought terrorist. Whether or not Al-Zeitun was killed in the explosion is not yet known. Though the blast broke several dozen windows on the west side of the luxury hotel where a number of Americans were staying, no one inside was injured."

Elizabeth sat at the edge of her bed to digest what she had seen. She punched the remote control until she saw Anita Eckberg cavorting in a fountain with Marcello Mastroianni. An Italian movie would be more comforting than the news.

———

Roger Shaw stood at the window of an empty Port of Ceyhan warehouse and focused his binoculars on the empty anchorages below. Shinning new pipes snaked among the tired corrugated iron buildings and the tugboat docks. The air stank of dead seawater and crude oil, the smell of money. Six years and three billion dollars had gone into the construction of the 1100-kilometer pipeline. Turkey and Georgia had their hands out for transit fees, but these were nothing to the profits the light crude oil pumped from Baku would make for British Chemical Enterprises.

Armenia remained angry over being excluded from the black gold rush and the Russians capitalized on the situation by selling them arms. Hell, the Russians were pissed for the same reason. Added to the mix was the Kurdish Worker's Party and separatist groups in Georgia yelling about environmental damage. Shaw had heard oil production in the Azeri fields was much lower than projected and weak oil prices made the Ceyhan line financially infeasible. Another boondoggle, he thought, for stripping a country of its resources for free. No wonder everyone except the people making the money was against the pipeline.

Shaw had security problems to consider. The bandstand and dais waited for the coming guests, and he counted at least ten clear lines of fire from the surrounding rooftops. He had to have men posted next to the dignitaries, in the crowd, on the roofs, and in helicopters for any kind of safety. He also needed to cover the water by ship and ask the harbormaster to close the port until the ceremony had ended. A new maritime scam had developed where hijackers took over legitimate ships and evaded discovery by constantly changing flags and identities. They got on board as passengers or boarded as seamen with forged papers. In one case he knew, a local patrol boat came alongside a cargo vessel and masked hijackers took over before the crew could stop them. When the crew resisted, several were shot. The gunmen stole sophisticated satellite communications equipment, laptop computers, night vision goggles, and anti-tank missiles in its original US army packing. They were well organized and equipped with the latest high-tech equipment, even satellite positioning gear.

Shaw's cell phone buzzed. Good, he thought, the interruption will slow my growing unease about the event.

"Devine here. Give me the bad news."

"Not so bad. I'm doing a recon on the buildings and in one right now. From this viewpoint, anything could happen. If you can have the Marines loan me the 82nd Airborne, we can secure the area."

"Shit."

"The port authorities have the main points covered already. They'll board every ship and check its papers, crew, cargo, and owner. The other day they boarded a German carrier and heard noises in the cargo hold. A stowaway was living very comfortably in a container, with a cot, hot plate, cell phone, and a well-stocked cupboard. He had a bunch of Canadian and American passports and entry permits for security men at O'Hare, Kennedy, and Newark airports."

"What happened to him?"

"He's in custody. The Italians want him."

"At least he's not your problem. Have LaGrange to keep tabs on the harbormaster."

"Will do. Is there any way we can cut and run on this, John? The whole setup is ready for disaster."

"The oil has to come through, for the region and the West, unless you'd like to fall back a hundred years and buy a horse."

———

Petrova Ivanovna Verkhovtsev stretched her languid figure across the silk sheets. "Take the pill and come back to bed, Grigory Parfenovich," she said.

"Stupid things. They make my heart race. How are you coming with Strauss?"

"The Americans are not responding as quickly as we hoped to the Taiwan threat," she admitted. "I wonder if there is another way to get the oil. Maybe the Iranians?"

"Get to him through his daughter."

"Too much trouble. Your kidnapping has interested the Americans. This means the CIA."

"So what?"

Petrova slapped his naked hairy chest. "Not fit for an afternoon fuck or thinking. What am I to with you, Grigory? Strauss may possibly stop the Chinese offer. I want another source who cares not about politics."

"Put more pressure on him. Mikhail and I can help."

"I can mind Burt Strauss. He thinks the Chinese want oil for a war."

"Why else would they try to obtain Caspian oil? They need a huge fuel reserve before they can start, especially with Kilo class submarines."

"Your idiots in the admiralty found subs for them, Dmitry Ogdanov and Sergei Ivanovsky."

"I was merely an adviser."

"Do not keep things from me, Grigory Parfenovich."

"Never, my wretched concubine. How much is our side if Strauss is able to supply the Chinese?"

"One hundred and fifty thousand hard currency, plus our consulting fee of one hundred thousand dollars. Tax-free in a bank of our choosing."

"I love the sound of numbers. Two hundred and fifty thousand is a quarter of a million dollars. We can play the currency market and multiply that amount into four hundred thousand dollars in weeks."

"Grigory," said Petrova. "I believe this talk of money has revitalized you."

He looked at his groin. "How better to celebrate our success?"

In the morning Petrova called Strauss to arrange a meeting.

"I'm not interested, Ms. Verkhovtsev. Tell Hoa Lin to find another pigeon."

"He has agreed to your finder's fee. This is an extremely generous offer."

"You can't get to me or anyone close to me. I've made sure."

"I will find them another source."

"How do you sleep at night, Petrova? The oil for the Chinese will go to killing people, and not only soldiers who know the risks. Farmers, teachers, bus drivers, and clerks will die. The ordinary people always die in wars. Economies are ravaged and mothers and children go hungry and homeless. Take responsibility for your actions. Don't help them."

"What of you, Burt Strauss? British Chemical Enterprises is not a philanthropic institution. Oil necessary to heat homes and fuel cars in the East will be taken to the West where every drop is squandered. Do not talk cheap humanist politics to me. The common goal we work for is hard currency. Your illusions disgust me."

Petrova slammed down the receiver. Men are assholes, she thought, the lot of them. For two pre-free market rubles she would have Grigory shoot Strauss, or do the job herself.

———

The bright teal awning over the storefront on Third Avenue and 23rd Street in Manhattan read "Viola Gelato" and "From Italy to America with Love." The manager at the counter, Franco Manzani, was a bulky man with a shock of black curls. Ali Massouf winced at the soiled apron hugging the man's protruding belly.

"Nice to see you again, Mr. Marshall," Franco said.

"You too, Franco. How's it going?"

"Always good in hot weather."

"Good. We have a delivery to the Garden this afternoon. I'm sending a couple of men over and they'll use the van most of the day for other errands as well. I'd also like to store some personal things in the back. Will that be all right?"

"No problem. I'll take out anything in the way."

"I need a lock for the room. Don't worry about the dog show this Sunday. Let me cover the concession and enjoy the day with your family."

"Thank you, Mr. Marshall, I appreciate that."

"If you have those payroll checks ready, I'll sign them."

Manzini retrieved a manila envelope from the cash drawer and Massouf took the checks into the rear office. He disliked giving him the Sunday off, as all routines should stay the same. When the mission was finished, he wanted the gelato business to look entirely normal. Whoever worked the last dozen events should work similar ones. Manzini should be at the Garden concession on the big day except Viola Gelato might be held liable or expected to pay his medical expenses should something happen.

Massouf finished the paperwork and returned to the front. "Franco, are you and the others covered by medical insurance?"

"Just Workman's Comp."

Massouf wrote himself a note to check out financial responsibilities in case of sickness, injury, or death at work. Business was a nuisance. He took the bank deposit from the cash drawer. "I'm going now," he said.

"Good-bye, Mr. Marshall."

"Change the dirty apron. I pay enough for the laundry service."

"Yes, sir."

CHAPTER 10

The six-story building on Greene Street in New York had a cast-iron facade, left over from when Soho was a warehouse district prone to fires in the nineteenth century. Banners fluttered to announce art galleries and cafes in the present day. Ali Massouf rode the complaining old elevator to the top and entered directly into a loft owned by a post-modern figurative painter who had moved his studio to Martha's Vineyard. He stayed away from Manhattan except for gallery openings and collecting rent checks.

"Samir," called Massouf. "Where are you?"

"Here in the back."

Most of the loft was empty. Floor-to-ceiling windows let in sunlight to play with the dust motes. In the rear were workbenches holding drills, a vise, screwdrivers, metal and wood saws, bits of plywood, lengths of pipe, boxes of connectors and washers, and a soldering iron. Wood dust covered the floor around Samir Mohammed. He lifted a squat, gray pump into an open plywood box, absorbed in his work.

"Are you designing a delivery system or making a bird house?" asked Massouf.

"This is for the portable sampling pump. We need an airflow and sample measurement at the Garden to see what kind of power they have."

Mohammed shifted the pump in its container. "Once we have an accurate picture of wind velocity coming through the vents, I'll know how to proceed."

"Sounds complicated."

"We should be able to tie in to their blowers. There is a device used for producing cotton dust aerosol I can adapt for our purposes. The one I have in mind utilizes a 12-inch loudspeaker driven by a 60-Hz sine-wave signal to vibrate a material membrane diaphragm, a powder re-suspension surface. The re-suspended powder is then entrained in an air stream for delivery to the exposure chamber.

"We'll work on a bigger scale and try several diaphragm materials, plastic film maybe, or a dental dam. The flow rate must be large enough to deliver a significant number of liters per minute into the exposure chamber. If the system in place can do the job, the next step will be to attach our device."

"Enough. This technical talk gives me a headache. Have you settled here? Are you keeping with your prayers and eating well?"

Mohammed wiped his hands on the front of his khaki pants. Outside jackhammers tore into the street in search of a cable line to repair.

"Manhattan is more pleasant than San Francisco, Ali. No one here gives a damn about my feelings and I like the distance. I pray five times every day, the same as when I was a boy, and the Papaya Garden nearby is good. I don't need much."

"I'll get out of here and let you work. We meet at the concession eight o'clock Saturday morning."

"Zaidan is taking the pump with the supplies this afternoon and storing them in the concession stand freezer."

"Be cautious, Samir."

"Only an extra drum of gelato."

Massouf wished him well. The project was becoming too complicated for his simple mind. He wanted a quick return to a straightforward killing field with weapons he could see.

———

The report on Marco Polo Imports did not impress John Devine, sloppy fieldwork turned sloppier as older agents retired and younger agents concentrated on promotions. The freight forwarder had claimed the container from the Sicilian ship and stored the contents in a bonded warehouse. Every company waiting for their merchandise was legitimate except for an outfit that appeared to be dealing in stolen goods. A late-night check of the warehouse showed a load of Gucci knockoffs taken by novice thieves who thought they had the real article.

Devine made his notes on the report and sent Howard Crumbly a memo to check on any businesses in the New York City area that had been sold in the last twelve months. Crumbly would yell when taken off the China desk, however temporary, but he needed someone he could trust. Devine shut off his computer, waved his pass through the security stations, and drove home.

Stephanie was quiet over dinner. Open take-out Thai food cartons filled the space between them on the scarred oak dining room table.

"What's on your mind?" he asked. "Don't like this elegant meal?"

"I love it. This is the first we've shared in weeks." She turned pensive. "I was thinking about your work. The station gets raw feeds from the White House for press conferences, you know. Today we had the Secretary of Defense making a statement about the bombing in Petra."

"This is why you're so silent?"

"Before we switched over to live broadcast I heard him mention your name to his aide. He said, 'I wish that asshole Devine had gone up in the blast.'"

"Don't worry, babe. The Department of Defense is playing politics. We're supposed to be sharing intelligence, then they change their minds and we're not allowed access to any nuggets they find. They don't know what they want and neither do we. Let's not spoil the evening by talking about work."

Stephanie reached for a spring roll. "I want to know if you're in trouble. No one threatens my man, especially after I bought tickets for the Bulls-Nicks game. You almost forgot last year."

"We'll take the train and stay at the Essex for the weekend."

"No excuses, Mr. Devine. Our anniversary comes before any world crisis."

"Yes, ma'am. I've brought something special for dessert."

"Don't tell me you drove to Filomena's for triple chocolate mousse."

"Yes, ma'am."

———

Kamal ibn-Sultan enjoyed being in Tehran after hiding in the rocky terrain of Afghanistan. The city sat at the bottom of the Elburz Mountains and close to the desert of Dasht-e Kavir. Outside the window of the rooftop apartment, Mount Damavand remained as a sentry against the Crusaders. Tehran had grown in eighty years, from two hundred thousand to fourteen million people. Most were Shi'ite Muslims, who adulterated the word of God, but enough were Sunni brethren that ibn-Sultan could move without the risk of capture.

With the increased population came the curses of the West, like air pollution. Automobiles ravaged the streets like Mongol horsemen and their fumes spoiled the sky. Ibn-Sultan took refuge in the Golestan Palace on the bad days, the former royal residence of the Qajars an oasis of silence. To return to the righteousness of the eighteenth century was his dream.

Five years before, Iranian President Mohammad Khatami sent his Law Enforcement Forces into the Khak Sefid, or White Soil, neighborhood of Tehran. Dark uniforms carrying truncheons, guns, and handcuffs kicked down doors, and fifty men involved with the heroin trade were tossed in the street for later retrieval. The people living in the shabby apartment buildings cheered the arrests. Parents and children no longer had to fear for their safety. When the price of raw opium increased from

$35 to $350 per kilo, new drug dealers took the place of those in prison but Khak Sefid remained out of bounds to them.

The back room was plain, small, and warm, with only cushions on the floor for furniture. A runner brought food from a local *chelokababis* and the smells did little to lessen the combined musk, dust, and street and traffic stench. None of that concerned Yakir Arvatian, the former colonel. He had traveled far for the meeting and missed two days' worth of meals. Arvatian tore into the bag from the restaurant. Ibn-Sultan watched him silently and admired his appetite. A man eating from intense hunger increases his pleasure in the food.

Loud voices and music assaulted them from the adjacent buildings. Arvatian opened foil containers and lunged at the kebabs and pita bread.

"I have information that might interest you," said ibn-Sultan. "Suleyman Ehmat contacted me."

Arvatian stripped a kebab and loaded meat into a piece of bread. "Where is he?"

"Ceyhan. He says the American Energy Secretary is guaranteed to attend the ceremonies for the new pipeline. An opportunity has opened for us."

Arvatian dropped his food. "How did Suleyman get such information?"

"A friend who works at the American embassy in Ankara. Some woman." Ibn-Sultan shifted in his cushion and his eyes darted to the door.

"You seem nervous. Are you expecting someone?"

"I have many things on my mind. Life is complicated and time is very short. I need your help."

"Yes, of course."

"I was disappointed when you lost the two Americans on Rebirth Island to Petrova Verkhovtsev. But you know my displeasure."

"American commandos came out of the sky and the Verkhovtsev woman had help from Russian thugs."

"To be defensive is unbecoming."

The reprimand silenced Arvatian and he folded his arms in front of him.

"I forgive the error. Our next operation is of greater significance and this time you must be prepared for anything. A large sum is yours if you succeed, since any contact with our organization will be a liability."

"The chance is mine to take," Arvatian said.

"One million dollars is on deposit in a Luxemburg bank account. The Americans will hunt you and they are improving at finding fugitives. Still, their new problems with the Chinese may divert their attention. You could die an old man of natural causes."

"Let us hope."

"There is another matter. The Americans are looking for al-Zeitun. He was not killed in the bombing at the hotel. Shafique has always shirked his duties and this time he sent in a young cousin. Make him dead."

Arvatian suppressed a sigh. Finding al-Zeitun when he did not want to be found was impossible. He would wait until the Americans captured him and tell ibn-Sultan the credit was his. The meal he wanted lay abandoned on the floor.

Ibn-Sultan left Tehran for two days and returned to preview the videos he had commissioned. The screening was held in an old factory. Sheared bolts poked out of pools of stagnant water and the remaining frames of conveyor belts held spider webs. Metal folding chairs were set in a corner around a television set and VCR, shielded with curtains to keep echoes from bouncing around the massive space. The curtains had been scrounged from a theater and reminded ibn-Sultan of a puppet theater he had seen as a child. Suyleman Ehmat the Turk came for the occasion, along with Abdullah, the director, and the five men of Abdullah's technical crew.

"Please," ibn-Sultan addressed the gathering. "Despite the humbleness of our quarters, our seats are comfortable and we have much to enjoy." The group clapped and he motioned them to sit down. Abdullah dimmed the lights and fed a cassette into the VCR.

"This one took longer to make than the others. We had the usual stoppages to evade the satellites, but on this day there were American planes going over. The noise interrupted us continually. A camel caravan forced us to run to move the equipment out of sight."

Ibn-Sultan cleared his throat, already bored by the narration.

"On this next one we had fixed our sound problems. By this time we were experts at working in the open. The text is self-explanatory."

Ibn-Sultan concentrated on the overall appeal of the video scenes, the intent of every chosen phrase, and the different yet unidentifiable aspects of mountainous and desert landscapes. These were perfect, he decided. His voice was steady, yet indicated the passage of time, as did his face and hair color. Ehmat's change in appearance too was excellent, and certain themes were carefully woven throughout but never said the same way. Extraordinary people had been picked for the job. The participants listened intently to the end of one of the tapes: "Though the Americans have elected a new leader, the war perpetrated against the Muslim world continues under a different figurehead. Nothing has changed and together we must continue to fight. Our land belongs to Almighty God, not the Crusaders."

After watching the videos, Abdullah turned off the VCR. "I think they are very good. I am pleased and hope you are."

"I am," ibn-Sultan said. "I credit your brilliant editing and aging us so remarkably year to year. To the rest, your help has been invaluable. Outside is a van to take you to the airport where funds will be distributed before your flight home. In keeping with our agreement, never speak of this, not even to your families, and all copies of your creative achievement must be left here. These videos may someday be important to our mission."

The crew was relieved to be done with the demanding project. "We are honored to have been chosen," said one of Abdullah's men. "We pray they will never need to be used and our group is brought together again to film a victory."

The men were in high spirits as they told Ehmat and ibn-Sultan good-bye. They gathered their equipment and left through folds in the heavy drapes. Ibn-Sultan listened to their footsteps cross the old factory to exit and board the bus.

"Yakir will meet them with everything he needs?" asked ibn-Sultan.

"The bomb is ready and he has the remote. He will set it off at the airport."

"The attack will leave many questions. Yakir will find out about the videos in the event of our deaths. Now we have other plans to make."

———

After a three-hour delay, Iran Airlines flight 32 took off from Imam Khomeini International Airport in Tehran and arrived late safe at the Ataturk International Airport in Istanbul, despite sudden air turbulence that caused a less than smooth landing. Yakir Arvatian walked into the terminal and joined the line at passport control. Two somber customs officials commanded a bulletproof booth to examine the documents of new arrivals.

Arvatian glanced over at the arrival lounge in the hopes someone would be meeting him. After clearing customs, he heard a page for Mr. Arventure. Arvatian went to the information desk and asked for the message. The clerk pulled a slip of paper from the mess on the counter. "Meet your party at the taxi stand outside the baggage area."

Arvatian thanked the clerk and toted his carry-on luggage outside. A man with a thick black beard speckled with gray, a black wool cap, and tinted eyeglasses read a newspaper. He wore a blue denim shirt and jeans. Arvatian asked him for the time.

"You're late," Ehmat said, and tossed the paper into a trashcan at the curb.

"Thank you for waiting. My flight was delayed by an accident."

"I heard a minivan exploded. Five passengers and the driver died. Air travel is not safe anymore with the violent people running loose these days."

Ehmat missed the irony of his words. He slapped Arvatian on the shoulder. "I have my car in the parking lot."

They settled in the silver BMW and pulled out of the lot. "I am surprised to see you at the airport," Arvatian said. "Is there a risk to come here?"

"We have much work ahead, Yakir."

"You sound like ibn-Sultan."

"We will eat and drink, and then go out to play."

Ehmat drove southeast from Istanbul. Several hours later after crossing the Sakarya River, he pulled off the main road. Forty kilometers went by before Ehmat stopped past abandoned three- and four-story buildings. Arvatian helped him carry dozens of bright orange targets from the trunk to a clearing. They laid them out in a 15-meter circle. The two worked in silence, then got back into the car and returned to the vacant buildings.

"Take the boxes," Ehmat said, and pointed to the tallest building. They hauled a dozen boxes up an exterior wooden staircase missing several steps between floors. On the flat baked-tile roof, Ehmat opened a box and took out a toy red and white airplane, the wingspan less than half a meter. White fuel powered the small motors of the planes.

"What new game is this?" Arvatian asked.

"These are for the opening of the pipeline in Ceyhan. Each plane will be packed with Cemtex. They can fly one kilometer with an altitude of 300 meters."

"Where did you get them?"

"We have a workshop. Got the idea from ones designed for Yasser Arafat of al-Fatah. His were steered by remote control, useless if the plane drops out of sight. Ours only launch by remote and then explode on impact. Let's try them out on the targets."

Arvatian looked over the side of the short barrier wall at the targets in the distance. Ehmat handed him a remote. "Make the plane clear the wall and head south."

"The targets are too far away."

"Practice, Yakir. Get used to sending them this distance over the targets. Think of the area within the circle as the dignitary stand."

Arvatian fumbled with the black control box. "This toy can lift off, soar, dive, circle, and land?"

"A small adjustment has been made in the engine. They are heavy enough so the wind won't toss them about like kites."

"How do I get these over the target before security agents start shooting them down?"

"When you master the planes, you will teach a team. Choose who you want. Launch many planes and the sun will be in the eyes of the security men, not ours. We have secured a building, a porcelain doll factory. The former owner has bought a shipment of the same airplanes. We will adapt as many as we need and switch them later."

"The payload is sufficient?" Arvatian hefted an airplane and turned upside down.

"One in ten hitting the target area are enough. You will see. Once you master flying these, you can try the real ones."

"There must be an escape route."

"After the planes are launched, your team exits the building to a waiting van. No one is going to know where to look, not from a kilometer away."

"I need a room near to the site."

"Comfortable accommodations are arranged within walking distance of the ceremonies."

"What about the pipeline pumps? To destroy them will take a shoulder-fired missile."

"We have a supplier who is a captain in an army unit stationed outside of Istanbul. They have the Igla-2 surface-to-air missile. He wants a large payment and we can take however many are necessary."

Both men knew of the Igla-2. The device was less than two meters long and weighed 13 kilograms, with a range of five kilometers and a maximum speed of 2,050 kph. Once launched, the remaining solid rocket propulsion for the Igla exploded on contact along with the warhead. The distance to the target was too far for a rocket-propelled grenade, and the Igla had greater accuracy and destructive power.

"Smuggling the weapon into Ceyhan is complicated."

"Not by ship. There will be plenty in the port. Where you want to participate is your decision. Realize this is most crucial to Kamal ibn-Sultan."

"That portion of the operation is mine."

"Very well. You are important to ibn-Sultan and the Cleric, soon to be admitted to the inner circle."

"The Cleric. I have heard much about him, yet I still know nothing."

"He is our guide to reclaiming the lands of Islam. This holy man has fought the infidel from Afghanistan to Bosnia. He shows us the true words of the *Qur'an*. To the Cleric, we are already victorious. He has seen the future with the help of Almighty God and we follow his lead in all things."

"I should like to meet this man."

"Be thinking of whom you want and get them here immediately. For now, we play."

Through the waning light of the afternoon, Arvatian tried to concentrate on getting the airplanes in the circle of targets. How should he greet the Cleric? The question disrupted his aim.

———

The bounty on Kamal ibn-Sultan increased as he traveled across the East. From one hundred thousand to two hundred thousand, the sum breached the half million mark until the amount offered by the American and British governments hit two million dollars hard currency. In Baku, Reza Deghani joined Suleyman Ehmat for dinner at the New Anadolu on Rasul Rza Street. The Iranian polished his rimless glasses to better see the broiled Dover sole fall under his fork. He ate the accompanying steamed vegetables with less relish.

"What news of the oil?" he asked Ehmat.

"Petrova Verkhovtsev is trying to get a new source for the Chinese."

"Always the damned woman. The American was not so easy to manipulate as she thought."

"Evidently not. She asks for your aid in acquiring Iranian oil."

"This is a good thing." He dipped a piece of boiled potato into sour cream before placing into his mouth. "Arrange a meeting."

"What do you have in mind?"

"Ibn-Sultan has an idea for the Ceyhan project, and I am told not to discuss with her but Grigory Pluchenko. We have had enough of the woman depending on her wiles."

CHAPTER 11

Grigory Pluchenko stumbled over the cobblestones of the Inner City, past the Mohammad ibn Abu Bakr Mosque and Maiden Tower. This latest development was not good. Reza Deghani, the counter-intelligence officer, asked for a private meeting. Pluchenko lived in warehouse, if the cavernous building filled with stereos, DVD players, and Kalishnakovs could be thought of as a home. His assignations with women other than Petrova were carried out at the Hyatt Regency on Bakikhanov Street, where the duvets were thick and room service waiters bribed to deliver hashish along with a late supper.

Modern pirate Grigory had no need for the dull routine of home, the shelves filled with ridiculous trinkets from packaged vacations, photographs of grandmother and grandfather staring down in black and white from the walls, and crockery in the cupboards. The Muslims wanted to see him at the home he did not have and Grigory gave them the address of Petrova Verkhovtsev. These fools and their religion. The problem hurried him along. His mother had been religious. She hid icons in the Moscow flat and prayed to them late at night with the window shades drawn. A real god would have given Grigory the riches he deserved. Instead he had to deal with the Muslims.

He rushed into Petrova's apartment without bothering to knock on the door. She lay on the large sofa with a copy of the *London Times*. He took in her lithe figure clad in a soft white wool dress revealing a pleasant glimpse of cleavage, her face flushed as if she had returned from a run on the beach.

"What is your trouble, Grigory?"

"Reza can help us find another source for the oil but he needs a favor. He wants to meet. The man is coming here."

"The oil deal is mine. I have put too much effort into accommodating the Chinese to be pushed aside."

Pluchenko shrugged. "He only speaks to me. Women are chattel to the Muslims."

"Not this woman."

The doorbell rang and Pluchenko admitted Reza Deghani. He wore a dark blue business suit and oxblood shoes. Two men stayed in the hallway as guards.

"Welcome, Deghani," said Petrova. "I am surprised to see you Azerbaijan."

"At the request of Kamal ibn-Sultan, I am to speak only with Grigory. A woman without the modesty of a veil is an insult to Almighty God. I cannot look at you or conduct business and be faithful to my beliefs."

"Do you think you could have gotten this far without my aid? Pluchenko trips over his own feet without guidance."

Deghani kept his head down and refused to look up until she had left the room. Pluchenko blushed in embarrassment under his heavy beard. Greed had stripped him of bluster. Petrova was used to winning battles with any man. She would not be moved, not in her apartment or anywhere.

"Petrova Ivanovna," pleaded Pluchenko. "Stop this foolish behavior. Everyone will benefit from ibn-Sultan."

To see the man who commanded her bed and body in such a ridiculous position made her weaken. "Make yourselves comfortable in your man's world. I have other matters to attend."

"We would like tea and sweet cakes," ordered Deghani.

Petrova left the room in anger. Pluchenko directed his guest to the sofa and sat across from him. His eyes revealed fatigue and streaks of gray ran through his goatee.

"The Chinese still need oil, despite your attempts to use Burt Strauss," said Deghani.

"Their bluff of an attack on Taiwan has not helped as they thought. We want to provide them with an alternate source, preferably from Iran. I understand ibn-Sultan has a proposition for us."

"Do you still have a friend at the admiralty in St. Petersburg?"

"Petrova's retired father retains some influence with the Russian defense ministry. There are few friendships that are not about money. The more money, the deeper the friendship."

"There is plenty for the right man."

"What do you want?"

"Tell the Chinese they can have oil from us. In exchange for the arrangement, I desire the use of a Kilo class submarine, including crew, and departure from St. Petersburg. We expect the price to be reasonable." He stood. "I will contact you later for your decision. No submarine, no oil."

"Your country already owns a Russian submarine."

"The exchange is for an individual outside political boundaries."

Pluchenko walked to the door with Deghani and saw him out. Petrova waited until she heard the door ease shut and came into the parlor holding a glass of Luksusowa vodka. To hell with Deghani and his tea and cakes.

"We can't do this without your father," said Pluchenko.

"The great brave and brutal Grigory is brought down by who? Reza, a corrupt official whose hand was always out for a bribe. Now he follows the Messenger of Almighty God and I dislike his new master."

"Money is to be had, Petrova. Our percentage from the Chinese and ibn-Sultan's people make any temporary discomfort worthwhile."

"Do not involve my father."

"You heard Reza. The Iranian deal is contingent on the submarine."

"Trusting the exremists is foolish. We have enough money, and my father is an old man. The proposal would not be of interest."

"The money, Petrova."

"He has made much from both of us."

"Making money is habit-forming. Contact the man and ask."

She sat quietly and played with a cushion. All men were damned to be weak and women damned to be bitter. Not this woman, thought Petrova.

"I cannot promise anything."

"An attempt is sufficient."

———

Retired General Nickolai Pavlovich Verkhovtsev in tweeds and thick sweater smiled at his daughter, who wore a somber black dress unable to hide her curves. The long tables at the Griboedov Club on Voronegskay Street were filled with revelers who clapped and swayed to the rhythm of the folk song, "Kazanka" played by two Balalaikas on a raised platform. White-haired and white-bearded Verkhovtsev drank Egri Bikaver, a harsh red wine from Hungary that caused a grimace with each swallow, and his enlarged pitted nose to glow brighter.

"Sing with me, Petrova Ivanovna," he pleaded. "I have not your voice in years. Come now, '*Vdol da po ryetschke, vdol da po Kazanke.*'"

"Papushka," Petrova said. "I am here for business with Grigory."

"The mafia ruffian from Moscow? He's a poor example of a man. I hoped you would find a better partner."

"You introduced us."

"An error I hope you would correct. In this situation, I offer the legitimacy and approval that can only be provided by a member of the old guard. Do not think I am doing this for more than my share of the Muslim's money. The people you work with disgust me."

Underneath the club's decor of tired lace bunting and strings of lights, the audience banged on their tables with empty liquor bottles, and shouted requests for songs at the bandstand.

"There is no nightlife like this in Baku. Return to Russia, my daughter. Leave the petrodollars to the Americans and let them revel in their own filth. Russia is still Russia, regardless of the free market economy."

"Yes, father."

General Verkhovtsev stopped his argument and waved over a waiter. A man in black slacks, white shirt, and brocade vest rushed in obsequious stoop to answer the beckoning.

"What do you need, General?"

"An end to this shit. You hear what the musicians are playing?"

"A song by Vladimir Vysotsky. He says he is sinking to the bottom."

"The Jew turncoat deserved a worse fate. Before our country changed from revolutionary to prostitute for hard currency, Vysotsky was not allowed to poison the ears of good Russians. You know where he is buried? Between the other stupid drunk, Yesenin, and the traitor Andrei Sakharov. Tell your musicians to find another song or none of their grandparents will receive another pension check."

"Yes, General. I apologize for the inconsiderate choice. Another bottle of wine?"

"And vodka for my daughter. Bring more glasses. We are expecting company."

The waiter left as Petrova rose from her seat. "Here they are." She waved toward Grigory Pluchenko and two companions. They pushed through the crowd and squeezed into the last available space at the table. Pluchenko shifted the leather attaché case he carried and extended his hand to the General.

"Good to see you, sir. This is Dmitry Ogdanov and Sergei Ivanovsky from the admiralty."

"My pleasure, comrades. You have chosen a grand night for the Griboedov Club, good Russian music instead of Western pap."

"Is that 'The Dashing Troika'?" Dmitry Ogdanov asked. "My mother whistled the tune when she ironed my father's shirts."

"A good woman, your mother. We shall drink to mothers."

The General filled glasses and the party drank. Ivanovsky stroked his trimmed beard and pursed his thick lips, while Ogdanov thumped his fingers on the table to the rhythm of the music. Verkhovtsev only had eyes for his daughter. He wished her mother were alive to see how beautiful she had become, compared to the tomboy she had once been.

"They still talk about Verkhovtsev in the admiralty," Ivanovsky said. "You had quite a distinguished career."

"Times have changed and I no longer have the influence I once enjoyed."

"You have kept your name and reputation," said Petrova.

"What do these mean to the new Russia?" the General replied.

Petrova noticed how old he sounded. He still had handsome features and his back was straight as an arrow. His bearing exuded authority, even with his white mane and beard, but his eyes were tired.

Pluchenko broke the advancing melancholy. "Sergei told me they have a new Kilo class submarine ready for sea trials at the admiralty shipyard."

"Yes, she is ready to leave the dock," said Ivanovsky.

"Petrova and I have an interested client," Pluchenko said. "An international businessman with lots of money."

The officers exchanged glances. "What does he want with our submarine?" Ivanovsky asked.

Pluchenko paused. "He did not share the information with us, but he is willing to pay a handsome price."

"What are the terms?" asked Ogdanov.

"A short term lease with minimum crew."

"This is a great risk for us," Ogdanov said. "The money better be worthwhile."

"More than worthwhile, Dmitry," Grigory assured.

The General shook his head and the white mane shone in the club light. His thick white eyebrows made a shelf across his deep blue eyes. Petrova took his hand and squeezed.

"We must return to our offices," Ivanovsky said.

"First, a toast to our success," Pluchenko protested. He raised his glass. "Here is to a very lucrative deal."

"My colleague and I are worried," Ivanovsky said. "We have respectable positions that could be jeopardized, unless we can count on a future retirement."

Grigory broke into a triumphant smile. "Gentlemen, your retirement is guaranteed." He patted his attaché case. "General Verkhovtsev is my witness."

"Depend on Pluchenko, comrades," the general said.

"We must know the name of this businessman," Ivanovsky said.

"Not knowing the identity of the lessee is more advantageous," Grigory said. "Just his terms." He placed the attaché case on the table and opened the locks. "This is twenty percent down. The remainder is forthcoming in cash as well, once the ship and crew are ready for service."

The officials nodded and accepted the case.

"To our success," Grigory said. Petrova watched with relief as the two officials downed their drinks.

"Tell your client we have a deal and get us a timetable for return of the submarine. We can fit the sailing into our schedule of sea trials and exercise tests."

"I will consult with him. In the meantime, enjoy the down payment."

The two men smiled broadly and stood up. Verkhovtsev rose from his seat and shook the hands of the two officials warmly.

"General, your presence helped us make our decision," Ivanovsky said.

"The money did the convincing," the General replied.

Petrova watched the unfolding scene. Her mind calculated the millions they stood to make. "Congratulations on your new business," she said to Ivanovsky. "Leasing is a lucrative endeavor for the admiralty. Imagine, five hundred thousand dollars of hard currency for a few days of work done by others."

Pluchenko shot her a scolding glance.

"A delight to meet you, Petrova Verkhovtsev," Ivanovsky said. "We hope to see you again." His companion nodded in agreement and the two left with the case.

Grigory turned to the General. "We couldn't have done this without you. Now to collect." He fished his cell phone out of his pocket and punched in a series of numbers. His face muscles remained tense until the party answered. "We have had a successful meeting. Please decide on a time schedule and get back to me."

Petrova frowned at him. "Tell Reza to get on that oil deal."

———

Necdet Shubaki had a ten o'clock appointment at the Port of Ceyhan offices of British Chemical Enterprises. The short, clean-shaven man in an uncomfortable gray suit sat on a chair covered with nubby green fabric in the reception area with a plain cardboard box next to him. His hands sweated, his hands always sweated, and he daubed at them with his handkerchief. Shubaki knew he would have to shake hands with the BCE man and he wanted to appear professional. This meant dry hands and a cool demeanor. Neither were Shubaki's strong points. He was a nervous and excitable man, more comfortable on the factory floor than an executive office. He waited patiently with a box on his lap. Just before eleven, the secretary called his name and he was escorted down a hall to a cubicle.

"Ruhi Jensrud," the man behind the desk introduced himself. He substituted a handshake with pointing to the only other chair in the small space. "Glad to meet a local businessman. What can British Chemical do for you?"

"As I explained when I made the appointment, I represent Ceyhan Doll Makers, manufacturers of the most prestigious porcelain dolls in the world, even to rival the Dresden. We've recently added a new line, a remote controlled airplane."

"You want sell us model airplanes?"

"Oh, no. Let me show you." Shubaki opened the cardboard box and removed a red and white airplane. A banner attached to the tail read, "Welcome to Ceyhan."

"I don't understand."

"We would like to fly these at the opening ceremony for the new pipeline. Other banners say, 'Bravo' and 'Congratulations' and 'Job Well Done.' "

"Very impressive, Mr. Shubaki."

"The pipeline is a godsend to Ceyhan and we want acknowledge the accomplishment of British Chemical on behalf of the local businesses who have profited from the venture. Adults and children will love the display."

"There's the safety issue. What if a plane should hit someone?"

"Our planes are quite precise and easy to fly. I taught myself in no time, just by playing in the warehouse and on the loading dock. They are programmed to fly above the stands at a height of five meters."

Jensrud frowned. "This should go through the Baku office. The American Secret Service and other security people have to approve."

"Tell them I have planes for their boys and dolls for their girls. They are valuable collector's items."

"Let me take your idea to the committee in charge of the opening. With the protests over the pipeline, everyone is suspect."

"Yes, I know," Shubaki said. "Thank you for your time." He paused and sighed. "I should have insisted on these new airplanes long ago, even train sets. Those would be fun."

"Never too late, sir."

"That's what my father said. He just recently died."

Jensrud looked at his watch. "My condolences. Now you can manufacture toys more to your liking."

"Yes, maybe I can."

Jensrud was impressed, Shubaki decided while walking to his tan Mercedes. Mr. Faisal would soon join the company instead of being a silent partner, and he could expand using the balloon payment due before transfer of title. Trains and planes, maybe even motorboats.

———

Ali Massouf, Michael and David, and Ramzi Zaidan met in the backroom of Viola's Gelato for an after hours strategy session.

"You have done good work," said Massouf. "Our mission is proceeding well."

"What's next?" Zaidan asked. "We have the uniforms, Garden employee IDs, and the truck painted American Systems."

"There are different events at the Garden for our project."

Massouf wrote several selections on a blackboard hanging from the wall. He read the list and erased one.

"What's wrong, Ali?"

"The business forum has the same time and date as the schedule for installing the anthrax into the apparatus. They have announced ex-President Bill Clinton as a speaker, and that means Secret Service."

After another half hour of discussion, the men agreed on an event.

Several days later found Massouf sitting in a rented Ford sedan parked outside the American Systems brick warehouse with "Plumbing Heating & Cooling" on the side of the building in Brooklyn. Samir Mohammad had tampered with the Madison Square Garden air conditioning system earlier in the day and they intercepted service calls in the hope the Garden would be among them.

David listened to the receiver linked with American System's tapped telephone and Massouf kept awake by organizing his thoughts on a yellow legal pad. There were two calls the next hour, one from a restaurant in Bensonhurst and the other from Manufacturers Hanover on Canal Street. The dispatch operator told them someone would be there soon, but the line remained silent.

"Liars," David said. "What happened to the 'immediate after hours emergency service' their trucks advertise?"

There were no reports from the Garden. David napped and Massouf joined him. They woke when a third call came in. The answering machine picked up and a female voice said, "Stevie, get some Polish sausage on your way home and I'll make breakfast."

Michael and Zaidan arrived after midnight. Michael stayed with the car and Zaidan drove Massouf to his studio apartment near the gelato shop. An hour later Massouf was getting out of the shower when his cell rang.

"David here. We got the call."

"You canceled American Systems?"

"I told them the problem was fixed. Zaidan went to get the truck."

"Who's picking up Samir?"

"I am going to the Garden with him. He says we have to get into the wiring to set up the resuspension apparatus."

"Remember to tell Garden security you will finish the job on the 19th when the missing part comes in."

Roger Shaw and Elizabeth Paige landed at Adana Incirlik Air Base on a British Chemical Enterprises private aircraft, provided by Burt Strauss. Ambassador Paige looked out the window of the airplane and remarked, "What fresh hell is this?" Troops in camouflage carried automatic rifles at port arms and held posts at every entrance and exit. Armored personnel carries rumbled over the tarmac.

"Dorothy Parker, right?" said Shaw. "This is security, Madame Ambassador. Between us and the Turks, there are about 10,000 men in town for the show."

Eric LaGrange waited at the gate in a black Mercedes SUV. "Welcome to Adana. This is as close as we get to the Port of Ceyhan. You're in country conquered by Alexander the Great, the Roman Empire, Caliph Harun ar-Rashid, and the Ottoman Empire. Adana's history is thicker

than the carbon monoxide." He drove along the Seyhan River, turned
on Haci Sabanci Boulevard near the second century Roman stone
bridge, and pulled into the gravel courtyard of the white and ochre
painted villa. LaGrange opened the passenger door for Elizabeth.

"The gear arrived last night and I've taken the liberty of assigning
quarters. We have ten rooms besides the general areas. Let me know if
you want to move. Energy Secretary Holbeck is down the road at the
Hilton."

Shaw and LaGrange toured the marble halls. The rooms were
sparsely furnished with beds here and there, cast-off divans and chairs
from another era, writing desks, and only the dining hall had a matching
set of chairs around the long polished wood table. Elizabeth installed
a temporary embassy office with fax, PC, and cell phones. LaGrange
stayed with the Special Forces team and Shaw wired his Special Ops
center.

The secure line rang and John Devine wanted a report. "All
accounted for, sir. Will the Army be with us?" teased Shaw.

"Too much room or not enough?"

"There's a suite for you if Washington is too boring this time of year.
The men are in, and the Ambassador. I brought her ahead of schedule
since I had a free ride courtesy of Strauss."

"Fine with me. How about Energy Secretary Martin Holbeck?"

"Secret service men are in place, as well as the Turkish security."

"Will the set up work for you?"

"I thought your idea was nuts, but we'll be fine. The men like the
Ambassador. They think she's cool, like hanging out with royalty. When
is the Secretary arriving?"

"I'll holler when I know."

Shaw established a routine of guard duty. The men came and went,
but LaGrange and Elizabeth stayed to the villa. LaGrange became the
cook and commandeered the wide counters, butcher block, deep sinks,
and copper pots and pans of the kitchen. He made a stir-fry of chicken
and vegetables, and carried platters to the dinning room with bowls of

steamed rice. LaGrange walked the grounds after dinner and returned to Elizabeth washing dishes.

"Couldn't sleep so I decided to be useful," she said.

"I didn't know ambassadors did dishes."

"This one does, though not for awhile. The help at the Embassy is too nervous about letting me in the kitchen."

"How about a nightcap?"

"Sounds good."

LaGrange opened a bottle of Medoc and poured her a glass.

"Nice dinner, Eric. Why is a man who cooks still single?"

"Marriage isn't in the cards for me. Maybe some day."

"Sounds like you haven't forgiven yourself for the Baghdad bombing. The weight must be crushing."

"Forgiveness is easy. My problem is I can't forget. Can we have a change of subject?"

"Sure. You were raised in the Middle East. Tell me how you see our situation."

"I categorize the players in the region according to religion. The meeting in Ankara had Muslim extremists of an organization known as Followers of the Cleric, who we only know as a veteran of the Afghanistan war against the Soviets and later in Chechnya. He went into hiding, more like hibernation, and emerged spouting a line of attacks against the West. The Cleric is angry the Muslim world has shrunk since the days of the Crusades, and believes too many Muslims have diluted their faith."

"The West is being held responsible for acts that occurred one thousand years ago?"

"Same players, different names, according to the Cleric. He wants the church and state to rejoin, and the West encourages them to move further apart."

"He should see Washington and how they are moving closer together. Our own religious extremists hold a great deal of political clout these days."

"They're not true believers. Besides the Cleric's followers, there is the religion of greed, like the Russians who engineered the escape of Strauss from Rebirth Island and tried to blackmail him into selling oil to the Chinese."

"We have Muslim religion and the religion of greed. What else?"

"Personal religions. Shaw's is the CIA. Strauss thinks his religion is British Chemical Enterprises and the corporate rah-rah, when his beliefs are actually in you and your daughter, Amelia. The same as you, Madame Ambassador. Maybe I should be less bold."

Elizabeth blanched at the personal turn the conversation had taken. LaGrange had no business talking about her daughter. Still, this haunted young man kept her intrigued.

"I'm listening, Eric. Please continue."

"Shaw told me about Strauss being Amelia's father and I haven't repeated our conversation to anyone. You rejected your religion of a diplomatic career for Amelia, a very brave move."

"What about Eric LaGrange's religion?"

"The dumbest faith possible, I'm afraid. I believe in my own guilt."

CHAPTER 12

Two kilometers from the villa, red and gold signs in downtown Adana welcomed the pipeline as "The Silk Road of the 21st Century." Dignitaries filled the hotels. Prime ministers, foreign ministers, and energy ministers joined the presidents of Turkey, Azerbaijan, and Georgia. Besides Holbeck, the United States sent the Deputy Assistant Secretary of State for European and Eurasian Affairs, and Assistant Secretary of State for Economic and Business Affairs. The European Union was also represented by a full complement of bureaucrats and diplomats.

LaGrange was bent over a pot of couscous when Elizabeth came into the kitchen. "Can I help?" she asked.

"Under control." He pointed to a bottle and corkscrew on the counter. "The wine needs to be opened."

She wrested the cork from the bottle. "Are we dinning alone?"

"So far. The guard is changing and Shaw has been sequestered for hours. You've been busy as well."

"There's not much to do. Mostly I'm staying abreast of things. Unfortunately, that means complaints."

"Like what?"

"Ruhi Jensrud from British Chemical says the whole town wants to get into the act for the port ceremony. A candy company approached them to distribute candies with prizes in them and a toy manufacturer wants to bring in remote-controlled airplanes with flags saying 'Congratulations on the Pipeline' or some such nonsense."

"Are these suggestions from crackpots?"

"I'm not familiar with the candy people but the other is Ceyhan Doll Makers. Their dolls are beautiful. I saved for months when I was a poor young mom and bought one for Amelia. I wonder if she still has the doll."

"I'm sure she does. How do you like your lamb chops?"

"Medium."

"Eating in is fine, but I bet there are several receptions and state dinners needing your touch of class."

"Let Holbeck wave the flag. You're a damn good chef."

"Part of being an inveterate bachelor. Most of the time I eat in cafes, especially when Shaw has me running around. Gets in the way of my culinariness."

"Eric, 'culinariness' is not a word."

"Sure is. The state of being culinary."

Elizabeth laughed. "I like seeing you lighthearted."

"My usual state is to be very intense. I'm responsible for the information I found in Ankara and I don't want anything else to happen to you."

"We're safe."

Shaw reeled into the kitchen, pulled in by the aromas wafting down the hall into his room. "I'm hungry and my brain is tired," he said. "How are you this evening, Madame Ambassador?"

"Fine, Roger. Have yourself a glass of wine and calm down."

Shaw accepted the drink and sat slumped on a high stool. His bloodshot eyes stared into the glass for a moment before registering its presence. He drank. "The Secret Service called with their panties in a knot. They said you approved a flyover of toy airplanes for the opening."

"I did no such thing," said the Ambassador. "They have to go through proper channels, especially for an air demonstration."

"Our problem is we have too many channels. Secret Service and the Agency are barely talking to each other, and when we do, we hold back. What is the name of the company with the planes?"

"Ceyhan Doll Makers."

Shaw turned to LaGrange. "You want to tell her or should I?"

"I'm only the chief cook and bottle washer. Go ahead."

He drained the glass and asked for more wine. "Rumors floated around a couple of years ago that Arafat's al-Fatah organization had come up with a new wrinkle in attacks on Jerusalem. Palestinian importers ordered hundreds of toy airplanes for distribution to kids stuck in hospitals and members of the European Union paid for this humanitarian gift giving. No one thought to ask how the bedridden kids were supposed to get outside and play with them, and who would supply the white gas needed for the engines.

"The airplanes came from all over Europe and sold to local shopkeepers. Not one reached a hospital. They were sent to workshops and packed with explosives. The Tanzim militia tested the weapons and found they could fly one kilometer at an altitude of 300 meters. When the airplanes ran out of fuel, they dropped and ka-boom."

LaGrange filled plates with chops and couscous, and laid them on the counter. Elizabeth spoke first.

"Were the weapons ever used?"

"The Israelis say maybe. We don't know for sure on account of they wanted al-Fatah to think the plan was a failure."

"Could this happen again?"

"Who knows. But we are going to check out the doll maker."

———

LaGrange entered the Special Ops center early the next morning. Shaw paced the floor between computer terminals and secure lines, and clutched a handful of printouts. White shirttails hung outside of his suit trousers and a blue and gold striped tie had yet to be knotted. He had a complete rundown on Ceyhan Doll Makers. The company had been owned and operated by Manana Shubaki for fifty years, until he recently died and left the doll makers' to his son, Necdet who continued to run the firm. Research from the Istanbul station showed no buyout activity or illegal connections.

"Here's the summary on the other buildings in the area of the ceremony," said Shaw, and handed LaGrange a section of the printouts.

"What's going on?"

"I don't know. I can't quite put my finger on the damn thing."

LaGrange scanned the pages. "Everything appears routine and nothing special jumps out. If you don't need me, I'm going to the market."

"Stay with the Ambassador. I have a trip to make."

Shaw drove the SUV to Ceyhan Doll Makers at the Port. He found space in the parking lot next to the reserved spot for Mr. Shubaki, filled by a shiny tan Mercedes. The offices were sectioned off from the main warehouse, a wood building with flat roof in need of repair and paint. An overweight man sweated in a light green short-sleeved shirt at the reception counter, behind a plaque reading 'Rafiq.'

"I'd like to see Mr. Shubaki," Shaw told the man.

"Buyers and distributors must have appointments," the man said, his head buried in a file.

"Rafiq, I'm new in Turkey and I understand Mr. Shubaki is interested in showing his toy airplanes."

The man looked up. "Damn things will never sell. Let me call him."

Rafiq whispered long and drawn out sentences into the telephone, the only audible word in the whole conversation was airplanes. For a company whose reputation was based in dolls, the airplanes stood out as a nuisance.

"Come with me." He led Shaw down a short hall and opened a door where Necdet Shubaki sat behind an oversized desk cluttered with papers and books.

"Welcome, Mr. Shaw. You wanted to see me?"

"Yes, I'm interested in your diversification into toy airplanes."

"We have yet to marketed them. How did you know?"

"A friend said you approached British Chemical Enterprises."

"Did they like my offer? All of Turkey should be proud of the pipeline."

"Most likely the proposal has gone to a committee and they work in their own strange and mysterious fashion."

"Let me show them to you. Right this way."

Shubaki and Shaw pushed through double doors into the warehouse. Rows of steel shelving were stocked with bins of small porcelain heads, arms, legs, and torsos.

"We are very enthusiastic about this new line." He opened a door to a large open area lined with more shelves holding hundreds of red and white airplanes.

"Break many windows with these?" Shaw asked.

Shubaki let out a giggle. "Oh, no. They're easy to operate." He handed Shaw a remote control unit. "This button makes the plane go up and this one levels out. This one makes it go right and this one left."

"How do you land them?"

"The bottom button."

Shubaki launched an airplane down the aisle and missed the light fixture. The plane hit a shelf of other airplanes. There was a terrific clatter and several stationary planes fell to the floor. The nose of the plane smashed and lost its propeller.

"Ouch. This bird is not going to fly home."

"No problem, Mr. Shaw." He opened a closet door to a jumble of airplanes in similar states of ruin. A few had torn flags with 'Bravo' in bold script.

"I have broken many with the flags I added. Maybe they throw off the weight. If British Chemical knew, they would never agree to my promotion scheme."

"What made you decide to do the airplanes?"

"My father, God rest his soul, left me Ceyhan Doll Makers in a terrible financial situation. Medical bills, mostly. I found an investor and he had the idea. We sell the planes and if they turn a profit, we manufacture them, or he will. I have other interests once the sale is complete."

"Meanwhile he's your silent partner."

"I'm thinking of getting into the mechanical toy line myself, in another city. Adana only has room for one toy maker."

"Where did the planes come from?"

"We bought wholesale in Belgium. You must have a big inventory to test the market. We should order more for a fair analysis here. These are prototypes. Mr. Faisal will not be making knock-offs. Maybe different colors."

"Where is he?"

"Mr. Faisal visits every six weeks. We have competent, faithful employees and the factory runs itself. I am quite tired of dolls. When Mr. Faisal made his extraordinary offer, I accepted."

"He also suggested showing the planes at the pipeline ceremony."

"That is mine. I have not asked his approval, but if British Chemical is interested, I will. He should be pleased with my ingenuity."

Shaw looked past the loading dock. "I'd like to have a confidential talk, Mr. Shubaki."

A tired Shaw returned to the house with arms full of packages. He rang the bell with his elbow and LaGrange opened the door.

"How generous. You brought presents."

"Yes," Shaw said. He walked through the foyer into the dining room and dropped the boxes on the table. "Where's Elizabeth?"

"In her office."

He took out two model airplanes. "These are for us."

LaGrange opened another box and pulled out a doll.

"For Elizabeth," Shaw said. "Are the men on watch?"

"Everyone. What's going on?"

"I need a blueprint of the plant for Ceyhan Doll Makers. Download the plans to the laptop and be ready for a show-and-tell. We have a guest for dinner."

"Muslim or Christian?"

"Forgot to ask. No pork just in case."

LaGrange made lasagna with ground lamb, green salad, and a pitcher of iced tea to replace the usual nightly wine. Four sat at the dinning room table: Elizabeth Paige, LaGrange, Shaw, and Necdet Shubaki. The doll-maker enthused over the Ambassador's daughter owning a Ceyhan doll. "A Spanish dancer with a black mantilla," recalled Elizabeth.

"Madame Ambassador, with your recommendation I may reconsider my waning interest in dolls."

"I hope you do, Mr. Shubaki. Even grown women treasure your fine work."

LaGrange cleared the dishes and set the laptop at the head of the table. "We have a problem in need of a solution," said Shaw. "Take a look at this floor plan, Mr. Shubaki. Here is the freight elevator. Has anything changed in the building?"

"No, Mr. Shaw, not since my father began the company."

"So you haven't done any remodeling."

"Mr. Faisal took an area on the second floor for an office. We keep this closed off unless he is in town."

"How about the roof access?"

"This goes through Mr. Faisal's office."

"From what I've seen, the roof is flat with a slight slant for drainage. Show me the side facing the oil terminal."

"Right here, less than kilometer away. The noise during construction made us close down for several days. Such racket you would not believe."

"Excuse me," Shaw said. "Eric, show Mr. Shubaki some of the infamous from our photo gallery."

"No problem," LaGrange said. "Where are you going?"

"I'll make coffee. We might be at this for awhile."

Shaw entered the kitchen and pulled down two brass ibriks, wide bottomed and narrow necked pots with long handles. He put handfuls of arabica beans into a matching cylindrical mill, known as the *kahve degirmeni*. Shaw had his best suspicions when his hands were busy, and wasn't intelligence work all about suspicions? He ground the beans into a fine powder, and filled the ibriks with cold water and set them on the stove under high gas flames. Shaw added spoons of coffee and sugar to the pots and waited. The mixture seethed to frothing three times before he took the ibiks from the stove and gently filled the four *fincans*, small demitasse cups. Elizabeth came in as he arranged the cups on a hammered metal tray.

"Mr. Shubaki identified Faisal," she said. "I recognize him from Rebirth Island."

"Show me," he said and carried the tray to the dinning room. Once at the computer, Elizabeth pointed to a clean-shaven man.

"This one. He had a beard and they called him Yakir."

"Yakir Arvatian is our Mr. Faisal," remarked Shaw. "This man is a member of the Followers of the Cleric. Arvatian has been implicated in many crimes in the Middle East and my bet is he's after the pipeline."

"This same man is my silent partner," said Shubaki. Consternation made his voice crack like an adolescent.

"Are you willing to help?" Shaw asked.

"Indeed, sir. I would not have entered into a business arrangement with him had I known."

"Here is what we'll do. Ready for dress-up again, Eric?"

———

The morning sun reflected off the pipes at the Ceyhan oil terminal. Less than kilometer away, LaGrange walked into the Doll Makers wearing a dark three-piece pinstripe suit and a false beard, and carrying a briefcase. He gave his name as Hassan Rashid Abbas to Rafiq, the receptionist. Today he sweated through an orange short sleeve shirt.

Shafiq referred to his appointment book and escorted LaGrange to Shubaki's office.

"I am behind schedule, Mr. Abbas," Shubaki said. "We have to complete an inventory report and these are always a bother. Please follow me."

Shubaki led him down the hall to a stairwell, and handed LaGrange the inventory list and a map of the second floor. He fumbled in his pocket. "Here's a skeleton key, Mr. LaGrange, and a flashlight. You might need this to find the light switch on the left side of the wall. I'll be waiting by the door."

"Watch for someone like Mr. Faisal," said LaGrange. "You'll have to alert me."

"I could set off the fire alarm."

"That will work." LaGrange left him and went up the stairs. He opened the fire door to the darkened second floor and located the wall switch. The skeleton key for Faisal's office door did not work, but the pliable wire he kept for such occasions popped the lock with ease.

Instead of a storage area for airplanes filled with explosives, the space was an actual office. The wide oak desk and leather chair, wall of bookshelves, three-drawer file cabinets, and waste paper baskets were the usual. The only non-office equipment was the workout equipment by the window.

LaGrange did a careful search of the employee files, manufacturing supply catalogs, inventory sheets, invoices, utility bills, accounting files, balance sheets, tax records, but they were too neat. The books were on business practices, history of dolls, encyclopedias, and trade magazines. Faisal had gone to through the trouble to make a very convincing front.

Next he checked the weight bench, stair master, and treadmill. The screws on the miles-per-hour counter for the treadmill were scratched, like they had been removed. He pried off the cover.

LaGrange took a final look around and departed. He descended the stairs to where Shubaki waited nervously. They returned to his office.

"I didn't find what we're looking for. Faisal will probably bring them in the middle of the night, and soon."

"This is not for me," Shubaki said.

"You're doing fine. I better get going. Plan B."

"We exchange clothes."

"That's right."

They stripped to their underwear and redressed. LaGrange peeled off the beard and helped Shubaki with the spirit gum.

"Very nice. The beard is you," LaGrange said.

"I just walk out with the briefcase and drive away in your vehicle."

"The white Toyota four by four. Here are the keys. No problem driving a standard?"

"Not at all."

"Drive to the airport parking and I'll have someone pick you up. He'll take you over to the villa for dinner. Shaw knows you're coming."

"Excellent, Mr. LaGrange. I so want to do a perfect job here."

"Pretend you're a busy salesman and walk to the truck without pausing. If you have to look at something, look at your watch."

"Here I go."

"Wait, Mr. Shubaki. You're forgetting one last detail."

He punched in numbers on his cell phone. "Rafiq, have the extra packers brought from storage and taken to the mail room. Hold my calls and do not disturb me the rest of the afternoon. I have a migraine."

Shubaki left the building. LaGrange called Shaw on his cell. "No airplanes but there are workout machines in the office. The treadmill is rigged for a bomb, maybe to get rid of the players if anything goes wrong."

"I'll get a man in there to defuse the device. Day and night surveillance on the building is in place."

"They are likely doing the same. Tell our watchers not to run into theirs."

"Right. Anything else?"

"Shubaki needs a ride from the airport."

"I hope he's a careful driver."

"Your expense account should cover any damages."

"This is the government. Don't count on it."

"I have to go," he said. LaGrange moved behind the door and listened to Rafiq humming down the corridor. He checked his watch: only an hour and a half until closing time.

Two hours later, LaGrange put on Shubaki's straw hat and drove the tan Mercedes to the villa. The next day, a Special Forces commando replaced an early arriving employee and was taken to the second floor by Shubaki. He disarmed the bomb.

CHAPTER 13

Petrova Verkhovtsev in her oyster Aquascutum overcoat walked the stairs to the third floor of Hoa Lin's hotel and knocked on the red door. She disliked this part of Baku, the unsteady stone buildings and trash in the streets. Baku had money for those daring enough to hold out their hands. The people in the slum were the unhappy byproducts of the free market. For every rich man in the new state, a hundred must be poor, or a thousand. The hard slum humbled Petrova and she went to her meeting with resolve never to falter like the men and women who cleaned homes, built offices, hauled garbage, washed cars, waited tables, and whored and traded in narcotics, and lived here. Only the children were happy. They ran along the curbs, played catch with mud-covered plastic balls, and chanted rhymes while skipping rope. Wait until their stomachs grow, thought Petrova, and the urchins will join Baku's criminal set.

Hoa Lin answered her knock in black jeans and Dallas Cowboys jersey under an orange hooded jersey.

"My dear Miss Verkhovtsev," he said. "Always such a pleasure."

"Anything for the daring man who keeps pace with fashion."

Another bottle of Johnnie Walker Red whiskey sat on a card table and the iron bedstead with sagging mattress had yet to be slept in. The drawn window shades, the lamps with bare bulbs, and the stench of mildew had not changed. Petrova wanted a bath.

"We are very pleased with the arrangements. Two tankers have arrived in my homeland from Iran as promised." He handed her a cream envelope. "Here is the final payment."

"I am glad there were no problems in switching sources."

"Not at all. The West depends on a pipeline we suspect will never be operational, and now we have a direct line to the Iran oil fields. Our promising future is due to British Chemical being unable to deliver. Join me in a drink to celebrate."

"Keep your cheap whiskey. What do you know of the pipeline?"

"An acquaintance shares my interest in Kilo class submarines. He said you were instrumental in securing a ship in time for the pipeline opening. Your pragmatism is refreshing, free of guilt or conscience."

"Be less obtuse, Mr. Lin. The subtlety of your English is confusing."

"Thanks to your partner's fidelity to money instead of ideology, the enemies of the West have a powerful weapon in the submarine. My country is not concerned with the religious jihad proposed by Followers of the Cleric, only the results. When the pipeline publicly fails, the West's delicate dependence is sure to falter. High prices at the gas pumps and lack heating fuel for winter are only the beginning. Armies on land and sea depend on oil. With our new supply, China has the means to become the world's major manufacturing center. Our labor force is accustomed to long hours and low pay, and the oil will keep the factories operating."

"I imagined you were doing this for your country."

Hoa Lin let out a rare giggle. "Oh no, madam. I have taken your example. My pockets are eager to be filled with Western currency. Favors have a cost. I may contact you with other propositions. Let us have drink to the bright and expensive future."

"Another time," she said. "This is a victory you should enjoy alone."

Petrova walked out of the slum under a dark sky with the bad company of her thoughts. When the pipeline was destroyed, Baku would lose its safety. She had to liquefy her investments spread between Switzerland, Luxembourg, and the Cayman Islands and run. The house she owned an hour out of Madrid would be her new home, and Spanish not a difficult language to learn. No more Grigory! The thought pleased her. He had benefited more from their association than she had. For lovers, she had a choice of battery-operated devices and the slender young local boys. What of the pipeline? Any action the Followers of the Cleric had planned against the pipeline would result in a horrible loss of life. She schemed only for money, never for a cause or anyone's death. Petrova was her father's daughter. He had told her conscience was a luxury, like a hot bath with perfumes and oils. Jean-Paul Marat had a knife driven into his heart while taking a bath and his conscience bled with him. If only she could be as cold as her father.

An hour later, Petrova argued with Madame Ahmadbayov through the intercom at the Park Residence.

"Mr. Strauss is going way on a trip. He is busy."

"Tell him Petrova Verkhovtsev is here. We must talk."

"No, no, I pack shirts. He not even have lunch and I make dumplings."

"Listen carefully, you Georgian bitch. Let me in right now or I will kick down this door and drive you back to the homely village you came from."

A silence, then the click of the lock, and Petrova was inside. Strauss stood in the doorway to his flat with two suitcases and his silver Haliburton briefcase.

"Petrova, what in God's name do you want? My housekeeper is ready to pop a blood vessel."

"No matter. I must know where you are going."

"To Ceyhan for the ceremonies."

"I am in time. The port will be attacked."

"By who, the Azeri? They don't use violence to get their message across."

"Much worse, the Followers of the Cleric."

Strauss pulled her down the hall to the living room. Petrova sat on the dark leather sofa and dropped her purse on the glass coffee table.

"Give me what you know," said Strauss. "The whole area is under heavy guard."

"Not against a submarine. I know this from a very reliable contact."

"Why give me this information? You've never been reticent to sell out to the highest bidder. The Followers of the Cleric is just another client."

"Grigory sells weapons to them, among other items. I have nothing to do with his business."

"Except when the price is right. The Followers of the Cleric kill innocent people and you've waited until now to think about consequences. Doesn't make sense."

"I do not want the pumps destroyed any more than British Chemical. If the pumps are attacked, the whole city will be in flames. Alert the Americans so they will stop this catastrophe."

"I'm grateful for telling me, but we're far from trusting each other."

"You must think I am totally debased."

Strauss laughed and Petrova walked out. Her father was right. Damn conscience and its attendant weakness. She hurried home to pack and reserve an airplane ticket for Spain.

———

Shaw slept curled in a mummy bag on the king-size bed. The villa's linen cupboard was low on bedding and he made do with a bag borrowed from the Special Forces commandos. The ringing of his cell phone woke him out of a welcome dreamless sleep.

"You a jogger?" asked Strauss.

"Only when my doctor is snotty about my cholesterol level."

"I flew in from Baku last night. Meet me at the port in an hour."

Strauss in white gym shorts and dark blue Harvard sweatshirt stretched his calves and hamstrings at the railing overlooking the

Mediterranean Sea. Time for a vacation, he thought, Crete or Sicily or Majorca. He wanted to be anywhere but in the middle of this mess.

Shaw came from behind with a tired "Good morning."

"I was beginning to think you were a no-show."

"I'm always a show, just not on time before noon."

"Let's go."

Shaw stumbled beside Strauss, his fanny pack bouncing, and the front and armpits of his thin tee shirt damp with perspiration. The port lay empty in the morning and quiet except for the cry of seagulls.

"Enough with this torture," Shaw said. "How about jogging over to that bench?"

Strauss slowed to a walk. "You tough guys."

"We're shameful. What's going on, Burt?"

"Petrova Verkhovtsev contacted me yesterday. According to her, there's going to be an attack on the ceremonies from a submarine."

"She's bullshitting you. Every ship near the port has been identified and registered, and that includes underwater activity. Between the Secret Service and the Turks, who don't want an international incident, everyone has done their job."

"I only deliver the news."

"Verkhovtsev is a sore point with you. Who's her source?"

"She wouldn't give me a name, only the attack comes from the Followers of the Cleric. British Chemical owes Caspian Works for drilling equipment, but Petrova has already been paid. There's no reason for her to tell me about the threat if it's not real."

"Altruism isn't part of her character. Nice how she let you off the hook on the oil deal."

"I know, and without the last temptation of making love like foreigners in a foreign land."

"Please, no cheap romanticism this early in the day. Is her information a show of goodwill or are we expected to pay later?"

"Probably the latter. She's a resourceful woman."

"There's been too much activity in this region among the Followers of the Cleric. I'll pass your news along and ask for quick action."

"Before you go, how's Elizabeth?"

"Doing fine and looking good. We have her in a villa where she runs an office on one end and I run Special Ops on the other. She makes my job easier by eating in every night. LaGrange does the cooking, best damn asset I ever recruited. You want to wrangle an invitation?"

"I hate to miss out on CIA cooking but I'd rather avoid her evil-eyed stare."

"I understand. We'll all be doing better once the ceremonies are over."

"Amen to that. Keep me in the loop if you can," Strauss said and took off running again.

"Don't have a heart attack, old fart!" Shaw dug his cell phone from the fanny pack and woke John Devine at home on his secure line. He repeated what Strauss had told him.

"This fits with the scattered reports coming in for the last month. We'll consider the threat to be real without confirmation. Even though we've frozen bank accounts wherever we could find them, the Followers of the Cleric still have access to the kind of money needed for a sub," said Devine.

"Like the kind the Chinese had in the Straits of Taiwan."

"Weapons are the international currency and Russia is chipping at its trade deficit by selling Kilo class subs. Silent, mean, and nasty ships from what I understand. A Kilo can sit on your back porch, drink your beer, and canoodle with your wife, before you hear the knock on the front door."

"The Chinese won't attack the port because they were refused oil."

"Anything's possible. From her slim case file, Verkhovtsev is in the game for her own benefit. Maybe a little of her hard heart has softened. Anyway, I'm on this and will get back to you."

John Devine kissed his sleeping wife, dressed, and drove into Langley before sunrise. The guards at the security stations were used to seeing him at odd hours and soon he swiveled in his desk chair in the Counterterrorism Center to consider his options. He called Howard Crumbly.

"Who the hell is this?"

"Your boss, Howard. Time to get back in the real work. The bad guys are on the move."

Showing up the Navy over the Straits of Taiwan debacle was bad enough, to hit them again was career suicide. The lines of communication between Naval Intelligence and the Agency had been cut since the old guard retired. No one in either office remembered the brief days of cooperation. Devine could only get to the Navy by going over them, so the warning from Strauss had to go into the White House pouch. Let the President and Joint Chiefs of Staff provide the pressure for action. If his career suffered from the move, fine. He preferred being pushed out and pensioned off to watching the Followers of the Cleric destroy the port of Ceyhan.

Crumbly stumbled into Devine's office, unshaven and dark hair mussed in every direction but the right direction. The black necktie looked incongruous wrapped around the collar of his salmon-colored polo shirt, and his khaki pants needed a wash and an iron.

"You're a disaster," said Devine.

"Sorry, sir. Your cryptic message had me throwing on what I had close to the bed. What do we have to do?"

"New intel has come in. There is strong possibility the Ceyhan pipeline will be attacked by submarine."

"Jesus."

"Throw in Joseph and Mary, too. We have to convince the Navy to act as if this has been confirmed. Pull up what's going on with the St. Petersburg shipyards. We're looking for a missing Russian Kilo class. Call your Navy contact."

"No luck there, sir. She's dropped a pay grade since the Administration figured out she helped with the China brief. I call, and she tells me to commit an unnatural act and hangs up."

Devine cursed being out of coffee and pulled out the keyboard. The brief needed a scenario. Unless he recommended a specific action, the brief would be lost in committee meetings. Sending in American ships was not an option, and too visible to carry out a sensitive operation. In 1969, Naval Research Vessel NR-1 was launched, and others followed with the same number. The submarine measured 145-feet long and held a crew of 11. She ran as deep as 3000 feet, just right for surveillance work. At present a revamped and redesigned NR-1 puttered in the Gulf of Argolis searching for Greek archeological sites. Perfect, thought Devine. About time the damn ship earned its budget.

"Find me the new specs on NR-1. We need to hit them with everything," said Devine.

"Classified information, sir, even from us. What we know of the ship comes from Washington being the worst rumor mill, loose lips from Capitol Hill to the Mall. Data about the NR-1 is confused. A crewmember wrote a novel about the ship's activities and when the Navy read the manuscript, he was transferred to monitoring whale pods off Alaska."

"We're going into harm's way on this brief. You want to keep working here, walk right now."

"You stuck with me on China, sir. I'd be gutless to quit. Who is the source on Ceyhan?"

"Man in the field. He doesn't exaggerate."

"How will they get a sub into the port?"

"My guess is the Volga-Caspian canal from St. Petersburg."

"Sounds right. The canal has been dredged in anticipation of being the major transport route for oil to Northern Europe."

"How can we stop a Kilo class sub if we're right? The NR-1 can be towed close to the port and motor into position on its own power. There are no armaments on board, only still and video cameras."

"We make our best guess. In the short term, they'll recall the Secretary of Energy."

"Along with the Ambassador and any American personnel. The

threat won't go away, because we're not the only targets. If an attack is launched on the pipeline, thousands of civilian casualties will go along with the port."

"How about we drag out the 'enlightened self-interest' routine, sir? We have to take responsibility for the safety of Cehyan. Send in the NR-1 for reconnaissance, with one of our battle subs ready to blast the intruder. Eastern Europe will jump for joy at having us as friends."

Devine looked at Crumbly with admiration. "I do like how your mind works, Howard, but taking the Kilo is the better option. We might be able to keep our paychecks with this approach. Now go find me a cup of coffee."

———

The seven-hour time difference between Adana and Langley was ignored as Shaw added suppositions and investigation results to Devine's brief. According to Shaw, the action on the pipeline ceremonies would be from two sources: the explosive-packed model airplanes had the dignitaries as their target while the submarine launched torpedoes into the pumps.

"The typical military maneuver is to triangulate and engage from three points. Do we have any intel about a third option?" asked Devine from the secure line at Langley.

"The Kilo can handle both jobs," answered Shaw. "The airplanes are likely a diversion. Followers of the Cleric are smart enough not to depend on toys."

"I'm sure you're right," Devine said. "Our only worry is the damn submarine."

"The problem belongs to the Navy."

"It's unnerving not to know how or if they will respond to this brief. If they don't stop the Kilo, Ceyhan spends the next decade cleaning the mess."

"The Navy will come through. You're the best paper-pusher in the intelligence community."

"I wonder if the Administration gives a damn about what we go through so they can safely show off in public."

"Cynical bastard. Get the brief in the pouch and make us proud." Shaw signed off.

An hour after the brief was presented to the White House, the stubby NR-1 pulled out from Greek waters and headed to Turkey and the port of Ceyhan. On board was the improved gear used for recording ocean topography and sample gathering, and underwater recovery and repair. The undersea research vessel was compact, nuclear-powered, electrically driven, and useful for locating ships lost at sea.

Instead of a missing ship, her two AN/UYK-44 military digital computers and Doppler sonar were on the hunt for a Kilo class Type 636 submarine. The Kilo was designed for anti-submarine and anti-surface ship warfare, and the dampened diesel engines enabled the ship to track other subs before the Kilo's twin screws were detected. Quick-loading computer-controlled torpedo tubes were rigged for firing by remote control.

Devine regretted his plan for the NR-1 when he heard of the ship's deployment. If the Kilo threat was real and used its torpedo battery, he would be responsible for any casualties among the research vessel's crew. He wanted to go home to Stephanie, break his promise and tell her what he had done. Devine wanted her comfort and forgiveness.

He reached for his telephone and called Crumbly, who had intruded on the Russia desk. "Tell me good news, Howard."

"Yes, sir. A Ukrainian captain named Vladimir Zylawy received papers on a Kilo submarine three days ago at St. Petersburg. He left with a skeleton crew on a shakedown cruise. Zylawy has no wife or children, and a minor arrest years ago for public drunkenness. He's been clean ever since. No connections to any political groups or criminal organizations. The analysts say Zylawy is an old-school sailor with a solid reputation."

"Forward what you have to Naval Intelligence and find out where and in what direction the sub went."

"I've already requested satellite thermal imaging. How long are you staying in the office?"

"Until we're done."

———

While John Devine fretted on the fifth floor of the CIA headquarters at Langley, four new workers joined the day shift at Ceyhan Doll Makers. Roger Shaw, Eric LaGrange, and two Special Forces commandos, Danny Greer and Dirk Lee, wearing shabby dungarees and thick sweaters like the other employees, shuffled in the factory door. Necdet Shubaki met the men and directed them to warehouse space on the third floor.

"Here you are, Mr. Shaw, everything you asked for, except we have no bathroom facilities."

"We're resourceful. The men can piss in a can," Shaw said. "Stop your worrying."

Shubaki nodded and an hour later returned with food, water, and a white plastic gallon bucket with a lid. Shaw shrugged. He thanked Shubaki and guided him out the door.

The commandos installed a video system to monitor activity in and around the building. Cameras set a mile away gave them the externals and cameras in the smoke detectors throughout the factory provided an adequate view inside. Even more important, the men had audio with the interior cameras. Shaw guessed they had several hours until show time. Better to be early and prepared, he thought.

"Don't forget to empty the bucket," Shaw told the men when he left.

———

The NR-1 lay on the floor of the Mediterranean Sea near the port of Ceyhan, exterior lights glowing in the dark. "This is the SSK Bukharin," sputtered from a speaker on the communications console. "We have you on radar. Respond and identify."

"Good to hear from you. This is United States NR-1 research vessel, Officer in Charge Charles Jurevics speaking. We are under command of the European Union to assess environmental changes in the Mediterranean seabed."

"We have not received notification of your efforts."

"Politics, I expect, also a bit of embarrassment. Who am I talking to?"

"Captain Vladimir Zylawy. Status, please."

"Since being towed into position, we've had more problems than a sturgeon has eggs. The wiring for the recovery claw on our sample basket is damaged, two of our video cameras are down, and we've lost most of our fresh water. Any help would be much appreciated."

"One moment, Officer Jurevics." Zylawy turned to the navigator. "What is this NR-1?"

"Pure research and no weaponry, Captain. Should I radio St. Petersburg?"

"No need, young man. This situation is under the rules of the sea." Zylawy depressed the send switch on his microphone. "Your request for assistance is acknowledged. We are on sea trials and have officers from the Russian Admiralty checking out canals and their depths for an oil transport company."

"Seems to be a light assignment for such a big ship."

"Oil people are competitive and secretive, and probably responsible for damage to the sea beds."

"Let's hope not. Our next shore leave is planned for Crete and I was hoping to get in some snorkeling."

"Spoken like a true seaman. Even when we rest, we must be in the water. Your accent is more than American."

"Yes, my grandmother was Russian from Novgorod. I grew up around the Upper Peninsula in Michigan. Lend us a hand and the party is on us."

"The European Union has stocked your ship well?"

"That's right. We have a surplus of Italian wine if you're interested."

Yes, the captain thought, full-bodied Chianti would be welcome. Only nuclear submarine crews were allowed red wine as a countermeasure against radiation leakage. "Prepare to surface," said Zylawy.

Dmitry Ogdanov burst into the command center and Zylawy turned on him. "You cannot come in here without permission. Any rank you have in the Admiralty means nothing when the ship is at sea."

"Our mission is for underwater trials, not to aid Americans."

"What is the problem? Sailors hold only citizenship to the sea. We are not enemies. Do not forget you are only a passenger on my ship."

Sergei Ivanovsky spoke from behind. "Our apologies, Captain. Come, Dmitry."

The men left the captain to his command center. "Sergei, we are almost in position to fire the torpedoes. The Americans must not board."

"We need to be cordial. Pluchenko may arrange other uses for the Bukharin if we are successful. Think of the hard currency we get for doing this job ourselves."

"I say we put a gun to the captain's head and show him who is in charge," Ogdanov answered.

"How did you ever rise in the admiralty with that hot head? Defer to the captain and smile at the Americans. The torpedoes will launch on schedule."

"Damn you, Sergei. This had better work."

Water poured from the dull steel vessels as they broke the surface of the blue Mediterranean. On top of the NR-1 hull, a bridge with plastic windshield protected the two-man bridge and the ship's access hatch. The SSK Bukharin fixed their gangplank between the two ships and helped six men from the NR-1 on board. Fresh water was pumped into the depleted tanks and exchanged in kind for a case of wine. Ogdanov and Ivanovsky watched the crewmembers of both vessels closely, despite their own pleasure with the wine.

Usually the crew of the NR-1 was composed of officers, enlisted men, and scientists. Navy SEALS had replaced the regular men. Once bottles had been opened and introductions traded, they removed Glock and Browning pistols from under heavy coats and took command of Kilo class 636, SSK Bukharin and its surprised crew. Ogdanov glowered at the combined stupidity of the captain and Ivanovsky.

John Devine cheered when the dispatch came from Naval Intelligence. Officer in Charge Charles Jurevics had radioed: "We have secured a major pollutant to the seabed of a Kilo submarine. Two live torpedoes were programmed to fire at the port of Ceyhan without the knowledge of Captain Zylawy. The Turks and the Russian Admiralty might like to know."

CHAPTER 14

LaGrange, Greer, and Lee monitored the video array in shifts. They slept and ate, and read by penlight. Throat mikes and earpieces kept them in communication.

"Hear that?" asked Greer. "Rats. Goddamn warehouse has rats."

"Quit being a pussy, Danny. My neighborhood in Baltimore had ones bigger than dogs," replied Lee.

"Must have been small dogs. You grow up with dachshunds?"

"Old man had a rotweiller, mean bastard. Mutt slobbered like an old drunk."

"There's another rat. Shit, the sucker must be a Norway. I get bit they better med-evac my ass out of here."

"Ask for a Purple Heart."

LaGrange's voice interrupted the conversation. "Knock off the chatter and keep your mind on the mission."

"Gee, boss," said Lee. "We didn't know you re-upped and got your bars."

"This is an Agency operation. Shut up and do your job."

The hours lapsed into silence until LaGrange's earpiece crackled with sound.

"We have a vehicle," said Greer.

Lee took his night vision goggles to the window and Greer put down his paperback to concentrate on the video monitors. They watched a truck appear at the back of the building. Two men got out and opened the freight elevator, then unloaded boxes from the truck.

"What do you think?" Lee asked.

"Let them unload," said LaGrange. "If they don't stay, we'll leave them alone. They may lead our men outside to a safe house."

The elevator closed with tired clanks and wheezes. Lee moved to the front of the building and LaGrange to the back, and left Greer at the monitors. The elevator began its ascent to the second floor, where the elevator door opened. Greer watched them on the screen as they moved past a camera to the false office in the dark.

Inside the office the intruders lined the boxes along one wall. They did not speak. One held the door for the other and they departed. Except for the old elevator, there was no noise. Soon they were outside and in the truck. LaGrange tugged at the grate between him and Faisal's office below, set the heavy metal screen aside, and jumped down to the second floor. He slit open a box with his Puma knife and hefted out several of the airplanes. They were heavier than the planes Shubaki had shown him.

"Packages received intact," he said into his throat mike. "I'm coming back."

Before daylight, the same deliverymen returned with another four. The cameras showed them bumping into doorways and shelves, like they had come out of bright light into a dark theater. LaGrange left the video monitors and looked out the window. Dawn was still an hour away from the horizon.

The six men entered the second floor office and settled down in the dark.

"Subjects taking a nap. What now?" Greer asked.

"Bring up the rear. Radio the boys below to give us fifteen minutes and then come on in."

Yakir Arvatian camped out next to the large air conditioning unit on the roof of a warehouse, a half-kilometer from Ceyhan Doll Makers. He had watched the brothers Anatoly and Hassan Abratov unload the boxes into the freight elevator, leave safely, and return with the other members of the team. Arvatian remained uneasy. Everything had gone as planned. He received delivery of the Igla-2 shoulder-fired missile from a fishing boat before the ceremony and had carried the weapon to the roof without passing a checkpoint.

The line of daylight in the east turned from red to yellow as Arvatian heard a vehicle. He retrieved his field glasses and moved to the western edge of the roof. A large van pulled into the parking lot of Ceyhan Doll Makers to stop at the front of the building, and out of Arvatian's line of vision. The van moved around to the back and parked in front of the freight elevator near his own men's truck. No driver got out of the vehicle.

Kamal ibn-Sultan regularly sent reinforcements on important operations, but the driver could be an agent of Turkish or American intelligence. He dared not use his cell phone. Besides, the Abratov brothers had installed explosives in the treadmill in the office. He was prepared to blow the treadmill and the model airplanes by remote control if the mission was compromised.

The other van was likely ibn-Sultan ensuring his success with a second team. Arvatian lay down flat on the roof and kept watch on the two vehicles.

———

LaGrange motioned for Lee and Greer to ready their gas masks. Lee stood at the window and watched the front entrance. He signaled the back-up team had entered the building. The gas masks went on.

LaGrange crawled to the air grate and the men below stirred, disturbed by the noise of his movement. Before they could react, he pulled the grate and dropped a squat canister of tear gas into the Faisal

THE VIEW FROM TIGER'S BACK

office, tidy but for the dozens of boxes. The three masked men followed the tear gas and landed with Glocks in hand. The six surprised sleepers flailed about trying to find the door. Before they could reach the lock, the door opened for them.

Within minutes the back-up team of dark-suited Special Forces commandos had the six men restrained, gagged, blindfolded, and on the freight elevator. Outside, the commandos removed their cumbersome masks to fresh, early morning air. LaGrange breathed deep, and watched the captives pushed into the white van and driven away. He returned to the elevator with Lee and Greer.

"We need to air this place out," he said. "Shubaki won't appreciate the new scent."

"Man should thank us," said Lee. "For driving the damn rats out."

"Put your masks back on," LaGrange ordered "Wear them until we open the windows on the second and third floors."

"Yes, boss. Must have been a real thrill under your command."

"We have more to do, Lee. The mission isn't over."

———

Arvatian saw men appear from the freight elevator and six pushing a like number to the white van. Who was who? He knew the operation had gone wrong. American or Turkish intelligence had every square kilometer near the pipeline under close scrutiny. Why had the men, especially the Abratov brothers, failed to see them?

He meditated on his dilemma and made a decision. Arvatian would complete his role and expect to be retrieved as planned. Turkish forces had not discovered his present location. Even his own men were unaware of his assignment. They had been told he was in Istanbul.

Arvatian put his head back against the wall to sleep until the ceremony began. He was tired, very tired. He had been unable to rest the night before, dreams of success and dreams of failure fought to keep him awake.

———

"The Silk Road of the 21st Century" read the banner above the dignitary stand at the port of Ceyhan, "Welcome to the Baku-Tblisi-Ceyhan Petroleum Pipeline." Turkish troops wore their parade finery and Secret Service agents dressed in the dark suits of Bible salesmen. Lines of armored personnel carriers from the Adana Incirlik Airbase brought officials from different governments to the wooden stand filled with folding chairs behind the podium, and decorated with flags and bunting. The crowd of four hundred onlookers included fans of the pipeline, workers, and journalists to participate in the festivities.

The night before, Turkish President Ahmet Sezer hosted a dinner party for two hundred guests in Istanbul at the Ciragan Palace. Much of the small talk concerned Ambassador Paige and Energy Secretary Martin Holbeck. Both missed the event and gossip circulated they were trysting at an undisclosed location, likely the Hyatt. This was discounted after a man who knew Holbeck described him as "florid, obese, bald, and stupid." Elizabeth Paige was too attractive a woman to bed such a man, even to further her career.

Fat gray pipes ran parallel to the left of the raised platform where the presidents of Azerbaijan and Georgia waited with other dignitaries for the arrival of the president of Turkey and the Energy Secretary Holbeck. Burt Strauss sat close to the front and scanned the crowd entering the stands. The day was a culmination of his work at British Chemical Enterprises. He hoped the port of Ceyhan would not turn into an inferno before his eyes.

Strauss admired the elegant figure of Elizabeth Paige moving in his direction. Her escort, Roger Shaw with government-issue earphone and lapel microphone, looked unusually tired. He directed Elizabeth to seats near Strauss. Even in a severe business suit, Elizabeth retained her grace.

"Nice day for a rally," Shaw greeted Strauss.

"Couldn't be better." He turned to Elizabeth. She accepted his hand politely and without warmth.

"Good to see you, Elizabeth. You look terrific." What a stupid thing to say, Strauss realized. She turned him into a bumbling fool with a cool glance.

"Thanks," she said. Strauss made room as Shaw pointed to the space beside him and she sat down. Shaw slid in next to her on the aisle.

"What can we do for an encore after the oil is flowing?" Strauss said.

Elizabeth shut down his attempt at friendly talk by not registering his comment. He doubted Shaw had passed along information about the SSK Bukharin. The confrontation between the NR-1 and the Kilo submarine sounded like a scene taken from a Clive Cussler novel, and Elizabeth stuck with her Anthony Trollope for fiction. Shaw had reassured him the threats to the ceremonies were under control, but still the Agency man showed the frown of anxiety. Strauss pointed toward the two berths and the black prows of the Very Large Crude Carriers about to be put into service. "This is your achievement, Elizabeth," he said.

She concentrated on the arrival of Ambassador Xiang when her attention turned an approaching armored personnel carrier. Secret Service agents rushed to open the doors and help out the passengers.

"Here comes Holbeck," Shaw said. "Living proof that political patronage keeps the halt and the lame off the street." He held a pair of field glasses and adjusted the focus.

The US Marine Band struck up "The Star Spangled Banner" and soon the Energy Secretary emerged and waved. Behind him came President Sezer, resplendent in his formal uniform weighted with gold braid. The band switched to the Turkish national anthem, "Istiklal Marsi," the strident cymbal-heavy martial air of "The Independence March" causing temporary nationalist fervor among many in the crowd. The two men walked to the stand, and met the Azerbaijan and Kazakhstan presidents who had been seated an hour earlier.

The heads of state faced the pipeline as the crowd cheered. Horns of the crude carriers ready to take delivery sounded loud into the afternoon air. A whining came across the sky, like a swarm of angry gnats demanding their share of the picnic. Strauss squinted at a red and white bird chopping the air. A model airplane! He pointed to the plane for Elizabeth, and she forgot her composed indifference to Strauss and smiled. Soon dozens of the airplanes were headed to the stand in ragged formation. The crowd waved at the demonstration and even the presidents followed the buzz of white gas engines. Strauss was alarmed by the sudden appearance of the airplanes, but not Shaw. People stood for a better look and began to laugh.

Flags trailed from the tails of the airplanes: "Bravo," "Welcome BCE," and "Job Well Done." Other slogans were too small to be read from their altitude. The airplanes flew over the crowd, then the dignitary stand, and crashed along the berths in a broken mass of wings and fuselages.

———

LaGrange laughed as Shubaki, Lee, and Greer flew the airplanes from the roof of Ceyhan Doll Makers. He had thought Shaw crazy to promise Shubaki payoff for his help, but he had to admit the wisdom of the display. Shubaki glowed like a little kid opening presents, and Lee and Greer joined in the adolescent fun. The occasional airplane crashed into the nearest building from a faulty engine or sputtered in the wrong direction. Shubaki had his moment, the Special Forces commandos a temporary respite from the seriousness of their jobs, and LaGrange had kept Elizabeth safe.

Shaw held his field glasses tight to his eyes. The glint of sunlight from the warehouse near the Doll Makers could be a scrap of tinfoil from a worker's lunch forgotten on the roof and the burn of fear in his stomach could be indigestion from last night's kebe. He pulled at his sleeve mike.

"Eric, Bird Dog, whatever I'm supposed to say. You have an extra guest at your eleven o'clock. Respond now."

"This line is not secure."

"Like I give a shit. Glass the target and go. This might be the third strike we've been missing."

———

Yakir Arvatian crouched behind the roof parapet and raised his head to scan the crowded field in the distance. His field glasses around his neck, he moved behind the air-conditioning unit and adjusted the glasses a second time before surveying the target from his position. He unzipped the long canvas bag and took out the light green tube of the Igla-2 missile. Arvatian looked at his target, an oversized valve wheel wrapped in red and gold ribbons ready to be opened for the first rush of light crude oil. The wheel was well within range of the missile.

He took a deep breath and hefted the missile launcher. Arvatian moved into a prone position, rested the launcher on the wall, and watched the model airplanes fly over the crowd below. The airplanes did not ignite their Cemtex payloads. He took a small black box from his jacket pocket, pulled out the antenna, and depressed the red button. Not a spark came from the airplanes. His cell phone rang.

"The operation has been compromised," said ibn-Sultan. "I expected to hail you with congratulations. The Cleric and I need your sacrifice. Do you understand?"

"We will eat mutton together in Paradise," he said, and cut the connection.

Former Armenian army colonel Yakir Arvatian, was full of sorrow for his life. He had been a good soldier, but had come to Islam too late. The reward of Paradise would be kept from him for the sinning he had done when younger. He had known women, drank liquor until stupefied, lied, cheated, and robbed. His sins grew in number until the Word of the Messenger entered his life. Prayers at the mosque relieved his pain at being a weak man, lifted his eyes to Heaven. Above was order and law older than the stones of his homeland. He embraced the refuge provided by Almighty God. The world should know such peace the infidels shunned in exchange for their dollars. When Muslim lands are Muslim again, ibn-Sultan had told him, the wars will end. In the crosshairs of the Igla-2 was an example of the infidel's hold on land not belonging to them, Caspian oil monopolized by Westerners who prospered while Muslims suffered. Arvatian adjusted the viewfinder and readied the missile for firing.

The rooftop door sprang open on torn hinges and three men hurried through the egress. LaGrange did not hesitate when he saw the crouched man with the weapon. He fired and the bullet knocked the man in the shoulder. Lee and Greer let loose their bullets until the receivers clicked empty. Terrible pain ripped Arvatian's chest as he framed his target and held the trigger. He fell backwards and the missile launcher slipped from his fingers and clattered on the roof beside him.

Since the purpose of the Igla-2 was to knock out a stationary target, its optical homing head with logic unit had been shut off. The missile had only its point of origin as reference and kept to a flat trajectory above the port of Ceyhan, across the bows of the moored crude carriers, and fell into the Mediterranean Sea five kilometers later when the missile ran out of fuel. No one on the dignitary stand saw the geyser when the missile detonated in the water.

LaGrange knelt beside Arvatian as the wounds bled out. The man whispered to LaGrange before a last shudder of living.

"Hard shit, boss," said Lee. "What did he tell you?"

" 'No Paradise.' He wanted someone to know."

———

Sitting in the kitchen of the Brooklyn brownstone, Ali Massouf leafed through his notes to check the details of the upcoming Madison Square Garden operation. The men must have the anthrax installed only hours before the event, though he hoped for more time. Basketball came first and the New York Knicks needed the court for practice earlier in the day. The management office rudely informed Massouf the air-conditioning must not be shut off until the practice was finished. He should have known and allowed for the extra time. An overlooked detail like this could ruin the operation.

The installation of the equipment had originally planned for three o'clock, with the anthrax set off at eight. They were pushed into the Friday rush hour and the men were unhappy with the news. Yes, he knew this cut down the time for evacuation to a safe distance. He spent a good twenty minutes bolstering confidence and calming fear among his crew by talking about adaptability, resourcefulness, and focus.

All else had better be in place, for he knew this operation had only one chance to succeed. Samir Mohammed had checked and rechecked the equipment with an inert powder to simulate anthrax spores. The contraption Mohammed designed to suspend the anthrax and keep the spores flowing before the huge blowers that cooled the Garden worked better than anticipated. Massouf pressed the scientist to test the timer for the anthrax device several times so they could be assured of its functioning. The most crucial part was before them. The killing chamber had to be filled no later than eight-thirty to infect the greatest number of the audience by the end of the Knicks versus Chicago Bulls game.

"Basketball," said Massouf to no one. "Men chasing a round ball, ridiculous as football." He left being a sports fan to the Infidels.

⸻

The white granite Beaux-Arts Union Station on Massachusetts Avenue in Washington, DC neared the century mark and did not look its age. Gold leaf shined on the 96-foot vaulted ceilings and two concourse levels were filled with boutiques, souvenir shops, restaurants, and a movie theater from the station's renovation in the late 1980s. Stephanie and John Devine were running late for their train to New York City. The Nigerian cab driver had cursed through the rain and early weekend traffic. Devine gave the man too large a tip and he and Stephanie skidded across the marble floors with overnight bags. They held hands like new lovers anticipating an illicit weekend.

"I told you we'd be here in time," he said, out of breath.

"You know I can't cheer on my Bulls without my man."

They found seats on the sleek Acela Express, possibly the slowest high-speed train in the world. When the tracks were dry, the train ran at a top speed of 150 mph but today's rain slowed the Acela to 75 mph. Stephanie and Devine enjoyed the slower pace with each other.

"Ready for the game?" he asked.

"Anything other than work. I want room service and no television."

"Not even CNN?"

"No news, no weather, not even Cinemax."

After writing lead-ins, voiceovers, and sound bites for WJLA-TV, Channel 7, Stephanie had started editing video, her first step to producing the news. The training began as the US President went on national television to denounce the threat of the Followers of the Cleric. "They are followers of an evil older than man," he said, and his hyperbole had stations across the country hurrying to compile packages explaining the menace. Stephanie pulled file copies of videos from Al Jazeera, the Arabic station with headquarters in Qatar, and ran through hours of footage to assemble a moving gallery of conspirators named by the State Department. She stared at images of Suleyman Ehmat, Ali Massouf, Yakir Arvatian, and the leader, Kamal ibn-Sultan, from the days when the Followers of the Cleric were another of many Muslim voices protesting the West's incursions on their lands. She looked behind their robes and beards for the men beneath who had turned to violence. Earlobes, eyes, and noses were her reference points to separate them in the Al Jazeera broadcasts. Arvatian had died in Ceyhan, Ehmet and Massouf at large, and ibn-Sultan rumored to be a dozen places at once, and dared anyone to collect the price on his head.

Stephanie spent long hours at the WJLA offices on Wilson Boulevard in Arlington, Virginia. She talked to reporters and gathered enough material for an hour-long documentary, and accepted the demands of the editorial director to cut the mass down for a manageable ten-minute slot. The special report shrunk to nothing special, and the questions she had accumulated were left unanswered. Did the followers really believe they fought a thousand-year-old war? Who was the Cleric and what hold did he have on the men who carried out his commands? Add to this the technological advantages of the US military being unable to locate ibn-Sultan and Stephanie's confusion grew. She wanted to ask Devine what drove the Followers, free of the State Department censors, but he had kept his promise not to tell her what he did at the CIA. The pact had held their marriage together. When the spot was aired, she had asked Devine what he thought. He said, "Pretty good," and Stephanie accepted the words as praise.

The Acela pulled into Pennsylvania Station and the Devines hailed a taxi for Essex House on Central Park. They left their bags with the concierge and sped back to the Station and Madison Square Garden. Masses of basketball fans poured in through the gates, ready to cheer on the Knicks. Stephanie and Devine handed over their tickets and passed through the turnstiles. This fourth version of the Garden had been slated for destruction and new one built across the street at the James Farley Post Office. Devine dreaded the eventual change. Every year they had courtside seats, once sharing a row with Spike Lee.

"Let's get something to eat," said Devine. "Who knows how much longer we'll be able to enjoy the hot dogs?"

"Men," she said. "Always resistant to change. There's a gelato stand ahead on the right."

"No argument there. The City has shuffled around the Garden since the last century. I like permanence."

"I like caramel or chocolate, John. We can gloat over a midnight supper."

Devine carried a plastic cup to his wife. Gelato, ice cream, one more expensive than the other, and who knew if the gelato really came from Italy. Stephanie turned from a program vendor and looked toward the concession with the sign, "Viola Gelato: From Italy with Love." She saw a clean-shaven man berate the skinny clerk who shook at the man's harsh words. He continued his tirade regardless of the waiting customers. "Zaidan," he called the clerk. Stephanie recognized the dark eyes and angry mouth.

"What's wrong?" asked Devine.

Stephanie grabbed his hand and whispered in his ear: "That man. He's Ali Massouf, of the Followers of the Cleric."

"No way. Massouf is in Syria or Iran."

Devine jerked his head to see who she was talking about, and she pulled him toward her. "He's bad, John. Be careful."

He strolled over and eavesdropped on the two men for a moment before completing a circle back to Stephanie. "They're talking about repairs to the air-conditioning. Are you sure it's him?"

"I've watched his face at work for the last week. He's Massouf, all right."

Devine pulled out his cell phone and dialed Langley where Howard Crumbly dozed on what he called the mini-mart shift, seven in the morning until eleven at night. He ran through the updates on the followers of the Cleric as he listened to Devine.

"The last confirmed sighting of Massouf was February in Kazakhstan. We had rumors of him in Milan, but nothing came of the news. He's been at large ever since, sir."

"This is when we call in every favor we think we have. Call the NYPD and have them liase with FBI and Homeland Security. Our man is at the Viola Gelato concession, about five-ten, 180 pounds, dark complexion and hair, and wearing tan slacks and a blue jacket. I'm staying with him."

"This causes problems with jurisdiction, sir."

"I don't give a great green goddamn about who is supposed to be in charge of what. The Feebies have been all over the Middle East and no one raised a ruckus. Anybody cries about jurisdiction, I'll give names to the media. Massouf isn't in town to see *The Lion King*."

"I'm only pointing out the obvious, sir. Tell me your location."

"On the right of the Seventh Avenue entrance. Have them locate the concession and hold the employees. I don't want the Garden stormed. SWAT team and bomb squad should stay in the background. They also need evacuation plans. Whatever is going on is happening now. We have no time. Viola Gelato may be the business we were trying to find. See if they have received an overseas shipment around the time the anthrax went missing. Call me back when the troops are coming." He hung up. "Stephanie, where is Massouf?"

"He's still at the stand. We have to stay with him."

"This breaks our agreement. We'll give New York's finest the job."

"I say we stay."

"On my lead, Nora Charles."

"I'd rather be Lois Lane. Having Superman at my side makes me braver."

CHAPTER 15

Crumbly bullied through the NYPD switchboard and relayed Devine's message. Homeland Security had cut New York Police Department's anti-terrorism budget by forty percent, and any opportunity to show up the bureaucrats was welcome. He still needed to find out the extent of the threat, and pulled a thick sheaf of printouts from the shelf in his cubicle, the silly check on businesses in New York Devine had ordered last month. The gelato maker hid deep in the pages as an Italian franchise bought by local investors weeks before Marco Polo Imports accepted a cargo container from a Sicilian carrier. The timeline worked.

The telephone rang on Crumbly's desk. "Devine here. How did you do with the cops?"

"Units dispatched, sir. I've been checking into Viola Gelato and they may have the anthrax."

"Shit. Do your wizardry and tell me who has delivered to the Garden today."

Crumbly tapped the keyboard until he entered the Garden mainframe, a simple hack. The firewall buckled like tissue paper under his fingers.

"ScanAm Imports, Southebys, East India Furniture, American Systems, African Art and Collectibles."

"Give me what you have on American Systems. They were on the Marco Polo Imports list."

"Plumbing and heating company in Brooklyn. They've been in and out of the Garden for two days."

"Find out why and what they had at the freight forwarder's."

"Right here, sir. Air-conditioning repairs. Marco Polo Imports have them down as taking a shipment of Persian rugs. Maybe they're redoing their corporate offices."

"Someday I have to teach you paranoia, Howard."

"Listen to this: American Systems has a contract with the Garden. According to their records, they haven't been inside for weeks. Maintenance isn't scheduled until next month."

"The pieces are starting to fit."

Devine and Stephanie walked around Viola Gelato in a wide circle, and stopped at souvenir stands to admire the pennants and foam rubber gloves with "We're Number 1!" printed in a close approximation of the Knicks' colors. Ali Massouf sat on a stool with a newspaper and "Zaidan" sold gelato to the line. Parents carried children on their shoulders, and hardcore Bulls fans strutted in black and red jackets ready to argue who would win this night. Jersey girls wore high hair and gabbed on cell phones, and Bed-Sty represented with oversized jerseys over hooded sweatshirts. Eighteen thousand Black, white, Hispanic, and Asian ticket holders mingled in the slow filling of the seats. The altered air-conditioner purred under the bragging and laughter.

"Ever done this before?" Stephanie asked.

"Surveillance is not in my line. I send other people to shadow and peek around corners. My worst fear is a paper cut," said Devine.

The police had yet to arrive when a man wearing overalls with "American Systems" on the back approached the concession. "Zaidan" scooped into his merchandise and handed him a large cup of vanilla. Massouf put down his newspaper to talk with the American Systems man. He paced around the small space behind the counter and glanced at his watch. Another man hurried down the hallway, spoke to Massouf, and walked from the concession with the American Systems worker.

Massouf put on a jacket, grabbed a briefcase, and headed for the exit.

Stephanie and Devine followed ten feet behind. He turned out the Seventh Street doors and stood outside for a moment. The street was crowded with commuters eager to get on subways and trains home. Massouf checked his watch and hurried into Penn Station. The Devines almost lost him. Once inside, he sat down, and concentrated on the overhead schedules.

"Keep him in sight while I make a call," said Devine. Stephanie sat three rows behind Massouf while Devine walked out of hearing range and hit the speed dial on his cell phone.

"Devine here. Our man is in motion and we're providing the tail. What have you got?"

"Sir, the NYPD have the concession but not you or Massouf."

"We're in Penn Station waiting for a train. Anything on American Systems?"

"Police have established American Systems knows nothing about the repairs. The Garden security people are looking over the work done to the air-conditioning vents. Otherwise, it's as quiet as a morgue."

"Find another simile, Howard."

"Yes, sir. Where's the suspect?"

"Front row bench. He hasn't purchased a ticket."

"I'll have the police right there, sir."

Stephanie waved for Devine and bolted after Massouf going to the train platform. The prospective passengers on the steps gave way without many complaints. He turned the corner at the bottom and caught sight of Stephanie boarding a train. He got out his cell as he ran. "Crumbly, I need the Feds to meet a Northeast Corridor train leaving Penn Station for New Haven, Connecticut, and Providence."

"Meet where, sir?"

"I don't know. Have them at every stop until you hear otherwise."

Devine ran to catch up and jumped into the train missing the doors close behind him. Stephanie stood inside the car. "I thought you'd never get here. Massouf is there," she said, and pointed at the window seat in the rear. "He's next to the old woman reading the *Post*."

The conductor asked for tickets and Devine paid cash for two. He scanned past a young couple, pairs of businessmen, a mother and child, and two women with Macy's shopping bags until he found the back of Massouf's head.

"Move to the next car, Stephanie. I don't want you near any line of fire."

"I stay with you. What now?"

"Feds are notified. We watch and wait."

Stephanie shivered as the electric train gained speed. "Wish we were at the game," she said.

"Not much longer, dear heart." He hoped he sounded confident. Devine knew his limitations. He could write briefs, stand before committees asking for multimillion-dollar budgets without a line item, send men and women overseas on perilous missions, but to have his wife in danger made him acknowledge how little he could protect her. Most men he knew in the intelligence community had progressed to wife number three, the string of divorces seen as an occupational hazard. Hello, honey, I'm home and I can't talk about what I do until you have the proper security clearance. Stephanie never asked, never wanted to ask, and concerned herself with the man inside the job. Devine believed she would have been happier if he was a postal worker, car mechanic, or florist, not the government spook. His profession had chosen him and already in place when he met Stephanie.

Devine's cell phone rang and he ignored the vibrating pulse. They watched for any sign Massouf was nervous as the conductor walked the aisle. He did not notice the conductor until the old woman handed him her ticket. Massouf gave his as well. Too cool, thought Devine, he is too goddamn cool and assured. The train slowed as it entered the New Haven station.

"Whatever happens, keep in your seat," he said.

———

Ali Massouf sighed with the exhaustion of a man who had run on adrenaline for a week and finally rested. The old woman next to him tapped the rubber ferule of her walking cane and clicked her teeth to the rhythm of the train tracks, an annoyance no Muslim woman made of herself. She moved away after several unsuccessful attempts to engage him in conversation and Massouf put his briefcase on her vacant seat.

He lay back and tried to sleep but the project nagged at him. For the third time since boarding, he reviewed his mental list. The rent on the loft was paid for a year. Ramzi Zaidan painted over the "American Systems" logo on the van and stored the van in a garage in Queens. Massouf told the corpulent Franco Manzani, manager of Viola Gelato, he was headed to Italy and left him in charge. The locked room in back of the gelateria was clean of anything relating to the operation and his gear sent ahead to Boston. The outbreak needed seven days to incubate. Eighteen thousand New Yorkers would wake to sore throats, fevers, and sore muscles. The disease progressed to coughs, chest pains, aches, and hard breathing. Doctors' offices and emergency clinics would fill with sufferers of this uncommon cold, and when the Center for Disease Control called the disease an epidemic, the videotapes would be released. Followers of the Cleric had defeated the infidels on their own soil. What monument would enshrine the dead sports fans, a giant orange ball stuck on top Madison Square Garden? He looked forward to reading the news in Berlin, where he would stay until Kamal ibn-Sultan called again.

Massouf took out his cell phone and punched in the number for Samir Mohammed at the Soho loft.

"We have a great victory thanks to your skill."

"I give my victory to ibn-Sultan and the Cleric," said Mohammed.

"Always so humble, as a good Muslim should be. Have you finished packing?"

"The remains of the device and any traces of our work are in the Hudson River. I have my bag ready."

"A genius such as yours will always have work with ibn-Sultan. Do not lose yourself as a servant to the Infidels. Enjoy your rest."

The next call went to the Brooklyn brownstone. "Zaidan?"

"No. I am David."

"Where is Zaidan?"

"He has not arrived. Neither has Michael."

Words came from him, like hauling a bucket heavy with water the depth of a desert well.

"Any trouble with the device?"

"No."

"Clear the house when the others arrive, and go to your different safe houses."

"We will."

"Consider Zaidan and Michael compromised if they are not there by midnight."

Again Massouf tried to sleep. Zaidan had lived too long among the infidels and grown soft. Put him in Afghanistan for several months training and he might be a dependable soldier. The mountains were the real battlefield, where the Kalashnikov reclaimed Muslim land one meter at a time. These elaborate plans fought the Infidels with their own weak weapons. A woman uses poison, he thought, a man uses the gun and grenade and mortar. He roused as the train slowed to a crawl for New Haven's Union Station. Massouf was thirsty and hungry, and hoped to find a decent eating-place before going to a hotel.

He felt under his jacket for the hammerless .38 revolver, a pleasant, nasty weapon good for making holes at close range. Massouf picked up his briefcase and joined the other passengers making for the exit.

———

Devine walked down the aisle without looking at the passengers. From one Union Station to another, he thought, what a goddamn day. Outside the platform was clear except for a scattering of dark-suited men and women ready to board. The train lurched on tired brakes and the passengers began to file out the doors. This situation called for field operatives, not a desk jockey. His choices of action dwindled as the car emptied. Massouf had to be taken before he entered the station where he could grab a hostage. The old woman fell into Massouf, her cane spinning along the floor. Devine pushed the woman aside and grabbed at the man.

"Leave me be!" demanded Massouf.

"Not a chance. I'm a government officer and you're under arrest for conspiracy."

He slid from under Devine's grasp and stuck the revolver in his ribs.

"Is that really a complaint under your justice system?"

"You're Ali Massouf, a follower of the Cleric. The station is full of Federal agents who are here to take you in. I want this done without any loss of life, including yours."

Massouf tightened his hold on Devine's neck. "You bomb Iran, you bomb Iraq and Afghanistan, you spend billions of dollars despoiling countries for oil, and now your concern is for saving lives. Excuse me if I reject your hypocrisy."

"Surrender and we can talk. This situation is only going to escalate. I don't want you shot anymore than me. Drop the gun and let me turn you in. I'll make sure you're treated fairly."

Agents quickly established a perimeter around the train and kept the platform clear. The only passengers left were Stephanie and the old woman. A calm infused Stephanie, a reverse adrenalin rush that steadied her heartbeat and flushed out the fear. She reached for the lost cane as Devine talked to Massouf, removed the rubber ferule. Let the man ramble, wait a moment until his back is turned, and make the move to end this charade. Bombs and wars mean nothing. John Devine means home, love, and compassion, and worth fighting for.

Stephanie stood and jabbed Massouf in the back. "Hey, crazy man. Let go of my husband go or I'll blow your nuts off."

Massouf turned. Devine knocked him to his knees and Stephanie banged the man on the head with the cane. The gun tumbled and four agents rushed the car. They pinned Ali Massouf to the floor, ratcheted handcuffs to his wrists, and led him out and off the platform.

The Special Agent in Charge greeted Devine and Stephanie inside the cavernous Union Station. "Mr. Devine? Your office called and said you'd like some help bringing in a bad guy."

Devine held on to Stephanie. "Thanks for holding back. I'm not exactly a field man but we managed."

"Nice work, sir. Crumbly asks you return his call. Is there anything else we can do for you?"

"Yes, get us back to New York. This is still our anniversary and we'd like to enjoy what's left of the day."

A car and driver sped them into Manhattan and the Essex House. The hotel welcomed them with quiet, hot showers, and room service club sandwiches. Stephanie toweled her damp chestnut hair and rummaged through the minibar for drinks.

"I'm having gin. What about you?'

"The whiskey, any and all." Devine paused. "You're still surprising, wife of mine. 'I'll blow your nuts off?' " He laughed. "Where did you pick up the mouth?"

"Comes with working in the news business. Cameramen are notoriously crude."

Devine's cell phone vibrated in his jacket thrown over a chair. "Mother Crumbly is calling. I have to get this."

"Gives me a chance to steal your french fries."

"Go ahead." He opened the phone and spoke. "Devine here."

"Sir, you are not going to believe this. I can't and neither can the bomb squad."

"Tell me and I won't believe it either. What's going on?"

"Okay. NYPD found a device in an air-condition vent in the Garden. The thing was pretty sophisticated and blew fine powder through the system. Anyone at the game tonight was going to be infected with anthrax by inhalation. Massouf's cell must have been working on the project for months, I mean with getting the material from Rebirth Island and setting up the different fronts. Anyhow, the bomb squad shut the machine down and sent a sample to their lab for testing.

"I did some research on how the Russians processed the anthrax before burying the canisters. The material is very hard to kill, sir. They had used a bleach wash and still the anthrax was active. Massouf had the stuff made into an aerosol by persons unknown and then smuggled into the Garden through Viola Gelato. This is where everything fell apart."

"They did evacuate the Garden, right?"

"No need, sir. The extreme cold of the gelato killed the anthrax. What bleach and Rebirth Island couldn't do, Italian ice cream knocked dead."

———

The waste of war marked the road outside of Mazar-e Sharif in Afghanistan. Due north sat Uzbekistan, the lax border open to whoever wanted to cross. The Taliban had lost the country to the Western influences and elections yet were able to leave a deeper mark than any explosive. Idolatry in Bamiyan Province had been routed by the destruction of two statues of Buddha, under orders from the Taliban. Let no sign be taller or sun brighter than Islam, they decreed. Kamal ibn-Sultan had participated in knocking down the false gods. Given another decade and all of Afghanistan would have been purified. Now the bands of the faithful had been scattered across the Central Highlands, Southern Plains, and Northern Plateau.

Ibn-Sultan and two armed men parked their sand-colored Toyota Land Cruiser next to rows of pistachio trees. Shadows stretched across the foothills and the sun slipped into the horizon. Soon the labored huffing of another vehicle came toward the Toyota.

The headdress and long beard of Abu Abdullah poked from the door of an old panel truck. He and his driver wore fatigue coats over their traditional robes, against the evening chill. Ibn-Sultan waved to Abdullah, "Almighty God be with you."

"Blessings of the Prophet on you," he answered. Abdullah stepped into the road and kissed ibn-Sultan twice on his cheeks. "How was the crossing at the border?"

"The border guards took all the money I offered."

"A greedy bunch as I suspected."

"They like your money, Abdullah."

"I was called foolish when I donated my family's wealth to the struggle against the Crusaders. No, I said, with the Cleric all things are possible. Now I see the rightness of my detractors in their judgment."

"What do you mean?"

Abdullah gave his successor a sad smile. "Not the cause, but who I have chosen for the mission. The lives of many good Muslims have been risked, and for what? The expense of the port of Ceyhan operation was too high for failure, and also the anthrax debacle in New York City. I give you the honor of taking the war against Islam to the Westerners and you bring me defeat."

"There were circumstances beyond my control."

"No excuses, ibn-Sultan. My disappointment cannot be healed with petty justifications."

"I accept your criticism of my mistakes, but this next plan is sure to be successful. What we have done in the past is nothing compared to we will do in the near future. Where are the goods you promised?"

"The plutonium oxide powder. Enough to make ten Hiroshima-sized bombs, you say. I do not have them. Your Russian, Grigory Pluchenko, has temporarily quit the armament business."

"We must find another source."

"There are none for the defeated. Look around at the fields of pistachio trees. In another nine years we will have our first harvest. While you lose the war for Islam, my brothers and I restore the lost tradition of nut farming. This is in praise of the Prophet and Almighty God. Islam sends its roots into the soil, and feeds on the water from beneath and the sun and sky above."

"I do not understand this turn to agriculture."

"A Jordanian from the gutters only knows fighting, not the reason for fighting."

Abdullah reached in his fatigue jacket for an inhaler. He breathed deep until his lungs cleared. The years of war marked him with pieces of shrapnel in his body no doctor wanted to risk removing, ragged stitch scars from bullet wounds, and hunger never filled. Abdullah was tired. He had wanted Kamal ibn-Sultan to be his warrior and lead the followers of the Cleric into victorious battle. The fight belonged to the young. Ibn-Sultan had been poor in *Qur'an* studies but adept at violence, learned in Jordan and refined in Iraq. With every report of his actions, Abu Abdullah regretted his decision to secede the leadership in favor of this criminal. Ibn-Sultan had an untamed meanness of spirit, and defeats made him demand more deaths among the Westerners. A true leader saw war as leading to peace, not to another war.

The driver of the panel truck handed a black attaché case from the front seat to Abdullah. "Here, take this."

Ibn-Sultan regarded the case with suspicion.

"No fear, brother. Open the locks."

Inside were stacks of banded US 50 and 100-dollar bills. "A final payment. Take the money and find a country you can learn to respect. I am not rejecting you, dear Kamal. We will be together again. For now you need to find safe haven from the price on your head and read your *Qur'an*. Purchase a piece of Almighty God's earth and plant crops. Let Islam into your heart."

Ibn-Sultan closed the case. "This farewell is foolish. How many times have I heard you admonish our soldiers to continue the fight against the Crusader? Your wounds have made you a weak woman, Abdullah. Followers of the Cleric have strapped bombs to their bodies on your promise they will be met in Paradise. They look down on you with shame for hiding in the fields."

Abdullah reached out a frail arm and slapped ibn-Sultan with surprising strength to leave a livid red mark where he had kissed his cheek.

"Speak to me again in this manner and my driver will shoot you through the dried organ you call a heart."

"Does the Cleric know you have abandoned him?"

"I can ask the same, ibn-Sultan. Take your leave while I hold back my temper. We will have need of each other, not today but another day. Until then obey my commands as if they come from the Cleric."

The Land Rover and panel truck started their engines and drove in opposite directions along the pistachio trees. The war was far from over. Kamal ibn-Sultan did not need Abdullah or the Cleric. He would fight into Paradise without being hampered by old men too long from the battlefield.

CHAPTER 16

E ric LaGrange looked across the dim cabin at the four Special Forces commandos sprawled inside the belly of the C-130J transport airplane. With LaGrange were Danny Greer and Dirk Lee from the Ceyhan operation, and two newcomers, the lanky Roswell Davis, and Philip Obermeyer, New Jersey's own. They wore jumpsuits stripped of identifying patches, paratrooper boots with soft rubber soles, com-links of throat mikes and earpieces, Kevlar helmets, night-vision goggles, and parachutes.

The monotonous hum of the four Rolls-Royce turboprop engines lulled him into a restless sleep. He dreamed of a woman whose long torso stretched against his naked body. LaGrange felt her velvet hand touch his belly and he became aroused. The last woman he had taken to bed was Suzanne DuMaurier, an Arabic Studies major from McGill University in Montreal, another lifetime ago. LaGrange found temporary peace in the woman from Quebec, her tresses of red hair and fair skin that burned too easily in the sun. For three days they loved in his Damascus rooms and then she left. "You want too much," she said. LaGrange feared he wanted too little. He looked for her face in the odd smokiness of the dream. Suzanne led him to a window where they watched a lit cloud of dirt and building debris. Explosions ripped the streets and he thought he was going to be sick. She poked him in the ribs and he jumped awake.

The muzzle of a 10mm Heckler & Koch MP5 belonging to Danny Greer jammed into his side. LaGrange carefully moved the weapon's barrel from him, so as not to startle the commando slumped against the cabin wall.

"I am dead tired," Greer said with his eyes open. "How much longer, boss?"

"Less than an hour until we jump."

The giant transport had left the Adana Incirlik Air Base at dusk, after days of training that had almost brought LaGrange to his knees. They had run, trained in hand-to-hand combat, and climbed mountains. LaGrange suffered along with the Special Forces unit. He missed his studies, the calm libraries of Damascus and cloistered life he had constructed. Shaw had ruined his careful retreat into the past by shoving him in front of an uncertain present. He had no place left to go.

"Any more intel from Roger Shaw?" Greer asked.

"Same as before. Ibn-Sultan is traveling in a four-wheel drive north of Mazar-i-Sharif, and our informant says he's down to two bodyguards and not much else. Shaw was optimistic or we wouldn't be trying this grab."

"I wish we had our regular commanding officer."

"You'll do fine. You're a capable guy."

Greer surveyed the interior of the aircraft. "Look at them in full gear and sleeping like babies."

"You kicked ass pretty hard to get us ready. I'm still aching."

"This is the Agency's show, boss. We're only along as security guards."

"And much appreciated. The beeper on ibn-Sultan's vehicle shows increased movement in the foothills. We take him and anyone else we find."

"Like the other camel jockey, Abu Abdullah?"

"I've spent my life in this part of the world and only heard scared men and white trash use the term 'camel jockey.'"

"Point taken, boss. You Arab-lovers are a sensitive bunch."

LaGrange looked at his watch. "Wake the men and tell the jumpmaster to get ready."

Greer touched the shoulder of Dirk Lee napping next to him. The soldier woke in a hurry and jerked his weapon. "Relax, we're still airborne. Let's be moving."

Soon the interior of the C-130J buzzed with men coughing and yawning. Greer grabbed the portable megaphone and held on the rope-web with his free hand. "We'll be over our target in less than twenty minutes. LaGrange will jump first, followed by Lee, then the rest of you. I'll bring up the rear. Buddy up to check each other's chutes and load your weapons with double magazines. Make sure you have spare ammo."

The commandos signaled their readiness and hooked static lines running from their parachutes to the cable hung down the center of the airplane. Greer looked to the jumpmaster and the aft-loading ramp lowered. Night air flushed through the belly of the aircraft.

LaGrange hit the cool air and dove in free-fall until the chute opened and he was temporarily jerked skyward until going back down. The brightness and magnitude of stars in the dry air above Mazar-e Sharif made the jump magical, if not for the weaponry strapped to his body. Once on the ground, any sense of the sky was gone except for watching the rest of the commandos land. His attention shifted to the sounds of the night.

The team members spread across in the rough tilled soil of the Northern Plateau. LaGrange felt a hand wrap over his mouth and a knee thrust against his back.

"Got you," Greer whispered. LaGrange slipped from the grip and laid the blunt edge of his Puma knife against Greer's throat.

"Nice try, asshole."

"Want to see if you still have the stuff. Where's everybody?"

"No sign yet." They crouched with weapons drawn. The wind was up and carried the noise of shuffling feet. Someone touched his shoulder and Greer turned to find a dark-clad figure crouching behind him. "It's Lee. All men accounted for, sir."

"Take point and stay off the com-link unless necessary. Dumb shit jumpmaster dropped us ten klicks from the target. We've got a long hump ahead."

The commandos filed behind Lee. They marched in silence and only stopped to listen. The silhouettes of the new trees were ominous, and they approached the occasional boulder with caution.

LaGrange thought of Suzanne and his dream. She would fit in the darkness of the region where who knew what awaited him. After she had left, he spent several days debating whether he should look for her. His indecision provided the answer. Suzanne was in Cairo or home in Montreal, making babies with a better man and not LaGrange.

The column stopped short. Lee crouched ahead and behind him the rest of the commandos. Greer stood and so did the others. He raised his hand for the column to fall back to its previous position. Lee had spotted movement.

LaGrange felt the assuring weight of the MP5 in his hands. Greer lay flat on the ground and crawled to Lee. The commando behind LaGrange, Roswell Davis, scanned the landscape looking for more surprises. They heard a cracking and thump, and Greer reappeared holding his hand in a thumbs-up position.

"Goat," he said. "Suppertime on the hoof."

"Knock off the bullshit. We're too close," ordered LaGrange.

Lee led the men along an irrigation ditch in the unfamiliar landscape. He had been on other missions for Shaw and expected to be pulled out like before reaching the objective. No, Shaw had told him, this time was different. The Administration was solid behind going after ibn-Sultan in any country he hid regardless of diplomatic problems. A little late considering the damage he had caused, but still satisfying to bring him down, Lee thought.

Submachine gunfire shattered the night silence. LaGrange dropped to his knees and Philip Obermeyer fell on top of him. Blood pulsed from a neck wound until Obermeyer lay still. Greer shouted to take cover as shadows ran across the field and shot at commandos. LaGrange stumbled along the ditch toward the voice.

"Two bodyguards? I'm counting at least five. Shaw's intel is shit, LaGrange. Do me a favor and shoot him."

"Save the blame for later. Get Lee and Davis ready for some real rock and roll."

They waited for footsteps to approach the ditch. In the parched air, LaGrange could hear Greer breathing next to him. A twig snapped and La Grange rolled a grenade at the sound. The four commandos stood in the temporary light of the explosions and fired at the illuminated enemy. Young pistachio trees candled in short pillars of flame and cries marked the dead and dying. Anonymous Kalashnikovs let loose rounds until the fingers holding the triggers went lax.

LaGrange crawled to the shelter of an outcropping a dozen meters away and came around the backside of a stone herder's shed. Inside were a dozen men, boys really, who gripped the plywood stocks of their weapons and were afraid to shoot. He tossed two grenades inside. Sorry not to warn you, he said silently, but Paradise will bless the brave.

The shack and its red tile roof blew upwards, the cloud of debris carrying blood and bone matter. Quiet enveloped the land and he lay on the ground to survey the graveyard around him. A few moments later he heard a familiar whistle.

"Is that you, old man?" Greer whispered.

"Still alive. How are we doing?"

"The ambush is over."

They joined the men. Davis found two of the enemy still alive and went looking for more. A pile of enemy guns shone in the slit of a new moon.

"We need to check the bodies for our man," LaGrange said to Greer.

"Dirty work. Some of the boys have been hit pretty hard." He called back Davis to stay with the captured, and he and LaGrange poked the bodies laid out by Lee. They worked swiftly but steadily, and shone flashlights on the faces of their attackers. Open eyes looked at nothing. Most were too young to be more than new recruits.

There were tire tracks on the dirt road and LaGrange swore he could smell spilled gasoline. Lee pulled a flare from his belt for more light. Bodies thrown from the shed explosion splayed on the ground, none who they wanted.

LaGrange prodded the torn fatigues and broken limbs with his weapon. One had to be ibn-Sultan. Obermeyer from New Jersey was dead and there must be a reason. LaGrange wanted satisfaction from the battle, beyond blood and loss, the stupid pride of nations and cowardliness of extremists. Shaw had seduced him, plied him with stories about how the capture of ibn-Sultan would end the cycle of hate. What a load of shit, thought LaGrange. We go against an enemy who has no remorse and believe we will prevail. Not unless we stop playing by our rules and start using his.

"Son of a bitch," he cursed. "The son of bitch skipped on his soldiers."

"Come on, old man, no war is fair," Greer said. "You need a few beers and a three-day sleep. I promise we'll run the bastard down. You'll see. We got to get to the extraction point. Keep up, my friend."

The two wounded soldiers of ibn-Sultan were transferred to a black site for interrogation. Bagram Air Base had closed down their covert detention center, along with "the Salt Pit" in Kabul, due to the deaths caused by ignoring the basic rules set down by the UN Convention Against Torture and Other Cruel, Inhuman or Degrading Treatment or Punishment. Wherever the men were held, they gave information gladly. No, they did not know the identity or location of the Cleric. No, they did not know where Abu Abdullah had fled after the skirmish in the pistachio grove. Yes, they did know about Kamal ibn-Sultan. He had gone into the west to release funds from different bank accounts and continue his jihad against the West.

John Devine sent an encrypted e-mail to Roger Shaw: Regardless of the failed attempt in Afghanistan, Kamal ibn-Sultan must be caught at all costs, budgets be damned. Shaw flew to Geneva and followed the money trail given by the captured soldiers. Clerks at the Swiss Bank Corporation on Place de Cornavin and Rue de Mont-Blanc referred him from department to department, each with thicker carpets and older furniture. Progressively quieter whispers apologized for being unable to help. Bank regulations were strict about releasing information on all depositors, regardless of current criminal status. Shaw consoled himself with dinner at Au Pied de Cochon, and filled his belly with the pork denied in the Middle East.

He took a Swiss Air flight to Zurich and hoped for better luck with Credit Suisse. In Geneva he had enough knife-and-fork French to navigate the city and the interviews with different bank officials were held in English. His bad-to-nonexistent German only transmitted his frustration to Zurich's Schwyzertüütsch, and he retreated across the Limmat River for the cobblestones of Old Town and the thirteenth-century Fraumünster Church. Years in the Middle East had knocked religion out of Shaw, yet Marc Chagall's five stained glass windows in the choir loft pulled at him. The red, yellow, blue, and green told stories out of the Bible he had forgotten. Jacob in a blue window wrestled with an angel until he was blessed. Shaw wrestled with that poor bastard LaGrange, who carried the weight of his guilt over firing on the wrong target in Baghdad.

Sending only Shaw and LaGrange after ibn-Sultan had been Shaw's idea, and Devine reluctantly agreed. Satellite photos, electronic surveillance, secure telephones, and every other gadget had proved useless in the field. One man against another gave them the edge they sought. LaGrange was ready. He wanted to finish the assignment begun with Ambassador Paige and stop the Followers of the Cleric. Be more realistic and less naive, Shaw thought, we take down an asshole like ibn-

Sultan and another replaces him in less than a week. LaGrange had the faith Shaw had lost and he wanted the scholar's blessing to make him human again, the boy who danced all night to "Gimme Shelter." He rose from the pew and plunked fat five-franc coins into the donation box before leaving the church.

Shaw walked across the Limmatt and entered the offices of Credit Suisse at Bahnhofstrasse 89. Herr Bernard, an official of the bank in his late fifties, arranged for Shaw to audit their list of foreign depositors. Numbers instead of names confused the different money transfers and made the search impossible. He left the bank angry in search of a cafe. The cold of Switzerland knifed through his light topcoat but the coffee was good and the beer even better. Awake and slightly drunk, he tottered along Sihlstrasse to his room at the Hotel Glockenhof.

Maybe LaGrange would find Samir Mohammad, thought Shaw. Ali Massouf did not need the threat of a black site and purred like a sleeping kitten in custody. He said Mohammad had contact with ibn-Sultan and traveled under the name Sammy Hammond, likely going over the southern border. Mexican authorities traced him to Mexico City, where he had taken a flight several days earlier for Marseilles.

Shaw dropped his key in front of his hotel room door, picked it up and tried again, when his cell phone vibrated in his pocket. He entered and answered.

"This is LaGrange. I have our scientist, Mohammad. Thought you might want to join the chase."

"Where are you?"

"Vienna. He's at the Hotel Wandi, not far from St. Stephen's. I've been with him since Marseilles. The intel you had was right. According to the desk clerk, he's a Turkish businessman named Ahmet Iskun and has the passport. How are the Swiss?"

"Too goddamn Swiss. I'll catch the next plane and be there soon."

"I'll met you at the airport."

"Thanks. Keep me posted."

"Will do."

Shaw packed his few things in an overnight bag and asked the doorman to call a taxi for him. Contacting Devine would wait until later when he knew more.

———

Smells of curly fries and bacon beef 'n cheddar burgers lacquered the walls of Devine's office as Howard Crumbly emptied the Arby's bags on the desk.

"Fifty bucks for dinner and you bring this? I was hoping for sushi."

"Here's the change, sir. I'm allergic to raw fish and Arby's was closer."

Devine grinned. "Of course. Hope you brought plenty of napkins." He shoved a few strands of curly fries into his mouth.

"What happened with the raid in Afghanistan?"

"Our commandos were ambushed and arrived at the campsite too late. Simple as that."

"I heard ibn-Sultan fled at the first sound of gunfire."

"He may have stuck around, but he'd already been planning to visit the devil West. Abdullah gave him a suitcase full of cash and he needed more for what, we don't know."

"Must have been a terrible mission."

Devine bit into his burger. He tabulated the calories and fats in his head, and made a silent promise to live on carrot juice for the rest of the week. "Special Forces lost a man and we captured two songbirds. Not an even trade."

"Do we have any reports on ibn-Sultan's whereabouts?" Crumbly asked.

"Now we go into the realm of politics. The attack on Ceyhan and the gassing of Madison Square Garden put the Administration into a vengeful state of mind. Money has poured into the Counterterrorism Center, more than Homeland Security. The White House thinks we can do a house-to-house search for ibn-Sultan, but you don't catch the man like that. You keep the situation very low-key so he thinks we're playing pocket pool while trying to make a decision. Only Shaw and LaGrange have the assignment, and need room to move. We'll keep the bureaucrats busy with loads of paper."

"The reason why you had me pulled off the China desk to help with the reports and dossiers becomes clear, sir. I have a question about your capture of Ali Massouf. Weren't you a leery of trusting your wife's ability to recognize him after only seeing his face on video footage?"

"Stephanie never exaggerates and she's always focused. I was hanging out there, but the possibility of catching Massouf made me reckless. I wouldn't recommend a stunt like that to anyone."

Crumbly gathered the empty wrappings, tossed them into the wastebasket, and carried the carafe from the coffee machine to fill Devine's cup.

"Sending an NR-1 after a Kilo submarine was even more foolhardy."

"Only if the mission had gone south. The bureaucratic mind thinks only in terms of results. We reached our objective and the Russian Navy has their boat back, except for Ogdanov and Ivanovsky. They've asked for political asylum."

———

Franz Josef marked Vienna in the nineteenth century with retrograde architecture, French and Flemish Gothic, French and Florentine Renaissance, and the stone buildings made the city look like a wedding cake confection. Frosting of white and gold loops and curls, and statuary decorated the buildings along the Ringstrasse and the monuments in Stadtpark. LaGrange and Shaw followed the mismatched big nose and miniscule ears of Mohammed. His hair was different from Agency photographs, slicked back flat against his skull, and he huddled against the cold in a loden green duffle coat.

The two men made a game of tailing Mohammed. LaGrange

walked ahead in jeans, rubber-soled boots, black hooded sweatshirt and leather jacket, and Shaw stayed behind wearing his usual suit, tie, and topcoat. Their paths twisted and twirled around Mohammed as he played tourist. He walked Naschmarkt to the Secessionist Building with gold ball on top and decorative borders hiding harsh corners, and through the Hofburg Complex of the former Imperial apartments and the faded whitewash of the Spanische Reitschule, the Spanish Riding School and home of the Lipizzaner horses. At three o'clock he took coffee at the Cafe Museum on Frederichstrasse. Groups of young Viennese argued and students studied at the tables and booths. Large violent abstract paintings hung on the walls stained brown by decades of smokers. Mohammed sipped coffee and read newspapers for an hour before returning to his hotel.

LaGrange and Shaw sat at a table in the Cafe Central near the Freyung shopping arcade. Thick pillars held the curves of the vaulted ceiling, scrubbed clean and brightened for businessmen and Japanese tourists.

"Lie to me," Shaw frowned over his *grosse brauner.* "With good news."

"He's like a clock. Mohammed waits every day in the same cafe at the same time. He returns to his hotel, orders room service, and stays inside. I've spread Agency cash around the staff so they watch him. If he goes out, I get a call."

"Has he made you?"

"Not possible. He would have varied the routine if he had."

Shaw swallowed the last of his coffee and harrumphed in the cup. "We know he's meeting someone and we don't know who or when. I'm going to ask for favors from the Embassy and arrange for backup. We're too close. Usually I can take the wait but tracking Mohammed will drive me nuts."

"You're getting old. We'll get our man only through patience."

"The Central is the right place for waiting. Leon Trotsky sat here over chess games until word came from Moscow that Kerensky's government was out and Vladimir Lenin was in. Bingo! Next stop the Russian Revolution."

"Stop reading guide books and buy a copy of the *International Herald Tribune.*"

"The crossword is too hard. You know something, Eric? I think I've gone native. I want back in the dust and grime of Istanbul. There's an honesty among the Turks I don't see in the West."

"Vienna is only Vienna. I ride the U-Bahn with Mohammed and look at the pinched, mean faces. Freud and Jung and Adler accomplished nothing. These people drink without pleasure and eat without hunger. Only the children save Vienna from being completely wretched. I've watched them run on the street and tease their parents into stoic exasperation. What I'll never understand is how they grow into such tight-assed adults."

"The schnitzel is the cause. Let's try the Italian joint on Neustiftgasse and eat a couple of yards of pasta. We have nothing until tomorrow anyway."

Secure lines from Langley to Washington to the United States Embassy on Boltzmanngasse buzzed with Shaw's demand for an armed force to be ready should Kamal ibn-Sultan appear. Vienna held the bizarre position of being a city-state, province, and municipality at the same time. Though cooperation had been promised, Shaw had to run through several layers of bureaucracy on a schedule he was missing. He bullied into the office of the Polizeipräsident of the Federal Police Department of Vienna, who referred him to the Generalinspektor of the uniformed police corps, the Sicherheitswache. A tired and confused Shaw pushed through the doors of the first district, Innere Stadt, on Deutschmeisterplatz for his appointment with the Inspector and was greeted instead by Karl Hoher.

"You are the American I have heard much about. Come with me," said the dark-suited man. He looked Viennese from up close and at a distance. Shaw put his age around mid-forties, in very good shape from what he guessed was a constant rigorous training program. Hoher had blond hair, tanned skin, and steel-colored eyes. He kept any sense of humor in reserve for the day he would be ordered to laugh.

"Am I that obvious?"

"We will go to my office."

They trooped in single file past the receptionists and cubicles to a stairwell, and several floors above the entrance to a clean and spare windowless office of generic desk, chairs, carpet, computer, and telephone. The only dash of personality was a red scarf hanging from a coat rack.

"Tell me the problem," said Hoher.

"A link to Kamal ibn-Sultan is in Vienna, and he might lead us to his boss. We want him captured."

"Is ibn-Sultan here now?"

"Maybe, maybe not. My partner is keeping an eye on his contact, a scientist named Samir Mohammed."

"I understand ibn-Sultan is wanted by several police agencies, but if you do not have positive identification of the man, we are unable to help. A crime must be committed for us to begin any action."

Shaw forced the frustration out of his voice. "May I speak frankly?"

"Certainly, Mr. Shaw."

"Neither myself or my man are armed. We wouldn't presume to enter a country with a weapon of any kind. The men we are after don't have the same compunction. Log on to the Interpol site and you'll see they are responsible for many deaths in the Middle East and abroad. We need your assistance to bring them in."

Hoher played with a yellow pencil on his desk blotter. "Very well. This is how we can aid your enterprise. Our counterterrorist unit is the Gendarmerie Einsatz Kommando, or GEK. They are better at shooting than thinking. For the city of Vienna and to protect its citizens from stray bullets, you should call on the Wiener Einsatz Gruppe Alarmabteilung, WEGA, our version of your SWAT teams. WEGA is more discrete and able to manage difficult situations."

Shaw slumped in his chair. "More goddamn runaround. Tell me where to go next."

"Here," said Hoher. "I am the head of WEGA."

———

Across Maria Theresien Platz in the Naturhistoriches Museum, LaGrange lagged behind Mohammed as he passed the mineralogy rooms without interest for rocks, and headed for the skeletons of saber-toothed tigers in pre-attack crouch and displays of dinosaur eggs. The Halstatt archeological enraptured the scientist with its glass cases of stone chipped arrowheads, crude knives, and rough pots. LaGrange kept his eye on his man until he came to the Venus of Willendorf. He let Mohammed roam the rest of the rooms while he stood with 24,000-year-old plump clay figurine. What am I doing, he asked himself, chasing after phantoms? What happened to living?

Three o'clock came and LaGrange sat in the far corner of Cafe Museum behind a copy of *Die Presse,* glad to be resting after the walk. Mohammed found a table, unbuttoned the wooden plugs of his duffle coat, and waved to a waiter. A well-dressed man entered with a leather attaché case and weaved around the tables toward him. He wore a dark suit with a herringbone pattern, possibly British and definitely not Italian by its conservative cut, a red club tie, and shined black brogue shoes. The man took a seat at Mohammed's table. His starched shirt was a brilliant white Egyptian cotton and he wore wire rim spectacles. LaGrange recognized him. His gray-streaked beard was black and trimmed to a goatee, and dark brown eyes had shifted to amber from colored contacts. Despite the changes, he remained unmistakably ibn-Sultan, and Ismael.

———

Kamal ibn-Sultan ordered coffee and stared at the paintings. Ungodly things, an insult to all that is holy. The city never should have been rebuilt after World War II. Better to have let the remains rot.

"Have you any idea what you have cost me, Samir?"

"The failure in New York was not my fault."

"Too many of our people have avoided taking responsibility for their stupidity. The attack on Ceyhan was a disaster from lack of purpose. The Americans hold the Russians we had paid for the submarine and oil flows into the West. Yakir Arvatian failed me and I am glad he is dead. I would have hunted him down and shot him myself for his inability to hit the target. Let me remind you: Jihad is mandatory for all Muslims, and true jihad demands we succeed in our battles. The Americans give money to the Jews so they can kill our children in Palestine. When the Americans are forced to take care of their own people, that source will no longer be available to the Jews. What has our jihad accomplished? Ali Massouf is in custody for the chemical attack you assured me would work and talking to the FBI and CIA."

"I did what you asked, ibn-Sultan. Massouf improperly stored the anthrax. The error is his."

"Muslims are dying in Palestine, Lebanon, and Iraq. Listen to your brothers crying. I question your dedication, Samir."

"Test me again. I have been and always be a loyal follower of the Cleric."

The waiter placed cups of thick black coffee known as *kurz* on the table. Ibn-Sultan looked past Mohammed out the windows facing Friedrichstrasse to the trees crowded in a small park. The oppressive pewter sky gave into the waning day and darkened. Students at a nearby table matched political theories in a language ibn-Sultan did not care to understand. He watched the nameless trees and their green leaves flap in a gust of wind. His coffee cooled before he added sugar.

LaGrange pulled out his cell phone in the men's room and hit the speed dial for Shaw's number. His hand shook and he hoped the tremor was from anticipation. The mission was for capture, not revenge. Stay cool, LaGrange, he assured himself.

"I've got Samir Mohammed talking with Kamal ibn-Sultan," said LaGrange.

"You sure?"

"One hundred percent. He's lost the mole he had when we first met. Whatever you're going to do, now's the time."

"We're set with the locals. Get out of there and meet me in the street."

CHAPTER 17

M ohammed regarded ibn-Sultan with caution. He had been
lucky to escape New York. With money drawn from his ATM
account, he took a subway to the Bowery and rented a hotel room of
peeling wallpaper and cockroaches. He stayed for a week and lived
slightly better than the bums on the street while the newspapers filled
with stories of Massouf's arrest. He took a Greyhound bus southwest
to Galveston, then Brownsville where his olive skin helped him hide
among the Mexicans. After checking his e-mail drop at a cyber cafe
and reading the message from ibn-Sultan, he walked across the border
at Matamoras and rode the bus for Mexico City, where he took a flight
to Marseilles.

Ibn-Sultan let his anger subside before he turned back to
Mohammed.

"Did you see that no one followed you?" ibn-Sultan asked.

"I took all the precautionary measures you taught me."

"I am pleased you want another assignment, though we have need
of further planning." Ibn-Sultan took out a thick manila envelope from
his attaché case. "Here is an airplane ticket to Frankfurt and a cell
phone. From there you will go to a remote area of Yemen and establish
a laboratory. You will be provided with anything you need including
a reliable vehicle. There is also enough cash for travel expenses and
immediate needs. Additional funds are forthcoming. I have yet to secure

the most important materials but they will be delivered once you are ready."

Mohammed fingered a chain of beads. "They say you no longer are with Abu Abdullah."

"He would rather have us plant seeds than regain our land. Abdullah no longer has the confidence of the Cleric."

"I have heard different from the brothers on the Internet."

He paused and sipped his coffee. "Samir, you are the best of our scientific intelligentsia, and my most able and trusted. Do not think the Infidels are above spreading rumors to divide Muslims from each other. We must remain steadfast."

Mohammed nodded and accepted the envelope. "I will not disappoint you."

"I know. Go to Frankfurt and meet with the brothers."

Both were quiet as they finished their coffee. Ibn-Sultan looked at his wristwatch.

"When this assignment is completed," he said, "The West will shake at the sound of the Prophet's name."

"May Almighty God bless the work we do in His name. Is there more information I need?"

"I will contact you soon. Carry the cell phone with you at all times."

Mohammed left the cafe with his package. Maybe the Muslims in Germany knew more about the rift between ibn-Sultan and Abdullah. He would ask them.

LaGrange left the men's room and recognized the dull pressure of an automatic pistol in his back.

"I'm unarmed and alone," LaGrange said.

"One is likely and the other is not," hissed ibn-Sultan. "I have been watching you since the museum when you stopped in front of the Venus."

"Tell me what you want. We aren't having this conversation out of comradeship."

"Walk with me to the door. If we are truly alone, I will set you free."

"My trust has worn a little thin. I believe you'll probably shoot me anyhow."

"Yes, and also the waiter and the young girl with her text books. Jihad is everywhere the Crusaders have polluted with their corruption. Almighty God calls for my resolve and watches over my actions."

"Bullshit. The Crusades were six hundred years ago and Almighty God sees ibn-Sultan as a murderer of the just. Check the *Qur'an*. Many devout Muslims have died by following your commands."

"Even so, they have taken Westerners with them. To end the life of an Infidel means less than swatting a fly." He shoved the pistol deeper into LaGrange's back. "Talking is finished. Walk."

———

Black buses with "POLIZEI" in painted white letters discharged WEGA troops at Operngasse and Kärntnerstrasse. They ran in full combat gear to barricade Friedrichstrasse from traffic in front of Cafe Museum. Shaw watched the methodical work, Steyr AUG heavy barreled automatic rifles slung across the troops' backs with 40-round clips. The 5.56 mm gas operated weapons would never be used back home. The trigger guard was too big and the plastic body parts made them look like spindly toys. As far as accuracy went, Shaw doubted the Steyrs were much good, except at close range.

The dull yellow stone front of the cafe house lay in the dark. Anyone coming out of the building would be in the line of fire.

Shaw pulled at Hohen's sleeve as he rattled commands into a hand radio. "Tell your people to watch for a man in a business suit carrying a leather briefcase."

"Yes, Mr. Shaw. They have the descriptions of ibn-Sultan and LaGrange. We have done this before."

"Sorry. In these close quarters, I'm more concerned about my asset's safety."

"As are we."

Shaw and Hoher stood across from the cafe and watched as WEGA teams crept along the street with Steyrs raised. LaGrange emerged, followed by ibn-Sultan. "Hold your positions," Hoher said into his radio.

Ibn-Sultan saw the empty street. There should be cars with people heading home from work and buses. Rage boiled inside the Jordanian, born of his beginnings in the slums. The Cleric and Abu Abdullah told him to channel his anger at the Infidels and he had, but too many plans failed. Not this one.

"Say your last prayer, young man. Offer your sins to Almighty God for forgiveness."

"After you. Whoever is out there won't accept a hostage situation."

"Neither will I." He turned LaGrange around and shot him. The first bullet sped through LaGrange's midsection and tore viscera before lodging in his spine. WEGA troops fired on ibn-Sultan, and the rounds tore red flowers in his white shirtfront. He held on his pistol and shot LaGrange again, this time through the sternum, before falling to the ground.

"Get an ambulance, goddamn it!" Shaw ran to LaGrange. He stripped off his topcoat and slid the bundle under the man's head. Kamal ibn-Sultan lay sprawled on the pavement nearby, still holding his attaché case and weapon.

"You got him, Eric. He's dead as you can get."

"Good guys won, that's us, the good guys." His eyes were shiny from adrenaline or shock. "Killing to stop the killing is a soldier's job, a nasty job, Roger. This makes me even. I'm not guilty anymore."

"Never were, son. Shit happens in the field and we find ways to cope. Don't torture yourself. Save your strength here. We can talk about this later."

"Have you ever been so ashamed you couldn't forgive yourself?

Those civilians killed in Baghdad were done by ibn-Sultan. I only pulled the trigger. Tried to stop the fucker who started this shit and made it worse. Another body for the heap." LaGrange lapsed into silence and closed his eyes.

"For Christ's sake, I need medical now!" Shaw barked.

Attendants dressed in whites ran toward the two men. They lifted LaGrange on a gurney, bared his chest, and applied pressure bandages to the leaking wounds. He opened his glazed eyes as he rolled through the open doors of the ambulance.

"Don't send my bones to Wisconsin, Roger."

"No one's dying today except assholes. You'll be fine. I've seen guys hit like you be up and chasing nurses after a couple of days."

"Only want Suzanne and she's gone. Make sure they bury me in Damascus. Don't want to be sent stateside. God is in the Middle East, all over. You believe in God, Roger?"

"I don't know."

"Me neither. Better to trust in people. Get a girlfriend, have a family."

"I'm too old."

"Never. Women love us no matter what. You need a life, Roger."

The ambulance driver hit the lights and siren, and sped along Operngasse to the hospital. LaGrange was quiet again and his breathing labored.

"Have we saved anyone?"

"Lots of people, Eric. Christians, Jews, Muslims, everybody."

He stopped breathing. The attendants pushed Shaw aside and started working to revive LaGrange. Shots of adrenaline and shocks of defibrillation paddles were useless. Shaw suspected LaGrange had wanted out.

His cell phone vibrated and jarred him back to the living. John Devine's number showed in the crystal display. "No more fucking calls!" he said and threw the phone against the wall of the ambulance.

———

Stephanie Devine sat in the newsroom of WJLA-TV and watched the CNN special report.

"Not thirty minutes ago, terrorist Kamal ibn-Sultan was killed outside a coffee house in Vienna by members of the local police. Former Special Forces Eric LaGrange died with ibn-Sultan, leader of an international Islamic extremist group believed to have headquarters in northern Afghanistan. Ibn-Sultan trained hundreds of recruits through the Nineties at a Hezbollah camp in Lebanon, and was considered to have masterminded the recent attacks in New York and the Middle East. State Department and intelligence community officials are debating on whether the death of ibn-Sultan will also result in the end of the organization."

———

Suleyman Ehmat held the remote and switched the television from CNN to Al Jazeera, the Arabic station. A similar newscast ran here as well, though unlike CNN, the announcer allowed suspicion to its veracity. Ibn-Sultan had been right. People of the Middle East would not believe such a thing. Suleyman hoped his cell phone would ring with a joke from ibn-Sultan about the report. One was not forthcoming.

He changed the channel and listened to a third version from the BBC. Finally he turned the television off. His duty was clear: he must carry out the instructions ibn-Sultan had given him.

———

Thick bound reports and dossiers flowed across John Devine's desk, and he had given up trying to keep pace with the materials. He bounced between Langley and the White House for a series of meetings where scenarios were exchanged about the future of the Middle East. A load of nonsense, he thought. No one could accurately predict the next step for the Followers of the Cleric. Other lunatics worse than the man who died in Vienna were expected.

He had been at his office on the third floor for less than an hour when Howard Crumbly rushed in with a black plastic case. "The package is here, sir."

"Let me get a cup of coffee. What are you talking about?"

"CNN in Atlanta received a videotape this morning, same time as Al Jazeera. We passed this through security checks and found nothing. The letter attached says this is from Kamal ibn-Sultan."

They sat in front of the console television. Crumbly inserted the tape into the VCR and played the brief message.

"Jesus," Devine said. "My Arabic isn't good enough."

"We have a translation provided by whoever sent the tape."

The tape ran three more times, and Devine stopped and started the message as he checked the spoken words with the sheet of typed text. Finally he was satisfied. "Yes," he said. "This is accurate as far as I can tell."

"Sir, what do we tell CNN?"

"Give them our thanks for their cooperation. They have to run the damn thing, so we'll let the State Department and Homeland Security handle the problem."

The television showed Kamal ibn-Sultan wearing traditional keffiya and white robes as he addressed the camera. Behind him rose steep hills of dust and rock.

"Praise be to Almighty God. American newspapers and television channels overflow with evident hatred against Islam and its people by the false reports of my death. This is a biased rumor, the purpose of which is an attempt to sow caution among the Muslims who sympathize with us, and to calm the fears of the Americans. Rest assured we are sure to continue our jihad and give America and its allies a painful beating.

"The Infidels tell Muslims ibn-Sultan kills civilians, yet what have they done elsewhere in the world? Vietnam, Iraq, and Afghanistan all show the marks of American bombs dropped by a people who have never understood the meaning of values. Muslims must be strong and follow our Prophet's mission to protect our land and people from the encroachment of the Infidels.

"Praise be to Almighty God who grants me good health. Praise be to all who continue the struggle to free our land and people."

Even from the grave, thought Devine, he's screwed us. The careerists and bureaucrats on Capitol Hill will look at the videotape and say the Agency brought down the wrong man, and this is proof. Devine fingered his scalp. He looked at the loose strands in his hands. Alopecia from stress guaranteed him bald patches before he hit fifty-five.

"We know ibn-Sultan was killed," offered Crumbly.

"Never underestimate the power of mass media."

"Would you like to be alone, sir?"

"Yes, Crumbly. Maybe I'll come up with a solution to this mess."

———

Suleyman Ehmat watched the news on CNN. An American journalist read over an image of Kamal ibn-Sultan:

"A video received at our offices in Atlanta suggests the man killed yesterday by the Vienna police was not ibn-Sultan."

The videotape was shot outside the Bekaa valley in Lebanon, if Ehmat remembered correctly. They made so many in different locations he was uncertain.

Sub-titles translated the Arabic spoken by ibn-Sultan into English. Suleyman knew the words well for this had been his leader's favorite video.

"The tape is being studied by several government agencies to determine its authenticity," the journalist continued. "Many Islamic extremists who reviewed the taped message say they will never take the word of American authorities that their leader is dead. Washington officials admit they have yet to obtain DNA or fingerprints of Kamal ibn-Sultan for positive confirmation of his death."

———

Sunlight streamed through the French doors of Ambassador Elizabeth Paige's office at the Embassy in Almaty. Her green eyes regained their lost sparkle as she spoke on the telephone.

"That was Roger," she told Burt Strauss. "He's meeting Amelia at the airport. It's such a beautiful morning. Let's wait outside."

She let loose the auburn hair tucked behind her ears for the call and took Strauss' hand. The foiled attack on Ceyhan had brought them closer, not as lovers but friends with possibilities.

Outside the air was alive with the smells of fresh turned earth, cut grass, and spring blossoms. They sat on a bench in the shade and faced the spot where Elizabeth had been abducted.

"I like the quiet here. The birds are louder than the traffic," Strauss said.

"Early morning is the best. What about Amelia?"

"I'm trying not to have any expectations and right all my wrongs to her overnight. Most of my life has been spent on things that aren't important, but I'm trying to do better."

"Like making money and getting ahead?"

"Yes, and forgetting about people and relationships, even fun."

"The older we get, the more we find to regret."

He laughed. "We can also learn to not be so hard on each other. Forgiveness has taken on a religious appeal for me. I want to stop hating my mistakes and enjoy the sunny days along with the rain."

"You're right. I've always wondered what happened to your ex-wife, Nancy. One day the two of you decided to divorce?"

"The process was longer and more drawn out. We had the house, the kids, and financial agreements to keep our lawyers busy."

"Did you tell her what happened between us?"

"She knew I was seeing another woman. Nancy liked the security of marriage and she stayed, not knowing where else to go."

"I was younger than Amelia is now and too immature to be a mother. Thank God for Tommy. He made me strong through the early years, and by the time he passed away, I had grown up enough to keep going."

"My fault, but I loved you and didn't know how. I'm sure you are a wonderful mother."

Elizabeth thought of Tommy dragging the reluctant Amelia through Macy's and Bloomingdale's for school clothes, him holding the video camera to tape dance recitals and plays, and bandaging small scraped knees from bicycle accidents.

"What? Sorry, I must have been wool gathering."

"My grandmother always used that expression when she was daydreaming. What is Amelia like?"

"She's fierce about her independence, compassionate and kind, and very bright. She has opinions on everything and owns them, especially politics. She's creative, too, and design her own clothes."

"She sounds like you."

"Somewhat, but she's definitely her own person. I think you'll like her."

"Will she like me?"

"I'm sure of it."

Roger Shaw poked his head out the door.

"Ah, the proud parents."

Elizabeth rose to greet him. They embraced and he kissed her cheek.

Shaw shook Strauss' hand. "Are you ready to meet Amelia?"

"Yes."

"Elizabeth's secretary, Sarah Edwards, has tea prepared in the drawing room or whatever the hell you call the place. Go on in."

Strauss looked at them. "Wish me luck."

Elizabeth waved him off and turned to Shaw. "I never thought this day would come. How is she?"

"She's a wonderful young woman, Elizabeth."

"Thank you. I appreciate you picking her up."

"No problem. Glad to help."

"Sit with me for a bit, Roger. Seems like the other day we were in Ceyhan and being buzzed by model airplanes." Elizabeth dabbed at her tears with a tissue. "I don't like being this emotional. I am so sorry about LaGrange."

"He was a good man, better than the Agency deserved. I tried to get him a star on the wall at Langley, but the bastards tell me no assets get the memorial."

"The man in Vienna, was he really Kamal ibn-Sultan?"

"LaGrange said so and who died doesn't really matter."

"Why not?"

"There'll be other fanatics."

"You sound like fighting the extremists is hopeless."

"We're not going after the cause. Dragging countries into the twenty-first century to create more markets for American business is stupid. Whole cultures are tossed and torn apart for the dollar. The unrest will continue unless we change our priorities."

"Equality and respect instead of disparity between rich and poor?"

"Madame Ambassador, you're too young to sound like an old time socialist. Start small. What's next for you?"

"I'll spend time with Amelia and do a bit of touring. I might see more of Burt. His job here is finished, but I think he wants to stay."

"This part of the world gets in the blood. Langley wants me in for an intense debriefing and I'm putting them off. I've had lots of questions about what I do and who I'm supposed to be since LaGrange was killed. The answers are slow in coming."

She smiled at him. "You know what the old bumper sticker recommends."

"Shit happens?"

"No. Commit random acts of kindness."

Shaw laughed, wished her well, and left.

—

WEGA chief Karl Hoher did not relent in his search for Samir Mohammed. The young scientist missed his flight to Frankfurt and was detained in Vienna. Hoher sent news of his capture to John Devine, and the positive identification of Kamal ibn-Sultan's corpse.

"You must be exhausted, sir," said Howard Crumbly.

"More like relieved. Time for us to write another brief to the brass," replied Devine.

"Where do we start?"

"We'll go through the operation from the beginning. The Ceyhan pumps are safe and the first loads of oil have already reached for Genoa. Other tankers are also ready to head our way."

"Wonderful news."

"Now we get messy. Circumstances the last few weeks indicated too well how the Followers of the Cleric network functions and uses any means to go after the West. They are organized, intelligent, and have access to funds we can't find. We have to become more proactive instead of reactive.

"The country is sick of war and the financial burdens we've assumed in the Middle East. What the general public doesn't know and shouldn't know is how tenacious the Followers of the Cleric are and how pervasive their movement has become. Ours must be the anonymous job of combating them. We won't make an issue over the identification of Kamal ibn-Sultan, only we and other agencies are satisfied the videotape is a lie, and he is dead. The next task is prevention, interception, and safety. We do this well, only we will know."

"Powerful stuff. Will the Administration listen?"

"Maybe, maybe not."